Afterlife

Poet, critic, playwright, broadcaster, anthologist and editor, Professor of Creative Writing at Newcastle University and Fellow of the Royal Society of Literature, Sean O'Brien grew up in the Hull and now lives in Newcastle upon Tyne. His six collections of poetry to date have all won awards, most recently *The Drowned Book*, which won both the Forward Prize for best collection and the T. S. Eliot Prize. *Afterlife* is his first novel.

A3 283 822 4

'Headily specific, with a strong sense of place and a subtle sensibility about the peculiar effects of the heatwave of 1976 on the British character, the continuing heat as potent as any narcotic . . . Rich, and almost tactile'
Times Literary Supplement

'*Afterlife* coheres into a crescendo whose most affecting moments have the ring of elegy . . . This is an erudite, entertaining novel'
Financial Times

'As a gothic tale of revenge and murder, *Afterlife* is a consistently compelling and satisfying page-turner. It is much more than that, however: it is a meditation on the proximity of hatred to love. It is a treatise on artistic authenticity, and an exploration of the link between madness and brilliance'
Irish Times

'*Afterlife* is a page-turner; full of sharp asides and cultural commentary. It's also a revenge fantasy, and will have anyone who has ever witnessed the idiocies of misplaced ambition cheering its cathartic final pages'
Independent

'A taut literary thriller that grips from the start and has a nice line in dark humour'
WBQ

'This is a dark story of jealousy and murder, but it's also very funny. The author is an award-winning poet and this is a merciless, absolutely brilliant unmasking of the poetic ego'
The Times

Sean O'Brien

Afterlife

PICADOR

First published 2009 by Picador

First published in paperback 2010 by Picador
an imprint of Pan Macmillan, a division of Macmillan Publishers Limited
Pan Macmillan, 20 New Wharf Road, London N1 9RR
Basingstoke and Oxford
Associated companies throughout the world
www.panmacmillan.com

ISBN 978-0-330-45567-1

Typeset by SetSystems Ltd, Saffron Walden, Essex
Printed in the UK by CPI Mackays, Chatham ME5 8TD

Visit **www.picador.com** to read more about all our books
and to buy them. You will also find features, author interviews and
news of any author events, and you can sign up for e-newsletters
so that you're always first to hear about our new releases.

For Ian and Kate Lawley:

on the side of the angels

Many thanks to
Sam Humphreys, Ruth Padel, Jo Shapcott
– and, as ever, Gerry Wardle,
without whom there would be no book.

I am grateful to the Northern Rock Foundation for
the 2007 Writer's Award which enabled me
to spend time working on this novel.

I wanna die in the same place I was born
Miles from nowhere
I used to reach for the stars but now I'm reformed
She's out there somewhere

The Only Ones

I am running across a field, then scrambling over a gate and stumbling down the road. It dips steeply towards a dry stream-bed that cars normally have to ford. I find that words are coming out of my mouth. I am shouting, 'Jane! Jane! Jane!' but this is no good. Jane cannot help me. She cannot help herself.

I smell of smoke. My hand stings and I realize the palm and fingers are burned. Now I see the cottage just ahead. I go on running and shouting. When I reach the pub I start shouting at Shirley the barmaid, who slowly puts down her magazine.

1

People ask if you're going to Hay, or Cheltenham, or even
Buxton, but those people are generally speaking your
novelist friends, for whom festivals involve holding forth
rather than reading their work. While the public are
waiting for the next ex-presidential candidate to show up
and fuck their collective brains out with sheer affability,
they don't mind hearing a few novelists blathering about
politics or the environment, as if it mattered. As long as
the sun shines and the catering's half decent, who cares?
The books wait quietly in their oddly chilly tent between
bouts of anxious acquisition. The bulk of these titles will
augment the furniture of holiday homes the summer after
next.

Divott is a different matter. Divott is a poetry festival
held in July, where nearly every event involves hearing
some poems read by a poet. The exceptions are lectures by
critics and biographers, but in these, too, poetry is in the
foreground. The programme is almost immune to celebrity
as that idea is generally understood. The festival originated
in, and has so far maintained, an interest in the work of
Thomas Exton. Exton was the parish priest of Divott from
1660 until his death by fire in 1680. He renounced life in

London for a rural parish, using his status as a member of the local gentry to find a living as far away as possible from the Babylonish temptations of the capital, where he had gone to study at the Inns of Court after graduating from Cambridge. As you can see, nothing could be further from fashionable concerns.

So at Divott the poetical tastes of that popular broadcaster X, like the Damascene conversion to culture of the ex-Tory minister Y, have had no effect whatever. Strangely, the events are rather well attended. The local economy, out of termtime, benefits in a modest way – hotels, bed-and-breakfast places, the handful of restaurants, the pubs that are normally comatose in summer except for the exploits of the local youth on Saturday nights. The audiences for the poetry festival are, for the most part, of mature years and know how to behave themselves quietly. So everyone is happy.

Almost everyone is happy. For poetry, like all other human activities, is subject to rivalry, jealousy and malice, though normally the matters in contention at Divott would at first sight mean little to anyone not themselves involved. The case of Jane Jarmain was different.

We live in an age of personalities, and in some sense Jane, or some versions of Jane as allegedly remembered, went on to thrive. Her work began to be written about and familiarly referred to. It was republished and became the subject of academic research. At the same time it connected with a readership beyond the core audience of critics and other poets and poetry victims. Poems found their way into university courses and, to the surprise of their teachers, me included, literature undergraduates began to view her as their special possession – an exceptional state of affairs for a poet at any time.

It was interesting and slightly eerie to watch talent turning into repute and repute evolving steadily into fame. Jane (after a while she only needed the one name, apparently) was name-checked by indie bands and used as a reference point for girly gloom by journalists anxiously surfing the wave of the *Zeitgeist* but not exercised by the need to read her work. By now 'Jane' was of course a good deal more famous than anything she had written, and the wider impression of her writing had little to do with the poems themselves. There was talk of the need for a biography, with some fairly discreet jostling for permission to gain the estate's blessing for such an undertaking. But the estate, by which I mean Alex Farren, had always declined to appoint a biographer, stating that the time was not yet right and, furthermore, refusing all co-operation to unofficial contenders (though one or two went ahead anyway, producing books remarkable for their earnest vacuity). Alex Farren, keeper of the flame and the keys, was far away, in America, enjoying some eternal quasi-academic sinecure that left him largely free to concentrate on the parallel course of his own growing celebrity as a cultural scene-maker of a generalizing kind.

There was also talk of unpublished poems in considerable numbers, of diaries and letters, of suppression. It was all very satisfactory from a contemporary point of view. There was life in the death, as it were. Then, as the thirtieth anniversary was noticed approaching, a couple of members of the committee of the Divott Festival came up with the interesting proposal that the remains of Jane Jarmain should be reinterred in the churchyard of St Bartholomew in Divott during that year's festival. It would help to cement – someone actually used that word – the tradition inaugurated by Thomas Exton and carried on by a few very minor figures up until the First World War. It was, undoubtedly, a radical proposal. It was also exactly the sort of moronic notion I would have expected of some of my colleagues – vulgar, sentimental, ignorant, and so forth: you name it. Had it not been for Molly and me, Divott would have been ruined long since. We kept the bastards at bay. You will notice the change of tense: Divott, the enlightened, unadulterated Divott, will soon be gone.

'Are there in fact any remains to *be* reinterred?' asked the Reverend Peter Langland, blinking in the sharp sunlight of the October dusk as it passed across the windows of the committee room.

'Yes, there was a body. Jane died of asphyxia rather than burns,' I said. I might have said a lot more.

'And where is she currently buried?'

'Her sister arranged it. She's near her family in Wales.'

'What do they think?'

'Most of them probably don't,' I said.

'Oh?'

I was about to reply when Simon Tunnock chipped in, anxious to keep a handle on his 'idea'.

'Her parents are long dead now.'

'Of course. The march of time.' Langland nodded as if agreeing to the proposal.

'And the other relatives – that's her sister and her brother-in-law – they have no objection.' This was Ginny Tunnock. 'We've written to them, so that's all right.'

'Have you now?' I said.

'They may come over from Wales for the event.' Ginny was never far from the reception class. Gold star for her, please.

'And what about Alex Farren?'

'We've sorted that out.' Simon nodded and raised his eyebrows. It was official, then.

'How?'

'Well.' Ginny glanced down demurely. 'He's decided it's time.'

'Time for what?'

'He's looked into his heart, Martin.'

'That can't have taken long. Did he find anything?'

'It's always easy to be horrible,' Ginny said, staring round in appeal.

'Not if you want to do a proper job.' Ginny and Simon looked patiently at one another. 'I see. Farren's finally written a book about it all, hasn't he? It's a matter of economics rather than mourning, then. Time to cash in.' It was many years since I had expressed any interest in Alex Farren's doings.

'If I may say so, that's a very ungenerous way of regarding the matter,' Langland said mildly.

'You may say so, Vicar, if it gives you comfort. I know Farren of old.'

'But people change – for the better, we hope, Martin. Is there any need to go raking over the coals of ancient history?'

'With respect, that's exactly what you're undertaking to do.'

I could see the writing on the wall – or, rather, on the tomb. For the rest of the meeting I kept my counsel. In the view of the festival committee, everyone would be a winner. Langland was sure that the diocese would raise no objections. The event would draw visitors to the church, as well, surely, as calling greater attention to the festival through media interest in this unusual act of literary reconciliation, as he put it.

'So we are in majority agreement,' said Langland.

I could have told the committee what they were going to do next. They would invite some twittering BBC arts presenter with a holiday cottage nearby to make the event official by somehow taking charge of it, bringing poetry to a wider public while somehow at the same time softening the edges and reducing the amount of poetry the public might actually be asked to encounter at the festival rather than vaguely talking about it or taking up space in its proximity. Farren's book would be everywhere, and so would he. *That Man who would see Harm done to what he Loves has but to be patient*, as Exton put it in his journals. I kept my mouth shut and went to the pub.

2

There have been plenty of dry summers. But that was the blazing sun in splendour among them, an unending season of pitiless bronze. The earth's waters sank back as far as possible into the dark, the streams and aquifers sucking on stones for comfort, far from the blazing daylight.

We were not so lucky in May Cottage, down Orphy's Lane, among the hopfields on the edge of the village of Summer Street, at the foot of Summer Hill. We lay on the parched lawn, trying to read. We sprawled uncomfortably in shorts on the ancient hairy upholstery in the sitting room. By night we waited restlessly on burning beds for the glimmer of dawn that would simply restart the cycle of discomfort.

At the same time – many who were young in those days will understand this – there were moments of intense happiness about the house. One world was ended and the other not yet born. We were all still young; there was time to play with and sufficient funds, more or less, to fuel the play. I see us in the garden, as if with the sound off, carrying our shadows lightly.

I keep referring to 'we'. I mean Susie and myself, and Alex and Jane. Except for Susie we had been at Cambridge together. We had declared ourselves tired of the place and its confining self-obsession. We needed somewhere to develop our own. Country life was the answer: we knew this without discussing it. Alex and I had decided to apply to do postgraduate work at the small new university in the Welsh Marches. It had formerly been a theological college, based in the ancient market town of Divott. Divott lay a few miles to the west of Summer Street, on the far side of Summer Hill. The Academy of the Marches was new, it was old, it was a long way away, it was near a frontier. They snapped us up.

Alex's subject was the American 'Confessional' poet Robert Lowell, then at the height of his fame; mine was Exton, the unsung poet of Divott and its surroundings. We'd got away with it again. We had also decided, without saying much about it, and certainly without informing the institution that had given us scholarships, that there would be something of an interregnum. We would be taking the money, yes, and we would not be entirely idle, but the world would officially start a little later, with doctoral theses (somehow) completed, and maybe jobs of some kind, if necessary.

Jane herself had no interest in further formal study, or in employment. She had access to a modest private income, apparently. She would use the time to write. Off we went into the west, our possessions crammed into Jane's Volvo and Susie's 2CV. Neither Alex nor I could drive; the condition is widespread among poets.

Susie was the exception in working for a living. She had already arranged to do some teaching at the local art college ten miles away in Willeford. Even then she was beginning to recognize that teaching, rather than painting, would be most of her living. She was a good painter but not an outstanding one, and she had the kind of dignity that enabled her to absorb this fact without the hysterical despair to which Alex and I would have swiftly given in if, at that stage, we'd had to face the same truth about our writing. We considered ourselves writers already. That we'd written little and published less was only a technicality: it was a calling, not a matter of objective proof, at least not so far. It was the world of *not yet*. Recently, when a literary agent came to talk to my MA writing students at the Marches (I've never quite escaped the place's somnolent gravity), I found myself smiling when she remarked encouragingly that even if none of them ever published a word (and she and I knew that hardly any of them would), they would still be writers none the less. There was, I swear, a just-audible sigh of collective relief. Desperate hope is as moving in the middle-aged as groundless optimism is annoying in the young. And imagine me – a dispenser of hope!

The world, then, could wait until we gave it our attention. The exception, again, was Susie. I knew that already she wanted a child and hoped we would now take steps to secure its future. *Ergo* I should find an academic job sooner rather than later. After all, it was what I seemed to want. Like so much else in our little nest of singing birds, this hardly needed to be said (or perhaps was hardly *allowed* to be said), but even I was aware of the discreet weight of longing, of pressure not being applied. Being young and stupid and selfish I chose to regard it as an eccentricity on Susie's part. In every other way she was so decent and, well, sensible. No one we knew had begun to have children. There was always time. What could she have seen in me? I see her melancholy grey-eyed, straw-blonde beauty now. She was the grown-up. She knew she must accept disappointment.

There were other things to think about. Poetry, for example. There was my own work, and there was Exton, and there was also the magazine we were editing. Susie had access to the art-college printing room and the publication fund. So the *Summer Street Review* came, very slowly, into existence. If it managed only a single issue, well, that was not without precedent, and a little magazine should certainly not outstay its time. I blame society. I blame the drugs. On the idle hill of summer, with the help of a bag of rather stalky grass, Alex and I sneered and guffawed our way through the stack of submissions that mysteriously find their way to even the most obscure, or in this case not-yet-existing, magazine. There was a sour, brassy-tasting pleasure in rejecting the work of people we'd known at university, who had themselves turned us down for their undergraduate publications.

'Give 'em a sniff of print and they'll suck your cock till Doomsday,' Alex liked to say. 'Hang this man. The law must take its course.' He would be crouching at the table he'd dragged out into the shade of a tree, where he happily spent hours exploring his gift for the uniquely offensive rejection letter. I remember: 'Dear Mr Tobler, There have never been and never will be any poets called Tobler. Here's your stuff back.' And 'Dear Miss Endacott, You really shouldn't send this kind of material out in public. Are you in fact mentally ill? Are you a nymphomaniac? Don't send poems: send a photo.' As I remember, Miss Endacott did exactly that, though the topless snapshot soon disappeared into what Alex referred to as 'the archives'. It looked like a sort of normality, out there in the sun, some of the time, in the meantime.

What we really wanted, although like most of the important things it could never actually be said, was a respectable context in which to publish some of our stuff. We hoped (I hoped) it might gain lustre, or at least an air of competence, from the company it kept. Careers have been founded on less. We knew the importance of the Little Magazine in the history of twentieth-century poetry. Severity, exclusivity, prominence and a refusal ever to apologize or explain would do for us, in our pastoral conspiracy. It had worked for others before us. Of course, as well as being arrogant we were criminally solicitous towards the poets we wanted to publish. Your Heaneys and Mahons and Muldoons were very generous: I mean, they had no need of us but still they let us have poems to include, their sole reward a free copy of the *Summer Street Review*, quite possibly mailed to them (supposing it ever was mailed – the records are regrettably incomplete) without sufficient postage. I still cringe to think of it. It was as though producing the thing was the point; distribution could take care of itself. To be hard to get was on the way to being a legend – and in recent years I've read knowing references to the *Summer Street Review* by people who've clearly never seen a copy

As you may have noticed, the magazine was a boys' game, though without Susie we couldn't have produced it. Jane herself took no interest. Writing this, I feel that reticence of hers, that oddly dramatic talent for not being there. She's not in these pages yet, but I need her to come in now. So: Jane had a cloud of dark red hair, and cloud-pale Irish skin. Her finely featured face and far-off green eyes combined delicacy with challenge. She most often looked as if she was asking something. People who didn't know her said she was fey, but there was nothing soft or sentimental about Jane. In her frequently silent and wholly unpredictable way, she was very determined. Yet she provoked in me (and probably in others, though not, I think, in Alex) a combination of desire and pity, whose result, which I could recognize but never learn from, was shame. You could never live up to expectations that seemed to her quite ordinary. She took a first and didn't care, wouldn't put it to work, except in her poems.

In the poems she had a subject from the start, as the best poets usually have. Subject is perhaps not the word: she covered a lot of ground, but she did so within a frame that might be described as the view from her window – into the woods and hills, westwards, a landscape haunted by a meaning it could no longer possess in our disenchanted times but that never ceased to lead her imagination out and away into its depths, the elsewhere around the corner and over the hill. There was no escapism about it, no nostalgia. The poems travelled towards a defining, sombre, unavoidable encounter. There was a faint kinship with Edward Thomas, another haunted taker of walks. As I try to describe Jane's work, I reduce it. Read it for yourself

When we were students we were told repeatedly, as though it were not blindingly obvious, that selection of significant detail was one test of the artist's capacities. In the case of Jane, selection is beyond me: it all counts – what she said, what she thought and felt, what she wrote, what she looked like, wore, drank, smoked, whom she loved, the tiniest gesture. Even a room she had recently left had its own melancholy-erotic interest. I admit defeat: she was simply more than I can hope to convey. But I have to start somewhere.

Jane was inclined to avoid the heat. She would go out walking before dawn or at dusk, but during the day she mostly preferred to stay in the bedroom, working by lamplight with the curtains drawn, perched on a stool at the dressing-table. Sometimes she lay down and went into a dead sleep for half an hour. I ought not to know this, but I do. I would stand in the doorway and look at her for a little while. It was as if she had gone away completely, leaving only the sign of herself, the cloud of hair spread on the pillow, her face empty and safe in the shaded room.

On waking she went straight back to her papers. She never grasped the notion of idleness, though she never commented on others' inactivity. She might not even have noticed. All those times she was 'just reading', which was what Alex said when I asked – no, she was working, putting in the endless time it takes to write a poem, or to begin to write one, or to come within hailing distance of beginning. People nowadays – my students, some of them – write poetry as if they think it's actually possible. Jane could have shown them otherwise. And in that endless meantime the boys were downstairs on the scorched lawn, rehearsing their extraordinary powers of procrastination.

Occasionally Alex would shout up to the bedroom window: 'Jane, make us a cup of tea.' It was as if he hadn't spoken. 'You lazy cow.' He would grin affectionately, and later I would see him staring up at the window, his expression unreadable. Everyone felt the lack of her presence. Everyone waited for her arrival, even Alex, and longed to extend her stay. But most of the time she was elsewhere.

Alex too was writing poems, of course, though it's hard to see when. And so was I, though it's equally difficult to establish exactly where and when I did so. (I have the files of cancelled drafts to prove it: but what I learn from them is how slender a pretext I had for continuing and hoping.) And though we were friends and colleagues and co-conspirators, he and I rarely exchanged work or read it to each other. We just talked, all the time. Or, rather, Alex did. He talks now, in a sense, in these pages, wanting all the air to himself. Jane, on the other hand, is always eager to be gone, out into the woods, back to her room.

Yet we were close, Alex and I, with the tight, exhausting friendship of the young. So I would have said at the time. It is as if I were someone else.

When I think back now I can't be precise about where

we met or how it happened that we spent the next few years in each other's company. Alex was simply there, somehow, as though fully formed, with the certainty that what the world needed now was him.

Our first encounter may have been at the welcome party held at the house of our director of studies next door to the college a few weeks into Michaelmas term. I remember sitting on one side of a huge punchbowl placed on the kitchen table while Alex sat on the other. We were both drunk and already we were conspiring as if we'd been in conversation since birth. We had chosen to sit somewhere that meant we were in the way of everyone passing through the kitchen. To maintain this station until the bowl was dry became a point of honour. *Épater les bourgeois*, I suppose.

We were still sitting there gone midnight, when the crowd was thinning. It was as if we'd won. I say 'we', but it would never have occurred to me to *do* such a thing had it not been for Alex. I was sucking the dregs from a slice of lemon, wearing it like a gumshield while Alex did the same. A sleepy-looking blonde girl had materialized on his lap. I remember she was a nurse. In a town as short of women as Cambridge in those days, the alleged nympho-mania of nurses was an article of faith, though I never found it borne out in practice. She smiled tolerantly while Alex enquired about the details of her uniform. He looked from me to her and back with proprietorial satisfaction: a job well done, as it were.

We went outside and smoked a joint in the tutor's front garden. The girl – Karen, Carol, Caroline – didn't want to come back into college over the JCR roof. In her heels and minidress she wasn't dressed for scrambling about. Alex pressed his cause with his signature blend of charm and insistence but she wouldn't budge. She was tired and needed to call a taxi back to Addenbrooke's. I hauled myself up the drainpipe on to the flat roof and bade them good night. A minute or two later I reached my room and found I'd left the gas fire on. The heat and the smell of a month's undone laundry turned my stomach. I opened the window in case I needed to throw up. I heard cries from below. When I looked down I saw Alex fucking his nurse against the wall of the tutor's garden. I was sure he knew I was there. 'Excelsior!' he cackled. I closed the window.

The nurse never reappeared in college. I remember my tutor remarking on another occasion that old friends often hate each other intensely. Now I wonder if I felt the same way about Alex when our friendship was only beginning. Perhaps in those days it was more important to feel *something* than to be able to give it a name.

But surely, I thought, Alex had gone too far in respect of the nurse – though here as at other times I sensed that he could make women conspire to do his will and think themselves lucky. More than one tearful note was pushed under his door.

'You shouldn't have done that,' I said, next day, at the bar of the Standing Pool. 'It was a bit, well, a bit cruel. You were sort of humiliating her.'

'Fuck off, man,' he said, affably. 'I'm not cruel. That's not what I am? Is it? Not cruel.' He might have been discussing left-handedness or the thickness of custard.

'Anyway, sounds as if you must have been looking into the matter rather too closely, eh, you pervert? Takes two to know, eh? She wasn't complaining, was she? And I got her a taxi, as she requested, afterwards.'

Alex, as you can tell, exhibited a Londoner's blithe confidence that the world would adapt itself to his requirements – or that it would at least understand when he punched holes in it to satisfy some immediate passing necessity. I, on the other hand, came from nowhere and felt that only a misunderstanding had admitted me to the world represented by Cambridge and London. I could be recognized and expelled at any moment and when that happened I would have no grounds for complaint. So I was happy to ride on Alex's coat-tails, to see what he saw and say some of what he said, for a while.

My parents were teachers in a northern city a long way away. We lived in a glum poky house on a dark Victorian avenue. Why would anyone visit my family home? It never occurred to me to suggest it, and neither did anyone ask. But we went to Alex's parents' house, in a tall, anciently leafy street of dark brick in a getting-on-for-loaded district of West London that I had only dimly heard of. There was a lot less information about in those days, unless you already had it, and I hadn't, and not to have it seemed to mean that you had no business to be wanting it anyway. You would be spotted and turned back at the gate – all for accepting a fiction, though the imaginary character of 'fitting in' was much of its power.

Knowing where people lived, and how, was part of it.

Closely related was the mystery of why, if Alex's parents had money, as they appeared to, he was about as broke as I was, though my parents made every effort to keep me afloat with beer money. Perhaps it was about self-reliance. Perhaps his parents were simply mean in some middle-class way I wasn't entitled to know about. I didn't mention these garbled anxieties to Alex. No doubt he was perfectly aware of them. He had a talent for putting you at ease if he wanted to, and of suggesting that this considerate approach was a better index of his true nature than any that previous events might have seemed to indicate.

We turned up for a party given by his parents. It was the eighteenth birthday of his sister, Lucy. I remember she was planning to read law. The father, Jeffrey, was a lawyer and his mother – 'I'm Helena' – clearly a beauty not so long ago, was some sort of writer, or had been, or was about to be again. There was an unspoken 'if' attached to the unfinished sentence, and a lot of nodding and thoughtful breathing. There didn't seem to be any of her books on the shelves.

That evening the big, bright house was full of the parents' friends, affable, frightened, complacent people who felt themselves sliding out of contact with their children but weren't sure if they were that bothered. The women seemed to be on the point of screaming and the men to wish they were at work. All of them appeared to be drunk. Someone kept trying to play a Stooges record and it kept being taken off.

Alex and I found ourselves a space in the chilly summerhouse at the end of the garden. At the height of the revelry,

Helena, wearing a creased, slightly grubby pale blue dress, her thin blonde hair slipping from its combs, came and joined us. She smoked a joint while clutching a bottle of wine that she then carried away, unshared, back into the house.

We stayed put all night, sitting on damp cushions on wicker chairs, smoking and talking with Lucy and her untouchably well-groomed friends from St Paul's in their velvety miniskirts and broderie-anglaise tops. They'd grown up with Alex and were all too aware that he was a bit of a lad, so they resolutely professed to find him sweet. That description, of course, is usually fatal, but he accepted it with good grace, perhaps because he was on home ground. Eventually the girls left and we sat on, braving the autumn chill, smoking, talking, smoking.

When the pair of us went back into the house, hung-over and in search of breakfast, Helena was sitting at the bottom of the stairs in her nightdress, drinking sherry and smoking Capstan Full Strength. It was seven a.m. Her husband passed her without speaking, on his way out to play squash. He affected not to notice me or Alex. I made Helena a cup of tea, which she very politely didn't drink. I was sweet too, according to her, and apparently Alex could learn a thing or two about life from me. While I found some bacon, grilled it and made toast in the vast neglected kitchen, he smoked Rothmans from the box on the unopened piano, watching his mother in silence.

'Alex is a poet,' said Helena. 'Aren't you, my lovely?' Alex looked at the floor. 'It's a hard life, I think.' She paused to remove a thread of tobacco from her tongue.

'It's a vocation. Many are called but few are chosen. That's what they say. Good luck to him, I say. Pass me the sherry, Martin. No, darling, don't look at Alex. Look at me. Alex can't advise you. He thinks I'm a bad mother. I dare say he's right.' I shrugged and poured sherry into her glass, cold with shame.

'Are you a poet, too?' Helena asked after a pause. 'It would be lovely for Alex to have a friend. Well, are you a poet?'

'I don't know, Mrs Farren.'

'I think you would know if you were. I think they always know in these cases. Alex knows, certainly.'

After a while, Lucy came downstairs, dressed to go out, and started shouting at her mother, who stuck calmly to her fatal task, occasionally looking up to smile forgivingly and sweep her lank hair out of her eyes. Lucy searched around, dug out her mother's purse and took twenty pounds, which I thought was a fortune. She brandished the notes before Helena's indifferent gaze, like a sort of fine, to be spent in Biba rather than the off-licence.

When Alex and I left shortly afterwards, he did not visit Helena's purse. As soon as we were out of the front door he returned to normal, gleeful, satirical, seeking objects for his energy. We walked to Shepherds Bush to wake up, then got the tube over to Notting Hill to score. After managing to do this in the terrifyingly blatant setting of Finch's, which seemed to me to be crawling with drugs-squad officers in Afghan coats, we spent lunchtime in another pub, then ended up at someone's flat (more nurses, Irish ones this time) where I watched *Mrs Miniver* on television with two of them telling me I'd lovely hair, wasted on a boy, while Alex was in another room with a third. We returned to Cambridge on the last train, drunk and exhausted. It seemed to me that although this might not be *War and Peace* it was definitely experience, and that I should try to gather more of it in order to be able to live up to the contents of my bookshelves. Mrs Farren, though, was difficult to think about properly. She might still be sitting there on the stairs, making her way down another bottle while her family got on with hating her. It was a strange form of privilege to kill yourself like that, I thought.

'There's nothing to be said about it,' said Alex, reading my thoughts. 'You don't have to try, and I'd rather you didn't.'

At least, I remember thinking, the unhappiness of Alex's parents had a certain swagger. My parents were unhappy on principle, it seemed: all that happiness business was a long time ago (my mother occasionally referred to a holiday in Belgium, apparently taken without or before my father) and, besides, there was work to do and there were people to help, endlessly. At the same time, in the teeth of their gruelling Labour principles, my mother and father paupered themselves to send me to a private school, because they had no intention of allowing me to enter the proximity of those in need of the help, still less risking my becoming one of them.

I had lived a long way away from life, it seemed to me, in a place where love was so absolute and everyday and joyless a medium as to be both unrecognizable and intolerable. It was clear to me that I could not deserve better:

I must take what I was given. I wondered why Alex befriended me. I had nothing to offer, no experience, no access to anything he needed or wanted. Perhaps it was quite simple: with me at his side it might seem to the world of nurses and other necessary females that he could not in fact be the bastard he so obviously was, not given the kind heart that let me come along for the ride. I was camouflage and diversion. And while I've been saying this, Jane has escaped once more, simply by being herself. She will not compete, does not recognize that there is a competition. That should be in the past tense, of course.

3

I remember it was a Monday lunchtime. In the garden at May Cottage we'd stopped pretending to work on the incoming submissions to the magazine and were sitting under the tree smoking a joint, when Jane appeared in the back doorway, wearing a short cotton nightdress. She was holding some sheets of paper, and seemed to be half offering them in our direction. 'Alex,' she said.

He looked at her with a negligent smile. 'Thought you were asleep. Have a draw on this.'

'I was working.' She shaded her eyes with one hand, took a couple of steps forward and held up the sheaf of papers in the other. 'Alex, what have you done?'

'It's very good gack. Isn't it, Martin?'

Susie had also now emerged from the doorway. She leaned against the kitchen windowsill with her arms folded. Her face told me she had known something like this – but what was this? – would happen.

'Why have you done it?' said Jane. She was standing on the edge of the lawn now.

'Don't you like it?'

'It wasn't yours to decide what to do with.'

'I take it the proofs have arrived. Susie's shown you, has she?'

'No, I came downstairs to get a drink. Susie was looking at them on the table.'

'Curiosity killed the cat.'

Jane went on in her tone of slightly baffled and anxious reasonableness. 'I wrote the poem.'

'Yes. You did.'

'So I should decide whether I want it to be published or not.'

'Published?'

'In this magazine.' She offered the pages again. In my stoned state I was struck that the parties to this exchange were still about ten feet apart.

'I suppose you might call it publishing, if you like.'

'What do you call it?'

'It's just a little magazine, Jane.'

'You didn't ask if I wanted the poem to be included.'

'Well. The editor normally decides that. In this case me. And Martin.'

'Did you know about this, Martin?' asked Susie.

'First I've heard.'

'Division of labour, you see,' said Alex. 'Right hand, left hand.'

'Shut up, please,' said Jane.

'As you wish. I was only trying to explain. Make your mind up, eh?'

'What are you doing?' asked Jane.

'I wonder sometimes, I really do.' At this point Alex stood up.

'Stop being an arsehole, Alex,' said Susie.

'You've changed it. You've changed a line, line six, look.' Jane held out the sheaf of pages.

'I could just see what needed doing.'

'You bastard,' said Susie. 'I can't believe anyone would do such a thing.'

Alex ignored her and continued, levelly, 'I didn't realize, Jane. I mean, I didn't realize that you didn't think the poem was good enough for the magazine. Honestly, I didn't realize that perhaps you weren't taking it as seriously as other people.'

'I don't know what you mean,' said Jane. Susie came forward and took her arm. 'You asked me for the poem. I told you I didn't want it to be included. I said you could pick something else.'

'Yes, this is what I was afraid of,' said Alex. He picked up his jacket from the back of the chair.

'Just fuck right off, Alex, OK?' said Susie.

'Fair enough, Susan. I shall do exactly that. I'm going to take myself to the Hop Pole while everyone sorts their heads out. I confess I'm baffled. Perhaps the foaming ale will clarify matters.'

The women had to stand aside to let him pass. He put out his hand and Jane, by now utterly bewildered, handed him the sheaf of proofs. He went away round the side of the cottage. I waited for Susie to return my gaze, but she wouldn't. We heard the front gate shut.

'Thing is, Martin,' Susie said, still not looking at me, 'you know what to say – you always know what ought to be said, and how to say it, and you know you ought to think it too, and perhaps you actually try to think it. But you don't know how to *do* what ought to be done, do you?' Only then did she meet my eye. 'Now you can piss off as well. Go on. Go after him. I'll see to Jane.' The two women turned and went back into the house and Susie closed the kitchen door behind them.

'Superstition' was playing on the jukebox. It always was, either that or 'Voodoo Chile'. In those days if you could find a jukebox with a couple of listenable tracks you were in luck. A group of older farmworkers stood in silence, drinking their mild in the brown gloom of the bar, while Shirley the barmaid sat in platinum-haired splendour on a stool by the hatch, reading a tattered copy of *Cosmopolitan* and smoking her long blue menthol cigarettes. At the dartboard four local lads played a game of cricket with bored intensity.

They took us for granted now. There'd nearly been trouble with them when we first started using the pub. Alex was so obviously instantly at home there that it stood to reason he must be asking for a good hiding. It wasn't the first time he'd provoked such a reaction among working-class boys who could imagine how this smart college cunt might look to their bored womenfolk; but luckily we'd been befriended by Gareth Pritchard, a local painter, and his younger brother Luke, an amiable layabout. Ten years older than the village malcontents, Gareth was apparently held to understand the ways of foreigners on the grounds of having gone to art school in Shrewsbury. Now we could play darts and bar billiards with impunity. What the girls thought was not recorded. They seemed to have little to say for themselves. They absorbed their crisps and lagers and occasionally exchanged nods and whispers. I could quite imagine finding the clientele in the same seats fifty years later, their lives resolutely unlived. That was the kind of ignorance I used to go in for.

'Yes, yes, yes,' Alex said. 'But can we change the subject? The woollybacks must be bored with it by now.'

'Stop talking so loudly,' I said. 'It's rude. It was wrong to include Jane's poem in the magazine.'

'Fuck, yes. Wrong.'

'You must see that.'

'I must, I must,' Alex said, tolerantly, spreading his arms in cartoon amazement. 'Everyone says I must. Here I am now, seeing it. What a fool and a Jasper I was.'

'It's not a joke, man. And you altered the poem too.'

'I quite see that. Believe me. Am I laughing?'

'Yes.'

'I can take a point when it's made to me in simple terms.'

'It was bloody arrogant. It was unkind.'

'Fair enough. But listen, man: was it cruel?'

'Why did you do it? Jane asked you that and you never answered.'

'It's a good poem. I exercised judgement. The Common Pursuit. Isn't that what we're supposed to be for? The Great Tradition and so forth. Scrutiny, man – that's what we're about. I should fuckin' coco.'

'I'm surprised you didn't just go ahead and *write* the fucking thing in its entirety as well. Or say you had.'

'Even I have my limits, probably.' He filled his mouth with cheese and onion crisps.

'And then there's the fact you did it without telling me.' This sounded mad and pompous. Alex spluttered crisp fragments into the ashtray. Shirley tutted behind the bar. It was hard not to laugh in the end. In any argument Alex kept moving the furniture around. He called it Taking the Opportunity the Language Provided. At the same time, he would never quite admit to agency, just as he could never be directly accused of doing anything as reprehensibly banal as walking down a street or entering a room.

'Let's have another,' he said. 'Let's have seven.'

'One more. Then I'll get back. I'll take the proofs.'

'Lend us a quid. You know she's a lesbian?'

'Who is?'

'Jane, of course. Who did you think I meant? I've had to save her from it. She doesn't know what she wants, or, more to the point, what's good for her. Thank God I'm prepared to make the sacrifice.' I left him playing darts and trying to charm the iron pants off Shirley.

There was no one in the kitchen at the cottage. Rather than take more fire from Susie, I sat down at the table and rolled a joint, then began reading the proofs. Alex was right, I thought, about Jane's poem. Not certain about the title, 'Visitation'. But the poem was strong. It was about the cottage, I inferred. There was night at the window, the movement of faces reflected in the dark glass, the door to the garden slightly ajar, and not much happening at all, just a convincing – and, once registered, rather clinging – sense of disquiet. It was not utterly original; it was the kind of thing many poets were attempting at the time, a form of minimal dramatic lyric, but Jane's handling of free verse that stayed discreetly in touch with the iambic was sure. And the central anxiety of the piece seemed anything but striven for, more like a visitation, which was of course the title. The disputed change involved the replacement of a colon with a full stop. I wondered if this was worth going to the stake for. The poem was certainly worth printing in the magazine. But: there was a but, though I couldn't name it.

'Where's Alex?' Jane had come up quietly beside me.

I resisted the temptation to scream and jump out of my skin. 'I left him in the pub. He was playing darts with the Pritchards. There's an afternoon lock-in.'

Jane smiled. 'Those boys. They're such innocents, aren't they?' she said, picking up the page containing her poem. It seemed an odd word to choose, though it was undeniably accurate. 'I like them, don't you?'

'They're decent blokes,' I said.

'They'd do anything for Alex,' she said.

'They'll have to join the queue.'

Jane shrugged, put the poem down and read it again. She didn't seem to be listening.

'He shouldn't have taken your poem without permission.'

'He can't help himself, can he?' she asked with a sad smile. 'He's the Lord of Misrule. It's not his fault.'

31

'Well, whose fault is it?' Again she shrugged. Then she put the page back in sequence and organized the proofs into a neat pile.

'It's a good poem,' I said. She looked at me without saying anything. 'I mean it. This one's a step forward.' It could be hard to compliment Jane: she rarely responded, and it always seemed as if you were the person being judged. It might be none of your business whether the poem was better than a previous one: she might have decided that you were in no position to know. The fact that there was no animus attached to these implied judgements served to magnify their authority. She knew what she was doing, and when there was time she might wait for you to catch up.

'That's all right then.' I was hoping for a smile but her expression didn't alter. She gave the proofs a final pat. 'Do you still think it really matters?' she asked. 'Poetry, I mean.' She continued to look at me steadily.

'Well, it's the thing I care most about. Always has been, since I began.'

'More than Susie?'

'Not the same thing.'

'No. I suppose.' After a moment, she added, 'I mean, it clearly doesn't matter. Hardly anyone cares about it.'

'More fool them.'

'What if they're right not to be bothered?'

'They're not right. They don't know enough to judge.' It was odd to be making this exasperated defence of a position I had assumed Jane would unshakeably occupy.

'In the end it might not matter at all, whatever any of

us prefers to suppose,' she said. 'In the meantime we'll still be here scrapping about a fucking colon. I do still think it needs to be a colon. Isn't it obvious? A colon. Never mind. No harm done.'

'Are you two all right – you and Alex?'

'All right? I suppose so. Why wouldn't we be? I mean, here we are, in the heart of the country, doing what we want to do.'

'What are you going to do about the poem?'

'Keep the colon.'

'No, I meant—'

'Well, he's got his heart set on using it.'

Not for the first time with Jane I had a sense of not being party to the conversation I was apparently involved in. It was as if the decrypted version were taking place in another room, nearby but not accessible.

'So you're going to let him get away with it.'

'You mean like you do? That's what he does, Martin. That must be why we love him, d'you not think? You're his human face for literary purposes. You do know that by now, I assume?'

'And what about you?'

'I'm what he wants to imagine. He's got no choice, has he, poor lad? He's smitten.'

I didn't follow this at all, but the words *He hates you* formed in my mouth. I offered her the joint but she shook her head.

'Now I'd better go and see if he's all right.' She pulled a denim jacket over her shoulders and went out. Much later, while I lay awake in the heat, I heard beery laughter as

Jane and Alex returned to the cottage. Everything was as normal, feet on the stairs, silence returning over the baking hills in the darkness. As I drifted off to sleep, I was thinking about how Thomas Exton made himself go walking by starlight in order to brave the demons. There were mutterings that he might be a sorcerer, but he was less interested in power than in confronting what he feared, in the hope that his torment could be ended by merciful oblivion: *I walk at Night to offer Invitation*, he wrote. *Meet me in the Dark and do thy will, only let it be Soon and let it end with a Forgetting.*

Believe it or not, there was a time within living memory when students in respectable numbers would attend poetry readings for pleasure. In Cambridge, the frowsty upstairs room at the Standing Pool, with its mouldering green flock wallpaper, velcro carpet and senile furniture, would often be packed on Wednesday evenings. Sometimes a published poet – Alan Brownjohn, David Harsent, Hugo Williams – would be supported by two or three drawn from the student body; at others it was all local talent, in particular Alex. After all, we were English students: this was supposed to be what we were interested in. Then as now the audience was predominantly female. And there was an atmosphere of mild rebellion against the faculty, which at that stage wasn't quite ready to confirm the existence of contemporary writing, preferring to see 1945 as the end of literary as well as military operations and professing never to have heard of 'Seamus O'Heaney'.

The stern Abbot Ale lent the proceedings at the Stand-

ing Pool a subdued Dionysiac edge, and at the end of the
evening an invited few would move on to the Indian
restaurant in Trumpington Street before concluding in
somebody's room with cheap red wine to guarantee the
kind of hangover that seemed to indicate this was the
literary life. The readings were run by a puppyish, enthu-
siastic bloke called Rory. Despised but essential, he did
all the correspondence and sorted out the cheques and
good-humouredly put up with Alex's sarcasm and Jane's
apparent failure to notice his existence. God knows what
would have happened if he hadn't taken the job on. Long
afterwards I heard he'd become a millionaire running a
mail-order clothing company.

Quite often on these evenings I sat with Jane at the
back of the room – the poet's girlfriend (Jane never read
there) and his loyal lieutenant – watching Alex deliver his
work. I say we watched, since he was at heart a performer
and the work a pretext for that. It was brash, aggres-
sive, entertaining and, I would now say, utterly empty of
the imaginative drive and sense of necessity to prove that
poetry is more than something you happen to be interested
in at the time. Not only is this true, it matters a great deal
to me that it should be so. Some people found his erotic
frankness exciting – plenty of organs, odours, tastes, scandalous declarations that sounded as though they had been
plucked from the pages of Verlaine and the freaks' agony
columnist Dr Hippocrates, but which were quite likely the
product of widespread sampling in the field.

I would be a hypocrite if I said I didn't admire and envy
his energy and confidence, but I was always waiting for

him to do the next, the real thing, to move on from the trailer to the main feature, and I'm pleased to say that, as it turned out, he never did. His party piece was not even a poem but a song, and the song was not even his own, but a classic from the dawn of rock and roll, Bo Diddley's 'Who Do You Love?', which Alex sang in a booming, studied bass.

It always went down well, though some of the visiting poets looked a bit startled by the idea of having to follow the graveyards and skulls.

In retrospect, it should have been obvious. Alex was marking time until success arrived, cutting out the middle-man of arduous labour. He professed a Restoration ruth-lessness and contempt for the order of things, wiping his cock on the curtains as he delivered his limiting judge-ments on the loved ones, or rather the bedded ones, who populated his verses. He was the poetic equivalent of the swaggering knob-rock of the day. He was, in fact, also the front man of an occasional band, the Rakes, who played not-bad-at-all Stones and J. Geils covers around the colleges – something a little harder-edged than the amiable pub-rock then in the ascendant.

For some reason I don't remember a word of his poetry, and you couldn't pay me to read it now. If he wasn't really a poet or a critic or even a musician, then what was he? I suppose you'd have to call him A Success, and in that sense perhaps he was someone born before his time. It wasn't a matter of what he would do, more whose attention he would attract. As a phenomenon he would be much more understandable now, not to mention commonplace.

On one of those nights we sat at a table towards the back and I realized at some point that I had tuned out and that Jane was looking at me. She placed her hand over mine. 'Don't worry,' she said. 'It'll all be all right.'

'Do I look worried?'

'Even more than usual. But you're not going mad.'

'You would tell me?'

'After I'd rung for the van.'

There was a burst of amusement around us at one of Alex's lines.

'You know he's unfaithful,' I said.

She shrugged and sipped her vodka. 'Why are you telling me this?'

'I don't want you to be hurt.'

'No, of course you don't. Well, perhaps I do. I wonder. Have you thought of that?'

'I don't understand.'

'No, you don't. Of course I know. And I don't know,' she said. She patted my hand, removed hers and went on watching the stage, once more absorbed in Alex's routine. They cannot be equals, I thought – one of them must fail – and filed it away as though it were a matter to be revisited and dealt with decisively at some later point when I had acquired a massive confidence in the field, whatever the field in fact was. The student press rated Alex as a face, a coming man. Somehow the fact he chose to involve himself in poetry didn't count against him. If they mentioned Jane it was as Alex's girl from Newnham. It would have been easier that way. Jane made no comment on this; as usual, whatever didn't interest her might as well not have existed.

What bothered me more at the time was that Jane never made any reference one way or the other to my writing. I had been brought up to wait to be acknowledged or asked, never to draw attention to anything I might be achieving. It had worked so far, to an extent, but it was frustratingly slow, and I was starting to learn that most of the people I was meeting had a rather less highly developed tendency to shrink from attention while simultaneously impaled by the longing for it. With Jane I saw no prospect of acknowledgement. She claimed my attention but the reverse was apparently not the case, and something in me recognized that this was a truthful if not an encouraging reflection of the status quo.

I rarely read at the Standing Pool – I told myself I wrote for the page, so that lonely neglect was a virtue, albeit rather inedible. Susie never went to the readings, preferring to work on those evenings. Her absence didn't matter.

4

I'm far clearer about when I first met Jane than I am about Alex. It was the spring of the first year, a bright gusty day. The outer door to the staircase was ajar to dispel the smoke. Alex was at the library. I was sitting at my desk at the window trying to finish an essay on Lawrence. It seemed as if it was all Lawrence then, him and his suave loins of darkness and his dodgy sexual politics. Anyway. For some reason I was writing about *Women in Love*, and had made a deal with myself not to smoke a joint before two o'clock. It was eleven thirty and I was struggling.

Look at the view, I told myself, *the gardens, the river. You don't want to lose this room like Cobb did.* Cobb was the original second occupant. He had retired hurt at the end of the autumn term, and was rumoured to be in a monastic retreat on the Lincolnshire coast, growing cabbages in the hope of becoming one. *Too much acid*, Alex had said. *Anyway, the place is yours if you want it.* So I had swapped my cell with its view of the tutor's garden wall for the impressively spacious, light, well-furnished surroundings where Cobb had lost his way. The view was great and my work suffered because Alex was never short of dope and I had no willpower. He, on the other hand, seemed to thrive on unsleeping indulgence.

I stood up to go and boil a kettle for coffee. There was a faint knock at the door. This was Jane. She seemed tiny. She wore a green duffel coat that somehow made her look like a sixth-former. Her cloud of red hair was Pre-Raphaelite. I had the odd feeling that I was being examined as if I were an interesting animal rather than the person I claimed to be.

'I'm looking for Alex Farren,' she said.

'I'm afraid he's out.'

'Oh. He said to come now.'

Here we paused for a few seconds.

'I'm not sure how long he'll be.'

She nodded.

'Would you like to leave a note?'

'A note.' As though this were some scarcely familiar novelty, the habit of a remote Aboriginal culture.

'Or I suppose you could come in and see if he turns up.'

'Yes, all right,' she conceded. I showed her to the settee, where she sat leaning forward with her hands crossed on her knees, a bulging shoulder-bag beside her. I made coffee and hoped I could leave her to it, but her very quietness made it impossible to concentrate. After a few minutes I gave up and turned my chair round. She had been watching me. The coffee was undrunk on the table beside her.

'So you're a friend of Alex's?' I asked.

'He was going to lend me a book. We were talking after a lecture.'

'Perhaps I can help. What was the title?'

'*Life Studies.*'

Lowell's most famous collection could easily have been found in the faculty library. So this was an assignation. Alex would be clear about that but would – I realized that, as usual, I'd failed to ask someone's name – the girl? 'Sorry. I didn't ask who you were.'

'My name is Jane Jarmain.' This was like a formal announcement. She plucked at a thread on the knee of her green tights.

'The poet.'

She looked at me carefully. 'You know that, do you? What's your name?'

I told her. She didn't seem to recognize it, although I'd appeared in one or two of the same publications.

'I've read some of your work,' I said. 'A little. In magazines. Interesting.'

She resisted the further opportunity to return the compliment. 'I'm going to disown it.'

'That's a bit drastic.'

'Is it? There's no point in not being serious, is there?' Seriousness was a near-sacramental term in those days. But you could tell Jane meant it.

'So are you – is your work developing?'

'I hope so.' She looked at her watch. 'Do you think Alex will be back soon?'

'As I said, I really don't know.'

'Perhaps I should take the book and go.'

'That wouldn't be a good idea.'

'I didn't realize it would be so complicated. I should have made a proper arrangement.'

'Perhaps. But Alex can be a bit erratic anyway.'

She lingered. I was at a loss.

'Well, have you got a copy of the book?' she asked patiently. In anyone else this would have been cheeky.

'Yes.'

'Well, then.'

'I thought you wanted to see Alex.'

'If you put your name in the book I'll know who to return it to.' She had spotted the paperback on my desk. She rose and came towards me. Given the excruciating course of the conversation so far, I could hardly refuse.

'I would like it back, though,' I said, and immediately felt like a toad.

'I'm very honourable.' She smiled for the first time. She picked up the book and opened it at the title page, then handed it to me to sign. Her perfume was faint, springlike, fatal. By this stage I wondered if I would be permitted to remain in my room or if she would require its exclusive use. She would get no argument from me.

She studied my pedantic signature, then looked at me again in that objective, slightly eerie way. 'Martin. You can take me for a drink if you like,' she said. Even at that date, this was an old-fashioned thing for a girl to say. I might add that she never returned the book, and that I ended up buying another copy.

I left Alex a note and walked Jane to the Standing Pool, on the other side of the millpond. In those days the pub still had its own small mooring, with a few ancient boats yielding slowly to the claims of the ooze. Though it was cool and damp we took chairs on the jetty and sat looking out across the fen towards the causeway beyond the clusters of willows. There was always something out of reach and heartbreaking about Cambridge.

'Tell me about Alex,' Jane said, and waited. My erection shrank away. She sipped a vodka and tonic.

'What sort of thing would you like to know?'

'Describe his nature.'

'Eh? Well, he's very bright.'

'Bright?'

'A quick study. Incisive.'

'And a poet.'

'Er, yes.'

She nodded expectantly. 'And as a man?'

I had not thought of Alex as a man, or that a girl would ask such a question, but I supposed he must be, now that Jane had done so. What could I actually say with authority? Nothing, it turned out.

'I suppose you could say he's a bit of a lad.' Was this disloyalty or the word of a pander? Jane sipped her drink and said nothing. I felt I must preserve us from the waiting silence. 'You know, a bit of a ladies' man,' I went on, thinking I was tailoring my vocabulary to hers.

'You mean he fucks a lot of women.'

I was worried I might blush. 'I don't know if I'd put it like that. He's certainly *fond* of women.' A lie, I thought, the first. 'They seem to like him too. They seem to like a bit of a villain.'

'Do they?'

'Or perhaps you don't.'

'Is he talented?'

'I think so. He's very ambitious.' Another qualification there. I realized I was already worried about Jane.

'He seeks fame, then.'

'He wouldn't turn it away.'

'And what about you?' *Do I fuck a lot of women? Not so's you'd notice. But, oh, God, I want to fuck you and now I'm going to have to spend the rest of my life not doing so.* 'What do you want?'

'I want to write good poems.'

'I didn't know you were writing as well. The place is crawling with poets, isn't it?'

'Infested,' said Alex, coming down the steps with a tray on which stood a vodka and a pint of Guinness. 'Vermin. In need of stamping out. That's the plan, anyway, Jane.'

A minute or two later Alex was in my chair and I was setting off back across the fen to my unfinished essay and the first joint of the day. I had swelled the scene as required. The eternal footman was bricking himself laughing. I had some harsh things to say about Hermione that afternoon. But in Alex's absence I got the essay finished. It was three days before he reappeared, with Jane, slightly dazed, at his side. In the interim she had become terribly sexy, I noticed.

5

It was hot from the moment I awoke the morning after the episode with the proofs, and it quickly grew hotter. The sky was a curdled white but it held no rain.

'The point is to intervene at the correct moment. Anticipate and intervene. Shape the tendency of literature for years to come.'

'Can you be quiet, Alex? I've got a headache,' I said, crushing a teabag against the side of my mug.

'Pound could always see the future of poetry taking shape.'

'Pound was a Fascist cunt. There's nothing further to be said about him.'

'Nevertheless.'

'Bollocks.' I went outside and sat in the early shade of the tall beech hedge. Summer Hill seemed steeper and more sharply defined than usual, like a stage flat positioned just behind the hopfield.

Alex was not to be prevented. He followed me and continued, skinning up on the table as he spoke. 'No Pound? In that case no Eliot either. Literature needs prophetic entrepreneurs.'

'Like you and Pound, right? You're not going to smoke that now, are you? It's too early, man.'

'Nonsense. Amid the dews of morning – what better time?'

'All we ever do in this bloody place, apart from getting stoned, is fucking talk. Especially you. Please, man, shut up. Or I think I shall have to go back to bed.'

He shook his head as he exhaled.

'How can you think of lying there fingering yourself in the humid murk of your pit on such a morning? It's disgusting.'

I took the joint and inhaled. Things settled back into their accustomed focus. The hangover looked away for a little while. But it felt as if the day was lost already and nothing would be accomplished. I let the smoke obscure the little knot of fear in my chest. Moon House, owned by the university and home of the Exton Archive, was a ten-minute stroll away, but the distance seemed continental.

'How's Jane?' I asked.

'It's all right.'

'Did she tell you that?'

'I think she knows she can trust my powers of anticipation.'

'That must be very reassuring for all concerned.'

Alex drew on the joint and squinted at me through the smoke. 'No need to worry, Martin. It's all in hand. As the actress said to the bishop.'

Susie came out with a stack of post that she put on the table between us. She did not meet my gaze. I followed her round the end of the house to where the 2CV was parked.

'You're still pissed off at me,' I said.

She opened the door and got in.

'Susie, don't just go.'

'Yes, Martin,' she said, finally turning to look at me. 'I love you. Yes, I am still angry, but mainly with Alex. And I'm also very worried.'

'About what?'

'I'll tell you when I work it out.' She looked away again and turned the key in the ignition. 'See you tonight. Your turn to cook, by the way.' The idea of preparing food seemed impossibly wearisome.

Back in the garden Alex had separated the post into two piles. In one there were a dozen letters to the magazine, in the other a brown A4 envelope that I could see bore the *TLS* frank. It was addressed to Jane. He was staring fixedly at it.

'What do you suppose that is?' he said, and held it out to me.

'Something for Jane.'

'Something for Jane. A postal item for our Janey.' Now he sniffed it.

'Leave it alone. Let Jane deal with it.'

'It might be a letter bomb. You hear about them.'

'We're not a government agency. Nobody wants to bomb us. Put it down. Or let me take it to her. You mustn't open it. Or even think of opening it.'

'Clearly I mustn't.' He'd put the envelope down again but he couldn't leave it alone. He moved it about, aligning it with a corner of the table. 'No, precious, we mustn't. Unless—'

'Shall I?' I said, picking it up. 'Just take it to her?'

'Go on, then.' He made a large, despairing gesture and turned on his heel. 'Get it out my sight, Martin.'

I went inside, up the stairs and knocked on the bedroom door. Jane opened it wearing only a T-shirt and knickers. 'Sorry. This came for you.' I handed her the envelope.

'I know,' she said. 'I heard you talking in the garden.' She put it on the dressing-table. 'Thanks, Martin. I'll be down in a minute. Let me get dressed.' Only now did I realize I had been expecting her to open it and reveal its contents to me. I went into the kitchen and sat at the table, rolling a cigarette. Sweat ran down my face.

Alex came in. He stood leaning with his back to the sink, nodding slowly, drawing on the last of the joint, then extinguishing it under the tap.

'Well, then,' he said. 'The long forenoon, eh?'

'I might go into the library,' I said. 'Since it's still early.' Occasionally, when I could raise the energy, I took the bus into town to do some uninterrupted reading. For some reason I never formulated this as: to get away from Alex's imperious anarchy, to avoid smoking dope all day, Moon House sometimes being too near as well as too far.

'You could refer to the extensive selection of newspapers, periodicals and journals of record,' said Alex.

'Right.'

'You could consult the range of supplements published by *The Times*.'

'I suppose so.'

'These include the *Times Educational Supplement*—'

'For fuck's sake, Alex.'

'The *Times Higher Educational Supplement*—'

'What's wrong with you?'

'What did she say?'

'Nothing. I gave her the envelope. That's all. She'd heard us talking. I dare say she can hear us now as well.'

'That makes it even worse.' He took a milk bottle from the draining-board and threw it against the wall. Mystifyingly, it didn't break but rattled its way down behind the rubbish bin. 'You see how I'm placed? Even the fucking dumb objects betray me!'

Jane appeared. Now she was wearing an emerald-coloured bikini with a batik skirt tied loosely at the waist. She smiled. 'Shall I make a cup of tea, Alex? D'you want one, Martin?'

'I was just thinking of going into town.'

'If you hang on I'll come with you.'

Dressed like that? I wanted to say. *They'll probably burn you at the stake outside the Assembly Rooms.*

'I'm off sort of immediately.'

'Okay,' she said equably, discarding the idea.

'What about me?' said Alex.

'I imagine you're busy,' said Jane, moving him away from the sink while she filled the kettle.

'Then you've got a very powerful imagination,' he said.

'Well, what *are* you doing?'

'Me? I'm fucking waiting.'

'Don't let me stop you.'

'Thanks.'

Sean O'Brien

'So do you want tea?'

'No,' said Alex, in a small voice. 'I don't want any fucking bastard cunting tea just now.'

I seized the moment to leave. I should have gone up to Moon House, but instead I ran for the bus. Half an hour later I sat down in the brown ecclesiastical murk of the university library in Divott among other semi-derelicts of all ages and began to examine the latest edition of the *TLS*.

There it was, 'Visitation' by Jane Jarmain, looking as if it belonged perfectly with the other poems in that issue, which I remember – still – were by Fleur Adcock and Peter Porter. I felt a strong vicarious excitement, a sort of referred pride, at Jane's accomplishment of this rite of passage. Young poets would give a lot to get a poem in the *TLS*. Now Jane had beaten the pair of us to it. How did that feel? Not so bad, it seemed. Jealousy was apparently not in the offing. I reread the poem, trying to identify the source of the unease it gave off. Hard to say. At least, I supposed, this was the poem as Jane wanted it to be read. Perhaps it was the sense that a problem – a threat, a sorrow – had been anticipated and that the anticipation had been proved correct. I took out my Exton notes and stared at them. Then it was lunchtime. I should look in at the Green Man, the preferred habitat of Professor Gwyther, scholar of the Metaphysical poets. It was he who justified my presence at the Marches.

As for Alex, I had no powers of prophecy. It was impossible to assess the scale or nature of his response to the publication of Jane's poem. I have often wondered since why I didn't simply leave the cottage, move nearer

the university and do some work. Moon House and its
Exton holdings were one obvious reason, but access would
not have been difficult from Divott. I think it was partly
an instinctive unwillingness to abandon Jane – that would
also have been Susie's priority. At the same time, to remain
at May Cottage also indicated a refusal, which I think was
characteristic not only of me but of the times themselves –
a refusal, that is, to recognize that what was taking place
was real and not a creaky kind of entertainment mounted
to distract us from our already distracted state. Domestic
strife? Vulgar but not uninteresting. Madness? We'd read
about it, or even observed it at one remove in the case of
Cobb. We'd also contrived some brief excursions to its
vicinity, of a kind obligatory in the period.

6

Much of my living, it seems, has been done through the life and work of a madman from three centuries before.

I had discovered that on my mother's side I was indirectly related to Exton, who never married. I felt a kind of proprietorial pride in this neglected figure. Like other, more eminent, Metaphysical poets – George Herbert, Thomas Traherne, Henry Vaughan – he'd gone into the west, but neither tranquillity nor grace awaited him there among the hills and hopfields and the little churches with the carvings of the Green Man and Shelagh na Gig. Over the years in Divott there grew on him the sense that he was irredeemably damned. His journals recorded an intensifying sense of torment, accompanied by terrifying visions, from which he went on to make the poems on which his reputation, such as it was, rested, the 'Hymn to God in My Affliction' and 'The Soul Cast Out'. Exton, as far as could be discovered, had died obscurely, perhaps violently, perhaps by his own hand, though he was not refused a Christian burial. While English poetry is rich in lunatics, not until William Cowper, writing almost a century later, do we encounter a comparable sense of inescapable perdition, when Cowper writes, 'I, fed with judgements, in a fleshly tomb, am/Buried above ground.' Exton would have understood. He had been buried in a cradle tomb in St Bartholomew's churchyard in Divott.

Whenever I had been seeing Professor Gwyther I would detour to visit the gravesite. I still go there quite often. The pale stone casket is raised on four clawed feet above a conventional rectangular tomb. It looks oddly like a deep Victorian bath, but it also reminds me of the tombs in the graveyard in the city of Dis in *Inferno* Canto X, from which the imperious Farinata rises to converse with his tribal enemy, Dante. He is succeeded, with terrible poignancy, by the beseeching Cavalcanti, who mistakenly assumes that his son must, like himself, be dead. This is a heavy burden of comparison for an (as yet) uncelebrated tomb in rural England to bear, but to my eye the candour of the stone invites it. And who is to know what I think, or to prevent me thinking it?

Perhaps strangely, since he offered little to comfort or console, I first turned to Exton during what I thought of as my recovery – the period post-acid and post-arrival of Susie. It was only by exerting a force of will I didn't know I possessed that I was able to stir myself from the sweetly narcotic consolation of Susie's bed and do something about my work. I would walk to the university library at nine a.m. and spend the day there reading with mechanical ferocity. One afternoon, I encountered Exton's work by accident, appropriately enough. Like his contemporary Andrew Marvell, he had attracted the interest of scholars assembling evidence for the canon in the dawn of academic English studies, but he hadn't received the crucial benefit of an essay by T. S. Eliot, and his work remained in a state of critical limbo. It was there, it was known about in a general sense, but few people bothered to visit. The big anthologies were happy to omit him. Although he lived and wrote before poetry was widely disseminated, perhaps Exton hoped for better, though he entertained few hopes for himself. In 'The Soul Cast Out', he wrote:

> This illness I must propagate
> To let all know my fallen state.

In my own 'fallen' and frequently paranoid condition, this seemed a very modern way of regarding the matter. The work itself was not, as often among his contemporaries, an affirmation of grace, but was *in itself* evidence of damnation. It was clearly compulsory for its author to write it but it offered him no way back through the gate by which he felt himself expelled from God's love. This would have made sense to Baudelaire, and thus to Eliot – which made it the odder that Eliot never even went so far as to mention Exton in his essays.

Something bit and held: I would be spending time in Exton's company. My interest proved permanent. I had found something that could be mine. Just after Christmas in my final year at Cambridge I met my director of studies to discuss possibilities for research.

'You should get as far away from this place as possible,' he said. 'From what I understand – and I'm not enquiring and you're not to tell me – you've done well to survive, but it's clearly done you no good at all. If you must continue your studies, for God's sake do so somewhere else. I'll write you an irresistible reference, alluding to your passion and your beguiling eccentricity, inventing the latter if necessary. I'll even mention your poetry if you insist.'

'Thanks very much.' I sipped his vile sherry. Through the window I saw two workmen replacing a window in the chapel, somewhere that in three years I had not entered once. The Master, a small silvery theologian several thousand years old, was out taking the air. He stood and watched, apparently offering advice with the aid of his stick.

'Think nothing of it. So what in fact are you thinking of doing?'

I'd like to go out and come in again with a more constructive attitude, I thought. I'd like to join the ADC and the Labour Club and go on freezing walks to Coton and not be stoned all the time and not have this accumulation of regret, and not be so fucking sentimental. I'd also like to lay hands on one or two of the legendary nurses before I die. I still probably wouldn't manage to visit the chapel.

'Well,' I said, 'as you know, I've become very interested in Thomas Exton.' A look of immense weariness passed over the face of the director of studies. It was part of the birthright of members of the English faculty, but he gave his features an extra squeeze to indicate that this time he really meant it. He had listened impassively on more than one occasion as I'd tried to formulate a view of this irredeemably minor poet.

'Are you sure, Martin?'

'Well, yes. I think I am.'

'I mean, look – Exton? Is there more than a fortnight in him?'

'Certainly. I would think so. That is, I hope so.'

'Well. It's your funeral.' He poured himself another glass. I declined a refill. 'I suppose you *might* get back in here.' We looked at each other for a bit. 'But not with Exton.'

Over his shoulder I could see the Master closing the door of the lodge behind him. The director of studies sipped his sherry and grimaced.

'Very well. If you must. As it happens, an old friend of mine teaches at this new place – God damn me, what the hell is it called? The Gallops? The Marches. He mentions in his most recent letter that they've acquired Exton's papers as a result of absorbing the old theological college into the new institution.'

'I had heard about this, in fact.'

'Yes? He seems to feel this constitutes a coup. A curious piece of fortune, he calls it. One might almost think this was a sign, except that there is, of course, no such thing. Anyway, Martin, off you go, and the best of luck.' He had no expectations of me. He thought I had already wasted my chances. I didn't blame him.

Yet there did seem to be work worth doing at the Marches. Whether I was the person to do it was, as you will appreciate, far from certain, not least to me. The director of studies's old friend, Professor Daniel Gwyther, with his wild halo of silver hair, his explosive purple face and his musty corduroy suits, preferred to conduct tutorials in the pub, leaving his secretary to run the department, what was there was of it so far, seven years after the place had opened. As he took his lunch of cheese and onion crisps and Wem bitter, the Professor declared himself confident: 'The field is quite open still – though you should make the acquaintance of a fellow investigator, Miss Elliot, formerly of Chicago, who should be with us soon, lodging up at Moon House. You will have made your own living arrangements, of course. Miss Elliot, who is here as a post-doctoral fellow, is going to catalogue the Exton holdings and will be nominally in charge of the archive during her stay, which we expect will be most fruitful. Miss Elliot too will be looking into some of the theological aspects of Exton's work.'

What other aspects were there, I wondered. Was I already redundant? Gwyther glinted at me, the sun falling on his rimless spectacles and sunburnt Longfordian head. 'You will see your way in time, I am sure, Mr Stone, um, Martin, and discover the true contribution you have to offer.' He gestured with his suddenly emptied pint glass. 'Now I think we could do with another of these.'

See my way? Would I? In plenty of time? Just in time? Gwyther, on the other hand, could barely see his hand in front of his face by afternoon closing, and was habitually assisted, by me or Sal, the affectionate, motherly barmaid, into a pre-booked taxi that delivered him to a vast Victorian mansion in the hills, there to recuperate and prepare for the next session in the Green Man. Professor Gwyther was one of the happiest people I have ever met, camping out in three rooms there in connubial bliss with his teetotal wife Lettice, a collector of wild flowers and medicinal herbs. There were worse ways to live, among them the one indulged at May Cottage. As often before and since, I felt ashamed in the presence of someone I liked and admired and whose good opinion I sought.

Exton had lived in a wooden house destroyed by fire, adjacent to St Jude's, the village church in Summer Street, but the climate of the archive at Moon House seemed to me indisputably his – a kind of cool, patient, inured apprehension, always on the edge of becoming fear. Perhaps I brought some of that with me. Perhaps places retain nothing of what passes through them, and the climate is wholly ours. Either way I didn't much like the archive – a long, low, dark-panelled room with narrow, oddly high windows looking out to the rear of the house through giant laurel bushes. One wall was entirely taken up with lockable cupboards holding the material. An empty fireplace occupied the opposite wall, and much of the remaining space was filled by a massive Jacobean table with black oilcloth laid across its surface. This was it: the mind's home for the foreseeable future.

Over the fireplace the most prominent item was displayed: the only known portrait of Exton, by Uys van Houten, speculatively dated 1670. Among the notables of the late Renaissance, Bacon looks as though in mid-plot, Milton addresses the greater picture and Donne is about to burst into action, but the bit-player Exton's clerical black half consumes him, and he seems to have forgotten that he's even sitting for a portrait. His melancholy gaze meets the viewer's eye but is none the less directed elsewhere, at something he has seen or is shortly going to see, as though accepting the grim inevitable. I didn't like the picture one bit, but it was hard to look away. Perhaps it was fanciful to suppose that van Houten had managed to represent a sinner turned ascetic, but it seemed that way to me. It also felt as though Exton knew his conversion had come too late – or perhaps as if he knew it had always been too late to mend his ways. Probably fanciful, as I say, but that word doesn't answer to the conviction I felt, however mistakenly.

If I had allowed my initial disquiet at the room to gain the upper hand, I might never have returned to Moon House. But I realized that if I actually stopped work altogether, even 'temporarily', I would be lost. So a couple of times a week I made myself unlock the room and the shelves and familiarize myself with Exton's literary remains. Yet the more I read his poems and the half-dozen large volumes of his journals, the less I knew what I wanted from the research. My provisional title was 'Exile of the Spirit: the "life retir'd" in the Poems of Thomas Exton'. All I was doing was immersing myself in his writing, without developing a particular perspective or strategy. In those days it was still just about possible to imagine poems in themselves and not as proxies of some other, allegedly more compelling and certainly more insistent, discourse in politics or theology or philosophy. There were grounds for undertaking a new edition of the poems, in the light of scholarship since Fenwick's late-Victorian labours in the field, but my mouth and the floor of my skull went dry whenever I even started to think about this. If I wanted to be a critic, did I have to be a scholar? Probably. And rather than either of those things wouldn't I prefer to be a poet plain and simple? Yes, but I might never be good enough and I could never expect to make a living at it. But Gwyther said I would find my way. And he was Gwyther, friend of my omniscient director of studies, so he must be right, surely. Yet Exton too had been certain of the truth of things, to quite another effect.

> Within the Stygian mines of doubt
> Mine is the soule, I fear, cast out.

You and me both, pal, I thought, turning this couplet over like worry beads in my head as I went back through the pages of his poems, looking for a way in. Fenwick had imported punctuation in some places 'as an aid to sense' – but suppose the second line of the couplet had been written without the parenthetic commas, that is: *Mine is the soule I fear cast out.* The emphasis would be altered. Rather than fearing that the soul *would be* cast out, the already outcast soul itself might become an object of fear, perhaps because of a new allegiance established with Satan and the powers under the earth. By this reading the soul is lost but by no means powerless. It appears to retain a degree of agency. But who would experience the fear? The individual whose soul was lost, enduring such a state through a form of spiritual derangement?

To someone uninterested in poetry (but how do such people manage to live from one day to the next?) it might seem strange or absurd to think that an entire afternoon can be passed in considerations of this kind, still more so that the curious reader will happily come back the next day and the next week and month without ever expecting (and very likely without wishing for) the matter to be resolved. God, or the devil, is in the detail, as that little couplet also suggests. But I suppose criticism can be as much a given as poetry: you do it because it's what you do.

Naturally I also investigated the reference collection in the basement, to which I took an immediate dislike. Reference collection? It was nothing of the sort. It was a literary dump, a place where books came to die and be interred, a mass grave, a war grave for the poor bloody infantry of the word. It contained a good deal of withered sermonizing and a substantial collection of bad nineteenth-century poetry beginning with Mrs Hemans and then plumbing the uttermost depths of unreadability – the kind of once-popular work that thirty years ago still occupied entire walls in second-hand bookshops. This virtually unsaleable material seems largely to have vanished for pulping nowadays. I miss it. I collect odds and ends when I come across them in dank anachronistic little premises in mid-Wales or the more neglected counties of the English Midlands. I like to smell the gutters of the books, the lifeless epics, the musings-in-a-library of dim critics, the vast three-decker novels gone like imperious cities under the deserts left in the wake of averted taste. I do this to register in imagination (one tribute for which failure may hope) the optimism in which their authors must have set out, and the awful soul-parching disappointment that the fate of their labours suggests; I like to think myself part at least of a tradition, be it never so despised and neglected. I suppose that is what Dieter was on about – but Dieter has yet to arrive in this story.

If my visit to the reference collection was as irrelevant as its contents, it was, none the less, a way of avoiding the most pressing matter: Exton's journals. His poems fascinated and haunted me, but his journals caused me an unease for which I could not properly account. These were the journals of a dead man, written almost three centuries before. He was a relative in name only. His beliefs were very different from mine, which is to say I didn't have any worth the name. What was there to worry about? What did we have in common? It was the fear of what he called damnation and I knew as madness. His terror drew me even as I wanted to turn away from it.

I had forgotten about the American scholar. The extent of my difficulties with Exton became the more apparent the day I turned up and found the archive already unlocked. I put my head tentatively round the door.

'Yes, can I help you?' said a female voice with an American accent. I stepped inside. A young fair-haired woman with a pale, determined face and heavy spectacles was approaching from the direction of the cupboards, unmistakably placing herself between me and the table.

'I was just looking for something,' I said.

'You might want to ask at the department in Divott. This room is occupied.'

'All of it?'

'Was there something specific? It's a little busy at the moment.' She glanced back at the table, much of which was covered with files and papers. But that was the problem: I had nothing specific in mind. I was just wandering in to read a bit more Extoniana.

'Never mind,' I said. I retreated towards the door.

She followed me. 'Right. You'll need authorization.'

'I'll come back.'

I raised a hand in farewell, but she had already closed the door. I had authorization, of course I did, but clearly I could never be as authorized as her. She had probably done courses in applied seriousness for extra credit. Why hadn't I made the position clear? I asked myself. Because I didn't think I deserved to be there, myself replied. This was Miss Elliot, from Chicago, and she was evidently the intended only possessor of Thomas Exton.

7

When I returned from Divott to the cottage at the end of the afternoon following the *TLS* incident nobody was in. There was a note from Jane on the table, held down with a milk bottle: *Dear All. Gone to visit my sister. Back soon. Love J xx.* I didn't know she had a sister. I did know there'd be trouble.

Alex didn't reappear at suppertime. Susie and I sat and ate a tired salad in not-quite-companionable silence. She was reading. I poured a glass of cider and she refused.

'Did you know Jane had a sister?' I asked, after a while.

'Yes, of course.'

'She's never mentioned it to me.' Susie shrugged. 'Have you met her?'

'No. I know they're twins and that Jessica lives in Aberystwyth. She's married to a clergyman.'

'Fuck. She's very young.'

'Perhaps. He's quite lot older.'

'Sounds like Casaubon.'

'Anyway. Jane will have gone to see the new baby.'

'I see.'

'A girl, called Angharad.' Susie turned the page.

'I wonder where Alex's got to?'

'Go and find him. I want to finish reading this. Don't wake me up when you come in.'

Susie. Why do I come to her last? Susie had rescued me. Away from home for the first time, timid and unanchored, I had compensated with pleasures and gone too far out without really realizing – stoned all the time, speeding through essay nights and taking acid with blithe frequency, despite the now-vanished Cobb, and the ragged, raving example of the former mathematician, Blow-Your-Mind-Pete, on his daily wanderings through the marketplace. It was as if I was trying to get somewhere.

The place where, in due course, I arrived, a week or two after first meeting Jane, was at the foot of a staircase from which one door led into the quad and another into the college bar. I had come down the stairs in an exponentially growing panic. I had been with Alex, Jane and one or two others. I had taken acid, and as it came on I was examining an LP sleeve for irony and, in what I would later recognize as an earlyish English moment of deconstruction, had lost my way. Meaning cancelled itself and deserted the image on the sleeve. Clearly, in some ultimate sense, I was wrong. Time I was elsewhere, before I turned into *un autre*. I became very frightened and muttered something to the group, wandered out of the room and down towards the bar. Now I couldn't think what to do, so I simply stood there at the foot of the stairs, treading the heavy ginger doormat, with the sense that the thrust of speed underneath the acid would shortly blow the roof of my head off, after which I would be obliged finally to disintegrate and lose my grip on the alphabet. Last to go would be the letter I.

'Come with me, Martin,' said a female voice, it seemed with the authority of the divine. Susie took me by the arm. She had been upstairs in our room, I remembered. She was a friend of a friend. She was a kind person, a guide for the perplexed, a stay against confusion. Before I lost my place and ran out of the room, I had been trying to chat her up, in an interminable, sidelong, drug-encumbered way, and she had seemed to enjoy indulging my clumsiness. She didn't mind me. It was as if we were already acquainted. She was there because she was a schoolfriend of Jane's. They were catching up. Alex had not tried any of his moves on Susie, which was very unusual. They seemed to avoid each other instinctively.

She led me outside. The buildings were shuddering and continually outlining themselves in glistening black. I looked down at the cobbles. They gleamed with rain, and they were seething, in a polite, impersonal way. Richard Nixon walked past, looking preoccupied.

'Oh, God,' I said. 'Where are we going?'

'Through here. It'll be fine,' said Susie, squeezing my hand. Now we seemed to be in the deer park, slipping between the immense green fires of the bushes. There was a gap while I thought about this, and next we were on the fen, which had grown immense and somehow central European.

'Are we there yet?' I asked.

'Not long now.' Susie led me over the footbridges and eventually, after I had studied the swans at some length, we went down to the jetty at the Standing Pool, where a couple of metal chairs stood out in all weather.

'Sit tight,' she said.

'Don't leave me.'

'I'm just going to the bar. You'll be better off out here for now. I'll only be a minute.'

When she'd gone I stared down at the pool full of last year's leaves. The problem, I could see, was not that I imposed meaning on phenomena, but that they were doing it to me. I could be such a leaf, a black tongue reclining on a bed of its brothers under the cold skin of the pool. I could be a howling prick as well. I was versatile, clearly. A cloud crossed the sun and erased the depth from the water.

Susie returned with a tray on which were several glasses of orange juice and a pile of individual packets of sugar.

'Drink all this. Then you can have a beer.'

'What do you think about all these leaves?

'I tend not to.'

I drank each orange juice greedily while Susie stirred sugar into the next. Very gradually, the horror diminished a little. She reassured me that the back of my head had not fallen off, and that it was not necessary for her to look again to establish that this was so. She advised me not to ring for a taxi to take me to Fulbourn Hospital on the grounds that they would be unlikely to let me out again when eventually I came down, met some of the actual madmen and changed my mind about being incurably deranged. When I finished the orange juice she encouraged me to drink several pints of beer. The world stopped stretching and bending. She spoke as if we knew each other well, as if this conversation was the natural outcome of many others, no more remarkable and no less enjoyable than normal.

Susie had come up from London for the weekend to collect some drawings. She took me back to her mother's little house in Newnham. Her mother wasn't there, as it happened, and we climbed into Susie's single bed and didn't get up for two days. I have never known exactly why she did any of this for me. Perhaps she thought that if I recovered from my damaged state I would be a more substantial creature than I ever turned out to be.

When I woke up, having weathered the comedown, I found that we were a couple, and I had a bulwark against self-destructive indolence. I got to work. There were anxiety attacks and fits of depression, but because of her I got by. I waited for the weekends we could spend together. I refined my selfishness to another level and pretended not to think of Jane. Exton, I was to discover, had travelled over this ground, too: *In Flesh and Heart I seem all Division, and if I ask, Why must this be a Torment? I must answer, It is Time that does this Work.*

Alex was seated at a table on the grass behind the pub, looking up at Summer Hill through the trees. It was still very hot and full daylight, though in that black-edged way of an English summer evening. The moon had risen.

He held out his empty glass. 'Gone to her sister's in Aber,' he said. 'Catch up with family news, see the new baby and so on. There's normal, wouldn't you say? Mine will be a pint of Tapeworm.'

When I came back with the drinks, I asked, 'Have you had a row?'

'We have not. We are adults. We are autonomous. We may fuck off to Aber if we wish, or we may stay here drinking Tapeworm or do any of a number of things, such as, for example, should I so choose, stick my knob in the mangle and turn the fucking handle, isn't it.'

'She'll be back. It'll be all right.'

'Of course. Of course. *Reculer pour mieux sauter.*'

'You must admit she played it pretty cool about the poem. Sending it out like that.'

He nodded admiringly. 'Plato's fridge, man. Fucking Electrolux. I have to hand it to her.'

'And, anyway, you were in the wrong.'

'I was, clearly, as you are kind enough to point out, not to say emphasize.'

'So don't save it up. Don't keep tending the rage.'

'I am reconciled to the situation. Jane has made me look a cunt. That's all.'

'Doesn't matter. Anyway, nobody knows. Except me and Susie, which doesn't count.'

'If there is a problem, and I'm not going so far as to say there is a problem, then the problem is that *I* know, Martin.'

We heard laughter. The Pritchard brothers and two women came out of the pub, busily talking. They headed for a table nearby. Luke was already well gone, staggering a little as he swung his platform-soled boot over the bench of the table, his rooster cockscomb emphasizing his wobbliness, while Gareth, as ever wearing his long brown leather overcoat, stood back in his gentlemanly way to let their companions sit down first.

The Pritchards were a melancholy pair, like many in the Marches. They had, you sensed, resigned their futures before beginning them. Better that than disappointment or rejection. Luke longed to escape into the deafening heavy-metal fleshpots of Birmingham, as he imagined them to be, but he never would; Gareth worked obsessively on his pictures but never dared hope to be taken seriously. The thought of them twenty years hence made me frightened, though we seemed to have little in common. Many things frightened me in those days.

Luke noticed us and called, 'These are Americans!' He was excited, as though encountering royalty. The women turned to look in our direction. One of them was the pre-emptive occupant of the archive. The other had a camera.

Gareth, still standing, considered and decided. 'You could maybe join us, then.'

'It would be discourteous to think of doing otherwise in the presence of ladies,' said Alex, standing up. He was immediately sober and alert. I had seen him do this before, shedding the weight of dope and booze, scenting the tang of possibility in the evening air.

'Behave yourself,' I said quietly.

'Behaving is what I do.'

'Hiya, boys,' said the dark one with the camera. 'It's a party, Marcie.' The blonde one seemed a little worried. She nodded quickly at me and looked away.

Diane, the dark one, the New Yorker with the tan and the teeth and the tits and the cascading black ringlets and the camera, was Diane Eckhart. She reminded me of a flamethrower on idle. She was over visiting her 'college friend' Marcie, the (as I now saw) nervous blonde one from Chicago, to whom this information was evidently news.

Marcie Elliot was delicately almost-pretty, with flyaway blonde hair and an air of impending retirement from conversation and company. She was staying, as Gwyther had told me, in the accommodation the university kept for overseas scholars at Moon House. Even from here we could glimpse the vast, grotesque but appealingly dank Jacobean-Regency-Victorian pile, through the trees on the upper slopes of Summer Hill.

Marcie and I were rivals. She was already a march ahead. I bet she'd found *her* way: a glance would show you someone rational, sensible, conscientious, quietly determined, implacably ambitious in an unimpeachably decent manner. I wanted to hate her, but it was hard, since she was so clearly the virtuous underdog.

Marcie was Diane's UK bridgehead. As to what Diane herself did, she was a film-maker, journalist maybe, a precocious (as a steel bar is precocious) contributor to *Ramparts* and *Mother Jones* (we nodded, having heard of but read neither) and something called *Outsider Movie* (which drew a complete blank). She was political maybe – talking vaguely of connections with the German Left; she was a poet if the occasion arose; she was going to make films; she was a scene-maker, manifestly. She also made it understood wordlessly, in passing, that she would be a great fuck.

Anyway, there she was, zeroed in on the other most powerful energy in the vicinity, the by-now glittering and aphoristic Alex. She had a Polaroid of him as soon as he sat down. We examined the result: somehow, unhampered by the then-primitive technology, he had contrived to pose – ironic, tolerant, not granting his entire presence to the occasion. And unlike the rest of us – our pictures taken after him as a matter of routine – he didn't end up with red, rodenty eyes.

Marcie, carefully sipping tonic water, looked in tiny alarm at the equally silent and abashed Pritchard brothers, who looked in turn as if their souls had been stolen by the talkative stranger with her box of dark light. Marcie was probably regretting being flattered by the interest the – one imagined – hitherto remote Diane had taken in her when news came about the scholarship. The big flat in Moon House was a draw as well. Plus Marcie had a car that Diane could monopolize. So it had all worked out. Moon House was a handy base. You got the rural life but not too far from the city. And when the contacts came along, London would be next – it had to be, if you were making films here, right?

Diane was so transparent as to be opaque. No one could actually be like that, could they? In the course of the evening her interest in poetry developed exponentially. She had heard Lowell read, and Anne Sexton and Elizabeth Bishop. I was surprised she hadn't been waiting on the ice with a net when Berryman went off the bridge in Minneapolis.

Here was someone it was quite simple to dislike: all she

had to do was turn up. But it would be a more difficult thing altogether to have nothing to do with her. She would always have an in, somehow. Perhaps Alex had found a soul-mate. I watched with fascinated dismay as he let her do her stuff, until she was seated opposite him, demanding his full attention.

'You take a good picture, Alex. Ever thought of doing something with it?'

'I've had offers.'

'You mean like *Playgirl*?'

'Mucky that,' said Luke, into his pint.

'A gentleman never tells,' said Alex, rolling Diane a cigarette.

'Well you can tell me.'

Alex grinned and went for another round. I followed to lend a hand.

'Americans, then?' Shirley said, getting down from her stool and reaching for a glass.

'Statistically inevitable,' said Alex. 'Even here, Shirley my love.'

'Aye, mebbe,' said Shirley. 'Had enough of them in the war. Up at Moon House, are they? What do they want, d'you reckon?'

Alex shrugged.

When we were out of her hearing, he muttered, 'Well, Shirley, one of them needs a good fuck and the other just wants one.'

'Don't, Alex,' I said.

'I'm just saying.'

'There'll only be trouble.'

'You mean action.'

'Well, anyway, don't.'

When we returned to the table Diane had got Luke to take his shirt off and was crouching on the grass to photograph him. Gareth seemed to have found an extra button on his coat to do up.

Like a good many evenings in those days, this one became a seemingly genial blur as the Tapeworm took hold. The local musicians settled in for a session in the bar. Harry the rarely seen landlord decided there was no point in closing, since by now Constable Jenkins would himself be fairly well gone in the Cat and Candle over the hill in Betterley, where he was also giving Julie, the landlord's daughter, a doing, a fact as yet unknown to Mrs Jenkins, who as luck would have it was a good friend of Shirley, Harry's all-seeing barmaid.

'I think we got off on the wrong foot,' I said to Marcie.

'I didn't realize you were who you were,' she said. 'I didn't, you know—'

'I do look quite, er, pastoral these days.'

'Yeah.' She gave a quick smile. 'Sorry. It's not very secure. Anyone could walk in—'

'And so it proved.' She looked worried. 'I'm joking. Anyway, now we've been introduced.'

'I don't mind sharing the room,' she said. 'I don't need all of it, not all the time.'

'I'm not there that much.'

Now she was puzzled. 'Okay . . . Is there some other material I should see that I don't know about? Is that where you are? I'm supposed to—'

'As far as I'm aware, it's all at Moon House. I just – well, I like working at home. Reading the poems, basically.'

She considered me carefully, as if I were a large animal that had wandered into the road and would need sensible handling. The conversation moved on.

I remember Alex saying to Marcie, 'And Luke, you see, Marcie, Luke is an exemplar of the idiocy of rural life.'

'Thinks I'm thick,' said Luke, smiling shyly, good-natured as always, ruffling his ridiculous Faces crop. Gareth shook his head: Luke might well be his real life's work.

'I wouldn't say thick. I might say curdled,' Alex went on.

Diane roared with laughter. Gareth looked at Alex while lighting his pipe.

'Yeah, man, it's like *Dead Souls* round here,' Diane said. 'Ripe for inspection.'

'Don't like soul,' said Luke. 'Soul's for girls, right? Black Sabbath, that's what I like. The heavy scene.'

'Shurrup, Luke. Talking daft,' muttered Gareth, his pipe clenched in his mouth. 'Take no notice of him, Diane. He doesn't know what he's on about. His ma dropped him on his head at the hospital. Must have been on account of she saw his ugly mug.'

'No, let him speak! Black Sabbath? Well, Lukey,' said Diane, taking him by the wrist, 'you never know. Maybe we can arrange it. Find a few virgins to sacrifice on the primitive altar when the moon is full, right?'

Luke's mouth was open.

'No chance round here,' said Alex.

'Really? There's always Marcie, I guess,' said Diane. 'Have to do a screen test. There's a kinda – I dunno – Eva Marie Saint ice-queen thing there, maybe. Need to do something with the hair.'

'I have to work,' said Marcie, and everyone burst out laughing. 'I mean I have to get back.' She blushed and gave an embarrassed smile. As usual I felt ashamed. As usual I went on watching.

'We should have a proper party, Marcie, right?' said Diane. 'We've got that big apartment – you know there's actually a ballroom there, with a sprung floor and everything?'

'I had heard that,' said Alex. 'I also heard they had a kind of Hellfire Club in the cellars. Hours of funless harm. Bored noblemen of the Restoration with lots of whores and servant girls and smoke and mirrors, all seeking the thrill marked X.'

'And what is that?' asked Diane.

'I imagine it varies according to individual requirements.'

'Well, what are we waiting for?'

'Actually, I don't know if I'm allowed to have a party,' said Marcie. 'I don't think I am. I doubt it, you know?'

'Who the hell's going to stop you?' snorted Diane.

'The administration.'

'You told me they're sleeping on the job.'

'Yeah, but still.'

'I've got a movie to make, remember?'

'What about, like?' said Luke.

'Whatever happens. People. What they do.'

'What about actors?'

'That's everyone. You, for example.' She took another photograph.

'Documentary,' said Gareth.

'Well, kinda, but actually not.'

'It's not that simple, really,' said Marcie. But she knew she'd lost. Luke watched eagerly: at last, a big chance.

'You wanna die worrying?' said Diane, her patience strained. 'Anyway, it's decided, yeah, okay?'

'I like a good party,' said Luke. 'Specially if there's lots of women. Nurses are good.'

'You'd run away if one so much as looked at you, you big girl,' said Gareth.

'You don't know what I'd do,' said Luke. 'You're no better, anyway.'

'But you're a sex king, right, Gareth?' said Diane. 'I bet you have your moments, you and your big lizardkingsnake overcoat.'

Gareth made a noncommittal noise and fiddled with his pipe. Diane alarmed him. She alarmed me.

I flatter myself by saying I tuned out. I was doing what I often did, trying to get high by all means at my disposal, with slowly diminishing returns. I still tried to imagine that getting wrecked was a way of actually going somewhere, of taking an early edition of the future, or getting sideways out of the confines of habit, expectation and neglected work. I was still very young, but not as young as I had been, if you follow me. There was a clock where previously there had been a vague sunlit sketch of a calendar on someone else's kitchen wall. These days nothing quelled the little advance party of fear in my chest – not dope, not music, not sex. Sex itself was turning into fear. In bed Susie would indulge me but rarely enjoy me. We were already an old couple, our roles established. She was waiting for me to grow up. I, too, was waiting, with great determination, working hard to be a patient, not an agent.

Marcie stood up hesitantly, fiddling with her shoulder-bag.

'Perhaps somebody could walk Marcie back,' said Alex, suddenly turning into the host. Luke tried to stand up but Gareth held him down. I thought I might as well help.

'Look, Marcie, a proper gentleman,' said Diane, wide-eyed with amusement.

Doing my best to appear unthreatening and reliable, I gestured towards the road. Marcie stepped away from the table with a nervous smile and gave a tiny wave to the company.

'Watch out for Reverend Exton,' Diane called. 'I bet he likes to take the air on nights like this.'

8

We walked in silence through the village for a minute or two until we reached the turn-off that ran up Summer Hill and past Moon House.

'Professor Gwyther talks about you,' said Marcie, eventually.

'Oh, dear.'

'No, really, he speaks highly of you. He says you have great potential.'

'What time of day was this?'

'I make sure I'm in there to see him at nine a.m.' She smiled. 'He's a sweet man, I think. Not quite in this world any more.'

'He knows his stuff.'

'He's the reason I came.'

'I love Exton,' I said.

'Right! I mean, who doesn't?' There was the American optimism. England had had nearly three hundred years to get to like Exton and still only a bare handful thought he mattered. The Americans had simply founded a republic and begun taking culture seriously. It seemed to involve them owning it as well, of course.

'And why Exton at all?'

'Oh, well, compared with a lot of people he hasn't been fully—'

'Exploited.'

'I prefer to say "explored".'

'Sorry – I was joking again.'

She looked surprised. 'Oh, okay,' she said uncertainly, after a pause. 'But I mean, I'm very committed. To Exton. To the seventeenth century in general.'

'Of course. To come to this backwater suggests it.'

'I also wanted to go to a – a really English part of England, if you know what I mean.'

'You made a good choice. One of the black and white towns. Though of course this is almost Wales as well. It's hard to see the border.'

'Wales isn't a country, though, right? It's a principality.'

'I wouldn't go around saying things like that. Keep it for thrones and principalities, orders of angels of the second sphere.'

'Every angel is terrible,' she said.

'Let's hope not.'

'Exton thought they were.'

'Perhaps he was just projecting his own anxieties on to the angel, using it as a white screen.'

'I don't know if you can read religious poetry as just metaphorical.'

'Metaphor isn't "just" anything. It's a bridge, isn't it?' I asked.

'What use is religious poetry if you don't believe?'

'I'm afraid I don't care about usefulness.'

'You know what I mean, though.'

'Are you religious?'

'Uhhh. Well, maybe. I grew up with it – church on Sunday.' She raised her hands in a gesture of impotence and defeat.

'Sadly we've run out of time for this week,' I said.

She laughed. Again the pause. 'If there was to be a God I think it would be here, somewhere like this. Is that sentimental?' she asked.

'Of course it is. But I understand what you mean.'

'Let me tell you that makes a change. I daren't mention the word "belief" with Diane around. She's in favour of free speech, you see. And movies, of course.'

We both laughed. The moon stood over the hill, enormous in the heat. The narrow road between the hedgerows was bright enough for us to see our way. I could feel the quiet settling around us as we moved beyond the village. If I looked back I could see the bedroom windows of the cottage.

'She's a livewire, your friend Diane. It's a bit much, all that taking pictures of everything.'

'She's hard to miss. She never stops – she's tried to photograph me in the shower, using the bathroom. She's crazy.'

'How did you get together?'

She stopped and turned to face me. 'We're not together, not like that.'

'No, no, I meant – well, you seem unlikely friends, I suppose.'

'Friends. Depends what you mean.' She took a couple of paces, then stopped again. 'I don't know why I should tell you this – we've scarcely met, have we? – but I really wish she'd move on. Do you know what I mean? I mean you only just met her.'

'I can guess.'

Marcie gave me her careful look again, what I came to think of as her American look, wanting to be clear and not to end up appearing foolish, but not minding if she seemed foolish at the outset. On no very strong basis, it crossed my mind that she was someone who, unlike many of her fellow citizens and mine, could only be herself in conditions of near-secrecy. If so, this conversation on the barest of acquaintances was a privilege and an honour. I knew there must be a world in which people behaved on such terms, but it seemed to associate itself with the nineteenth century and Henry James, and I had no idea how one gained membership.

'She's a wrecker, I think,' she said. 'I only knew her from a distance in Chicago, knew some of the same people, but, you know, I heard things, kinda ugly, people being used, ending up hurt, all for the sake of her projects. And now somehow she's here. In the room. All the time. Using up the oxygen.' Marcie shrugged.

'You could tell her to go.' *What things?* I wanted to ask. *Exciting, depraved things?*

'What? Look at me. I'm going to tell *her*? Apart from anything else it would be very rude.'

'She wouldn't care. She seems quite well versed in rudeness.'

'I guess. I don't know. And she kinda scares me, Martin.'

'You're a free agent. You've got work to do. She should be able to understand that.'

'Hmm. You're very decisive.'

'Sorry. It's not my business.' Marcie smiled and shrugged again. 'But she has an effect, and you end up responding. Like this, for instance.'

'Respond away. I don't mind.'

'So, understanding's not the issue, then.'

'Not really. It just doesn't matter to her. Other people behave conveniently, or she just kinda does what she wants. You end up where she puts you, somehow, and, like I said, she's hard to say no to. You feel as if she deserves to be right, since whatever she wants at the time she wants so absolutely. Oh, listen to me – am I gabbling? Sorry!'

'Of course not.'

'Okay. You're sure?' I nodded. 'And this' – she gestured at the night – 'this is such an opportunity for me, to come here and work on Exton when no one else – sorry, I mean, almost no one else – is really doing it. I'd hate to waste it.'

'You won't,' I said. 'You're clear about what you want.' I sounded strangely rational, like a grown-up.

'Kind of.' We went on a little way. Then she stopped. 'But I mean, a party?'

'She seemed very determined about that. Which is odd, since presumably she doesn't know anyone.'

'That won't slow her down. People will want to know *her*. That's what she assumes. It seems she's right. She's the scene-maker. Things happen around her.'

'Well, she'll get bored. She won't stay long, will she?' It

struck me that the only person capable of getting Diane to leave was Alex. No good looking in that direction, then, not till he'd had his fill. Me, she had seemed hardly to register, which was a relief.

'I just wonder if Moon House will still be standing when she's finished. And she doesn't care about literature, about poetry. She thinks it's history. Now there's just film and music. She doesn't listen – about poetry – and I can't see the point of trying to tell her any more. She's just all confidence. She's what Europeans think Americans are like.'

The road grew steeper and the beech trees met overhead. We went on more slowly.

'You know *Comus*?' she said. 'It's kind of like that here, isn't it?'

'It was first performed not far away, you know.'

'Yeah, I have to go visit Ludlow Castle when I get a chance. But it's creepy here, isn't it? I keep waiting for something to jump out of the bushes.'

'Sabrina fair's abduction. Would you like that?'

She smiled to herself. 'I guess it would depend on the something doing the jumping. With my luck it would be Luke Pritchard.'

'He's not very demonic.'

'Alas, not. I'm sure he's a nice boy, really.'

'He's just a bit dim. He can't help it.'

'And his brother has to look after him all the time? Difficult.'

We reached the pillared gateway and stopped. Creepered and turreted, early Tudor but repeatedly augmented and disfigured since, Moon House stood glittering in the moonlight like an Atkinson Grimshaw painting. A great place to write stories or do evil, it seemed to me.

'Do you know the history?' Marcie asked. For a moment I had forgotten she was there. Her smile showed she knew this to be so.

'Only vaguely.' I was fibbing because she was relaxing a bit and enjoying herself.

'Yeah, it's great, isn't it? Like condensed Gothic,' she replied. 'Let me see if I can get it all in the right order.' She began counting off the episodes on her fingers, like a schoolgirl practising for a competition. 'A wastrel – I just love that word – lost the place for a bet. It was eventually inherited by another wastrel. Then he went mad and died of syphilis and his son took it on but he was crazy too. And then one time – did you know this? – Aleister Crowley and McGregor Mathers came to dinner and had a fight and tried to turn each other into flowerpots or something. Then it was an asylum – just like some place in a book, right? Then the army got hold of it during the war. Then a girls' school. Finally the university. Decline and fall, I guess.' She laughed. 'Did I miss anything?'

'I shouldn't think so. Only about three hundred years.'

'Well, I was doing it in captions. After all, I'm American.'

For a minute or so we stood looking at the pillared front of Moon House as it reared heavily from the hyper-trophied laurel bushes and heavy copper beeches. The building looked indifferently back.

'I have to go and work for a little while,' Marcie said.

'She'll move on,' I said. 'She'll get bored, won't she?'

'I hope so, yeah. I just wonder what she'll do in the meantime.' Marcie smiled and shook her head. 'Listen to me, telling a stranger my troubles.'

'You should come and meet Susie. She's my girlfriend. We can have something to eat. Do you like very limp salad?'

'Thank you. That would be nice. But remember, you get me, you get Diane. Are you ready for that?'

'We'll cope.'

'And, actually, you know there's a pool at Moon House?' I nodded. 'Well, please come and use it. No one else does. It's actually got water in it. Come on Saturday if you like.'

'A swimming party – think that might pacify Diane?'

'I don't know. What do you think?'

Not a chance. I returned to the cottage along the paths at the edge of the hopfields, which brought me into the garden by the back gate. Marcie was the real thing, I could tell, so what did that make me? A dabbler in the margins?

Although I was exhausted and light-headed with heat and drink I knew I wouldn't be able to sleep yet, so I took a chair outside in the light from the kitchen doorway to roll a joint. There were faint voices in the trees – little conspiratorial snatches of laughter, scarcely there but somehow intended to be heard. The church clock struck one. I heard Luke's wooden platform soles stumbling by in the road. Summertime.

I held the last draw deep in my lungs for a long time. Then I went upstairs and made love to Susie, who was only half awake but didn't seem to mind. When I came I wondered if she was still taking the pill. The future seemed a long way off. Afterwards, still far from sleep, I lay listening to the deeper silence after the cackles and the merrymaking. I waited. After a while something made me get up and go to the window. Diane stood on the lawn staring up at the house, holding what looked like a movie camera. She didn't seem to see me. After a minute or two she turned and let herself out by the back gate. There was no sign of Alex. Exton took up his intermittent commentary in my ear: *Seek not to comprehend Desire except ye fear it.*

9

When Saturday came, Marcie's invitation to go and swim in the pool at Moon House was received with something close to enthusiasm. Susie had had a hard week in college, and for Alex and me it would be something to mark one day out from the others, as if the weekend were a rest from our ceaseless labours. In fact I'd been struggling out of bed early to read and make notes, but I didn't tell him that. He was bearing it well, but Jane's continued absence would have made it difficult for him to tolerate any divergence from habit on my part. Anxiety had settled on me again with nothing in mind but to remain.

In the event it was mid-afternoon by the time we arrived. Susie had made a picnic. She came to get us out of the pub and instructed Alex and me to carry the baskets of provisions up the hill. The parking area in front of the locked main doors of Moon House was empty except for Marcie's blue Mini. We wandered around the side of the house, along the edge of an old kitchen garden with a vast greenhouse built against a wall, filled with leaf skeletons, then across what was still just recognizable as a topiary chessboard. There were voices through a stone archway.

We came out again into the sun's full glare. There was

the large, marble-edged pool, and beyond it the woods and wild gardens, thick with green-black heat.

In a blue one-piece costume, Marcie sat reading at the side of the pool, with her feet in the water, while Diane lay on the diving board in a bright red bikini, smoking a joint and staring down through the viewfinder of another expensive camera. She looked like a supercharged version of one of those languid girls from an Alma-Tadema painting, smouldering on the battlements of antique pornography. The pool itself was quite large, edged with flagstones. It seemed clean but very dark, as though of uncertain depth. The overgrown garden was reaching the pool's far side, grass and dock finding its way into the gaps in the paving along the edge.

For a moment neither girl noticed us, then Marcie glanced round.

It was evident that she had been crying, but it was equally obvious that no one was to refer to the fact. She came pattering over.

'You must be Susie. I'm glad to meet you. Is that a picnic you've brought? That's wonderful. Susie's brought a picnic, Diane. Susie, do you want to come inside and unpack it in the kitchen? I think we have some outdoor plates.' Susie had taken everything in as usual and seen where the need lay. I don't think she ever actually had a conversation with Diane. Marcie led her indoors, and Diane watched them go, then uncoiled herself from the diving board and approached.

'Hiya, boys. You palefaces like the heat?' She took a photograph.

Alex grinned, accepted the joint from her and drew on it, then courteously handed it back, took off his clothes to reveal a pair of tiny black trunks, ran to the pool and threw himself in head first. The length of time he took to surface was slightly worrying. Diane watched the water with a smile.

'Thirsty work,' he said, when he reappeared.

'Marcie will bring something to drink,' said Diane. She stood there gleaming slickly in the light, like something just about to happen. A gold disc hung from a chain around her neck, decorated with a figure in relief.

'It's Diana,' she said, seeing my gaze. 'She's the goddess you don't fuck with, right? Actaeon – you know that story?'

'Of course. I didn't mean to stare.'

'Stare away. The view belongs to everyone.'

'Not after what happened with Actaeon.'

'Take pity on the ignorant,' said Susie. 'Tell us what happened.'

Alex grinned. 'Actaeon was a hunter. He saw the goddess bathing. She turned him into a stag and his own dogs dismembered him.'

'Cruel but fair, then.'

'It may have been a misunderstanding,' said Diane. 'Wrong time, wrong place. Wrong guy maybe. Here,' she handed me the camera, 'take my picture.' She struck a cheesecake pose and after some fumbling I did as instructed. Then she stepped off the rim of the pool and vanished into the water.

'She's got you at work, then,' said Marcie, more cheerful now and dressed in shorts and a T-shirt, appearing in the doorway with a tray of drinks. Susie shook her head and smiled at her.

Marcie and Susie set up a table on the flagstones while I found a large, tattered garden umbrella in a shed that was a cemetery of flowerpots. Which were Mathers and Crowley, I wondered. The story fitted, though – Moon House was the kind of place where rock-star dabblers in the occult were found floating face down by amnesiac friends who had seemed oddly slow to call in the constabulary. But all that was years ago, surely.

I noticed I was grinding my teeth like a speedfreak. Just because I was anxious, though, did it mean something would have to happen? That would be magical thinking of the kind by which Exton was obviously afflicted as he strayed restlessly over Summer Hill and back to the rectory, carrying the vast impedimenta of the symbolism and more than symbolism he found waiting for him everywhere in the landscape. Moon House was just an odd, superannuated place eking out its afterlife with the aid of state funding. It was atmosphere. The third dimension was, fortunately, bound to be missing, wasn't it? I went on grinding.

I sat with Susie and Marcie, drinking lemonade, being unstoned, occasionally glancing at the list of urgent but unbegun tasks listed afresh every day in the notebook I'd brought with me. Most of all though I looked on with a sinking sense of the inevitable as Diane and Alex made their moves around the pool, swapping the camera back and forth, getting through a couple of bottles of wine with no effort. Susie, her face hidden by her blonde curls, was sketching, while Marcie, pale in the shade, watched admiringly as she worked.

'She's very energetic, that Diane,' said Susie. 'Full of beans, isn't she?'

'Yeah,' Marcie muttered. 'You haven't got a Mickey Finn in your bag, have you?'

'I'll see what I can find.'

They laughed. They had made friends in a moment. It's a gift, they say. I can watch it happen and recognize it. I can even impersonate it. But no further.

'There'll be trouble,' said Marcie. 'She couldn't help it even if she wanted to. Something has to happen. Lights, camera, action.'

'I'm afraid so,' Susie replied. 'Alex is the same. They're a match.'

'He's got a girlfriend, though, hasn't he?'

'He certainly has,' said Susie. 'A lovely girlfriend, Jane. He doesn't realize what a lucky lad he is. But he's a man, isn't he? He thinks with his dick.'

Marcie giggled and looked at me.

'Don't mind me.' I said. 'I'm just the despised and loving creature. A humble logman.' There was a louder splash. 'Anyway, what can we do?' I asked.

'Well, as usual we can look after Jane,' said Susie. 'Try to, anyway.'

'What's Jane like?' asked Marcie.

'I imagine you'll find out soon enough.' Susie smiled and cast her gaze heavenwards. 'Complicated.'

'Diane will like that. A mess, something full of possibilities,' said Marcie.

There was another splash, then an inviting scream.

'Where does the water come from?' Susie asked.

'One of the owners, this guy Lord Bromsgrove, had a big underground tank put in,' said Marcie. 'It draws off a deep spring in the hill, apparently. For some reason it doesn't dry up.'

'Where streams not fail,' I said.

'They failed for Exton,' said Marcie, indicating her copy of the poems, which she seemed to take everywhere.

'Oh, bugger Exton,' said Susie. 'Sorry, Marcie – I know he's your topic too. He hasn't done Martin any good, I can tell you that.'

'That's okay,' said Marcie, nodding. 'Exton can be very intense.'

I hadn't known until then that Susie had read Exton. Not that I'd asked. She put up with poetry for Jane's sake, not because it had any intrinsic interest.

'I just hope all this' – Susie gestured around – 'this country living and so on, will get it out of his system.' She sounded matter-of-fact and almost maternal, as if I wasn't there, a bit like my mother with one of her washed-out women friends comparing notes on their children, as if I wasn't listening.

'He's a great poet,' I said. 'Well, not great, but . . .' I looked at Marcie for help.

'Historically significant,' she said, which didn't make the case I was after.

'That's fine,' said Susie. 'I don't deny it, but Exton's just – it's as if he's, I don't know, some kind of magnetic anchor under this place, tying everyone down. Like a huge excuse. I'm not sure what I mean. "Poetry makes nothing happen," right? Well, it's true. It doesn't. Spending your time with nutters.'

'Philistine,' I said.

'Fuck off, darling,' she replied affectionately. Marcie blinked.

'Believe me,' she said, 'I follow you very clearly. I sit in there in the library' – she pointed at the house – 'squirrelling away with my notes and the papers and I keep thinking, let me out! Let me get back to somebody normal, like – like Emily Dickinson!'

'But it matters to you, this research,' said Susie. 'It's – I mean, obviously, in your case – not just something to do, or not do, in the meantime.' Susie looked at her sketchpad: always busy, waste nothing.

'Oh, no, it's everything. I must be nuts.' Marcie laughed. She seemed almost to be awaiting instructions.

Susie smiled and covered Marcie's hand with hers. 'Martin's the one who's nuts,' said Susie. 'Aren't you, darling? Fucking barking when he wants to be.' I seemed to be standing in for Alex as the convenient object of her disapproval. 'And he's got the Doubts, of course. The ontological ones, I mean. Very nasty, can be. Needs a lot of ointment and bed-rest.' She poked me in the shoulder.

I shrugged, enjoying the attention despite myself. 'You make it sound like constipation,' I said.

'Better out than in, Mother says,' Susie replied. 'Syrup of figs, that's what these poets need. A good clear-out.'

The two of them laughed, a suddenly established conspiracy of girls.

'What's that in your drawing?' asked Marcie. 'There. Is that a *snake*?'

Susie held up her sketchpad. There was Diane, voluptuous in her scarlet bikini, reclining on the diving board. Camera in one hand, she appeared to be embracing a serpent with the other. 'Well, the pool and the underground tank and Diane being there made me think of *Salammbô*. And obviously, since she's the temple priestess, Salammbô needs a nice large serpent.'

'What for?' said Marcie, snorting with laughter now.

'I dunno,' said Susie. 'Why would a girl need a snake? For company, I suppose. Something to snuggle up with of an evening.'

'Don't you think it's getting a bit crowded?' I said.

Susie looked at me directly for the first time in an hour and said, 'Speak for yourself.'

'I meant crowded mythologically.'

'I think I'm becoming a polytheist.' She went back to adding detail to her drawing, with Marcie leaning in close to look.

Feeling suddenly restless and surplus to requirements, I got up to go for a walk. Only now did I notice that the pool had fallen silent. The revellers were gone. The woods of oak and birch beyond the pool were green shot through with gold. Who could resist their invitation? I took a path at random into the green, bird-haunted shade, light-headed with unaccustomed sobriety.

The woods were populated with a variety of erotic incitements. I paused for a while to look at a life-size statue of a naked bacchante teasing a satyr. Chipped and fissured, the male creature's tangle-bearded face was contorted with lust as he waited through a moss-grown eternity of impatience. A little further on, the path came to a circular crossing where several such statues were arrayed for the diversion of the stroller. There was something heartless and almost industrial in this erotic display. Further on, steps led down to a dank grotto with an oddly biological smell. Did they enjoy themselves at play here, the wastrels, chasing the maidservants in the hot green evenings? Or did it pall? Or was that the point, to exhaust the impetus finally? Did they get religion, like Exton – exactly the person I was taking this walk not to think about? Was this somewhere he would have avoided, a Restoration pleasure garden stiff with temptation? Or would he have made himself brave it, to do honour to the great creating nature that underlay and would outlive these transitory human indulgences?

Although it was opium and syphilis that did for him, the second wastrel, the Victorian one, Henry Bromsgrove, was actually quite industrious as rakehells go. His ruin was achieved partly in the service of enlightenment. He was passionately interested in whatever innovations the age could offer. Nowadays he'd have been involved in nano-technology and cryogenics. In his own time he was fasci-nated by hydraulics, heat and light, transport, methods of printing. He was one of the first of his class to install hot water and electric light. He had his own railway halt built at the end of a spur from the main line. You could still see the course of the tracks, and I followed them to the little yellow-brick villa of the station, where I walked along the mossy platform and peered in through the creepered windows of the ticket office and waiting room. I wondered if anyone but the servants had ever actually sat there in earnest.

At the far end of the platform a wooden staircase reached uncertainly up to a signal box. This stood close to the gated mouth of the long-disused tunnel under Summer Hill, which the local kids presumably used for smoking, sex and whatever other rites of passage they could dream up. There was no one about this afternoon. I climbed the sun-bleached steps gingerly and found the door unlocked. The signalling equipment had long gone, but there was an easy chair, a paraffin heater, candles, an ashtray and a stack of *Men Only*, so clearly someone was getting use out of the place. When I was a small boy I would have given my right hand for such a den. A den *with a door*. I'd never given up looking.

I shut the door, sat down and leafed through one of the magazines. Those were more innocent days. Pubic hair had only recently been invented for the mainstream, though the fantasies allegedly sent in by readers revealed an immutable and tyrannical banality. I put the thing aside and drifted in the heat, wishing I'd brought something to drink. I wanted to wake up properly from this muddled Arcadia, to take stock and move on to decisive action. But I was suspended just out of reach below the surface of the world. Although I was managing a bit of work – that was surely a good sign – my habitual anxieties were so generalized and confining that I was frightened I would never escape them. It seemed that ultimately, by the logic of my imprisonment, having released me once, Susie would have no choice but to escape me. That might happen very soon. What would it be like to be alone again? It would be like forgetting how to speak a language.

I closed my eyes on that prospect and let Exton take its place: soon the period of reading and considering would have to end, and it would be time to define the direction of my work. Gwyther had every confidence in me. Maybe that was part of the problem. Maybe I needed someone to wave a big stick.

Exton had come to the Marches desperate to serve. He longed to be a parish priest of the selflessly imaginative kind described by Izaak Walton in his life of a much greater poet-divine, George Herbert, whose ministry so lovingly sustained and inspired the parishioners of Bemerton in Wiltshire in the brief years before his premature death in 1633. Between Herbert's death and Exton's maturity stood the Civil War. More personally, Exton faced an insoluble crisis of a kind Herbert seems never to have had to deal with. Exton's particular sense of damnation was based on the fact that he had lost the power to believe. This was not the same as God having ceased to exist. It was also in some sense, Exton thought, his own fault, perhaps (the journals he kept were not specific on this matter) because of the life of sensual indulgence he had enjoyed in his youth. His punishment might be to wish to return and be prevented by his own failure. The spiritual predicament was not unique, but it was terrible. I could not see what it had to do with me, yet at the same time it exerted an apparently unbreakable grip. Now I might say it was a case of adolescent identification on my part. I might.

Much of the time, as well as bearing his burden of guilt and fear and isolation, Exton led the normal life of a parish priest – visiting and comforting the poor and the sick, officiating at the sacrament and other ritual occasions. More than that, on his regular walks over Summer Hill and the neighbourhood he began to make notes amounting to the beginnings of a natural history of the area, as well as describing features of antiquarian interest. Thus at the same time as expecting to be consumed at any time by fires 'issuing from the Adits of the Earth and stoked by Satan's Mine-men', he was describing and making quite decent drawings of local flora and fauna. His little owl is especially striking – the creature sacred to Minerva, goddess of wisdom. I knew only the names of the commonest plants and trees and was too clumsy and unobservant to see whatever creatures were passing by among the hedges and undergrowth. And as far as I was concerned, my antiquarianism began and ended with Exton.

As I sat drowsing in the signal box, though, a perspective opened up down which I caught a melancholy yet slightly clearer glimpse of the links between me and the landlocked drag-anchor of Exton's work as increasingly resented by Susie. Exton's beliefs had failed him. He was unlucky and could not get back to the shore from which he had innocently set out. What did I want with him? Perhaps to do him justice, as an act of the imaginative sympathy whose existence I grew later generally to doubt. But Marcie was probably better equipped for that task. Accidie, the noonday devil, seemed quite unknown to her.

> Blest be the man that Christ will save.
> For me there waits a fiery grave.

It was getting hotter. I thought about making a move.

When I woke up, the glassed-in signal box was like a furnace. My watch said it was seven p.m. I'd slept for two hours. I was dry-mouthed, nauseous and thick with sweat. I went down the steps, crossed the track and headed off through the woods, thinking this would be a shorter route back to the house. The disorientation of unexpected sleep remained with me, and soon a different, velvety order of seething evening quiet fell into place among the ferns and birches, which now assumed a distinctly Lawrentian cast. I remembered Birkin going for his naked constitutional among ferns like this after Hermione (Eleanor Bron) tried to brain him with the paperweight. I could see clearly the luminously pale, sickly English skin of Alan Bates as he staggered about doing the scene, playing half delirious but careful not to show the camera his willy either then or during the subsequent fireside wrestling scene with Gerald Crich in the formidable form of Oliver Reed. Everything reminds me of something else and nothing is for its own sake, I thought, knowing as I did so that such an unre-markable train of associations could lead back to horror and confusion unless I was careful now. Think of what is simply there in front of you, I told myself, but what came out was relentlessly literary – the drowned lovers in the drained lake at Crich Hall, the nightmarish sex scene between Birkin and Ursula in the laurel bushes, the blood-choked death of the ancient Max Adrian's character. I tried again and got Housman: 'The cuckoo shouts all day at nothing/In leafy dells alone.' Even 'heartless, witless nature' came out of a book. Better perhaps 'Annihilating all that's made/To a green thought in a green shade.' Though Marvell was never in the same place at one time, his lines from 'The Garden' are often read as an imagining of ecstasy, a transfer from the realm of the corporeal towards pure consciousness. So, fine. The problem with acid, though, I had found, was that it greatly magnified the force of verbal association, so that the arrival of the word 'annihilated' in my head invoked a sudden unmoored horror of dissolution rather than literary curiosity. Now I was really lost. It was like old times.

Indeed, though the distances involved were small – the walled core of the estate was nowhere more than a couple of miles across – I began to feel uncertain of my actual location. I couldn't seem to understand why I'd got there. Then I began to fear that this was a flashback rather than simply (fearsome, but lower on the Fulbourn scale) an unsettled episode of idle reflection. If so, it would be the first in a year. Just to think of this made me afraid. Normally, given the warning signs, I made sure I wasn't alone. Now it was as if I'd been looking for trouble. I was sweating but cold. There is a taste in the back of the throat

Sean O'Brien

that acidheads liked to say was dead brain cells, and it seemed to be with me again. Visually, everything was normal, almost artificially so, as if charged with imminent mutation, but I felt that thirst would soon drive me mad anyway. Was it safe to drink from a stream, supposing I could find one that hadn't dried up? I was doomed to fail. I would never complete my work. I would be arrested here for ever. They would put me away until I was simply the voices wittering and sneering in my head.

I crouched on the grass, closed my eyes and breathed deeply, aware of the heavy hum of life up close, waiting all around me. Finally I lay down in a ball and tried not to think. The evening watched me with close indifference. I might never find my way home. I had drugs, Exton had religion, but the outcome would be the same. I turned my face to the parched earth. It smelled like the garden in my childhood.

I'm not sure if I slept again. After a while – time is hard to register in those conditions – the panic receded, passing through my brain like the spectral barricade vision accompanying a migraine. I sat up and looked about me. To my left the ground rose sharply. I decided to climb it to try to spot Moon House. The parched soil powdered underfoot and I scrambled up, clinging to exposed roots. The slope ended abruptly above a forty-foot drop. I was standing on a broad tongue of rock projecting out over a dry pool that contained a shoal of earth and leaves. On the far side of the pool was what appeared to be a Greek temple built mostly of wood. Someone had painted it pale blue. Against one of the pillars stood Alex, his eyes closed, his hands wrapped in Diane's black curls as she knelt before him. As I turned to move away, I saw Jane in a short denim dress, emerging from the woods to one end of the pool. She saw what I saw, but none of them saw me. Jane retreated the way she had come. As I made my way back down the slope I felt sane and sober but frightened all over again. *After the Fit is passed I am returned into the World I know, yet it becomes more strange and terrible in its Familiarity.* For God's sake shut up, I thought, but Exton was as powerless to stop himself as I was.

10

Suppertime had been declared when I found my way back to Moon House. There were stereo speakers propped on the kitchen windowsill. The music just beginning was John Martyn's *Bless the Weather*, the Glaswegian boy-god in the beauty of his youth, with the girl-melting voice and the miraculous light, silvery touch on the acoustic guitar and Echoplex. A heavy white cloth had been laid on the table, with candles for later, cutlery and more wine. Susie and Marcie came busily back and forwards from the kitchen with bowls of salad and plates of cold meat and cheese.

Susie gave me a glass of wine and pecked me on the cheek. The heat showed no sign of breaking. 'You look awful,' she said. 'Are you OK?'

'Just a bad moment back there,' I told her. 'Nothing to worry about.'

'That's not like you.'

'I'm okay, honest.'

'I can tell, you know, Martin, when you're not, like now. Have a drink and think about something else. Have you seen the others?' She looked at her watch.

'Not along the railway track.'

'Jane's back.'

'Good.'

'Let's hope so.'

'Where is she now?'

'Gone for a walk. I thought you might meet her.'

I put the wine aside and drank most of a jug of water. Then I stepped out of my shorts, walked over and slid into the pool, under the surface. It was cool, dim and seemed very faintly oily, as if many bodies had passed through it. Staying close to the side, tracing the rough stone with my hand, I followed the floor. Two-thirds of the way along there was a sharp drop-off in which nothing was visible. I made myself dive and hover over this darkness for as long as I could hold my breath. This, too, was like something else – the grim, shadowy South Bay pool from childhood holidays at Scarborough, a pit of monstrous, scabby depths. In winter the sea broke over it. At least that would clean it, I thought, and let myself drift back to the light.

When I surfaced Jane was sitting on the pool's edge in her emerald bikini, her legs drawn up, drinking a glass of wine. Her skin glowed in the reflections from the water. I noticed she'd painted her toenails a matching glittery green. 'Welcome home,' I said. She seemed perfectly at ease.

'Thank you, netherworld visitor. You reminded me a bit of Geryon swimming up to meet Dante and Virgil. D'you know that passage?'

'I take it that's not meant as flattery. D'you think I'm the actual embodiment of falsehood, then?' She gazed at me across the rim of her glass.

'No, you haven't got the tattoos for it, or the scorpion's tail.'

'Have you been in the water? It's a bit weird but it's lovely and cool.'

'Perhaps I'll swim later, when Alex gets here. We ought to have something to eat. Where is Alex, by the way?'

'Haven't seen him for a while. I imagine he's around. How was Wales?'

'Oh, you know, over there.' She pointed westwards. 'Was he very cross when I went off like that?'

'Oh, you know. He'll live.'

'I'll just have to make it up to him, won't I? That's what people say in these situations, isn't it?' She stood and walked over to the loaded table, pulled her dress on over her head and sat down. I lingered in the pool until my erection subsided.

The four of us began to eat. Marcie showed a rather touching respect for the fact that Jane was a poet; without affectation, Jane took this as her due. She was vague in her replies to Susie's questions about Jessica and Angharad, preferring to look at Susie's drawings of Marcie and Diane.

The record ended. I went indoors to change it and met Diane coming through the kitchen, towelling her hair, dressed now in a long T-shirt and sandals, camera in hand.

'Christ, you Brits and your fucking plumbing,' she said, good-naturedly enough. Newly applied scarlet lipstick consorted oddly with her clothing. 'There's no pressure, just lukewarm dribble. I'd have been better standing on my head and peeing.'

I imagined she was perfectly capable of this and much else besides.

'Well, feel free to try. There is a heatwave, of course.'

She shrugged. 'But that's no reason for civilization to collapse, right?' She peered past me at the others. 'So, is whatsername out there? Pollyanna?'

'Who? You mean Jane? Yes, she's back.'

Diane opened the fridge and took out a bottle of champagne. 'The gang's all here, then,' she said. 'Don't put that on.' She put the bottle down and took *A Love Supreme* from my hands. 'This is better. You like Miles?'

'Of course.' No girl had ever interfered with my selection before.

'Correct.' The anxious churning of *Bitches Brew* began.

'Almost,' I said.

As we went outside, Alex came strolling out of the woods. No one spoke as he came quietly up behind Jane, then leaned down to kiss her neck. 'Hello, my love,' he said. 'And where have you been?'

She shivered. 'Welsh Wales, *cariad*,' she said, and turned to embrace him. As she did so, she touched the disc that hung round his neck. 'What's this?' she said.

'I found it in the woods. There must be a story attached to it.'

'Whose is the face?'

'That of a goddess, obviously. Here. I brought it back for you.' He pulled the string over his head and placed it over Jane's. Now it lay, a drop of gold, between her breasts. 'One goddess should adorn another.'

Diane had watched impassively. 'Bravo,' she said. 'I like a guy with class. Where are we going to find some more like him, Marcie? Place needs shaking up a little. It's like a fucking nunnery.' She popped the champagne cork and took the bottle to Jane first. Jane watched her with the strangely innocent expression that I knew meant she was bypassing the opinions of the object of her scrutiny in order to make a proper assessment. Untroubled, Diane returned her gaze. 'It suits you, the coin,' she said. 'You should try to hang on to that. You're Jane. I've heard a lot about you.'

'Which means you must be the exciting-sounding Diane who's been leaving such an impression during my absence. Cheers,' Jane said, and touched her glass first to Diane's, then to Alex's. She raised it to her lips but didn't drink. 'I'll save this for later.'

'It'll go flat,' said Diane.

'Never mind.'

Diane raised her camera.

'No, thank you,' said Jane. 'No pictures at the moment.' Unusually, Diane did as she was bidden.

Slowly the dark came up around the table, though as midsummer neared it seemed it would never be truly night – there would always be a faint blue fanlight somewhere to westward. Despite the heat and a recurrence of the worrying detachment I'd felt earlier, I concentrated on drinking and let the conversation pass over me, aware that at one point Susie was sitting next to me and holding my hand, then that she'd moved away again and was talking to Marcie, their heads close together, their faces animated, like people who'd known each other for years. I remember Nico singing 'All Tomorrow's Parties' and the Flying Burrito Brothers doing 'Ain't That A Lot of Love'. For some reason I stood up and joined in tunelessly with the chorus, which produced what seemed to me unwarranted hilarity from the company. The evening drifted woozily on, like a reminder of happiness, something that had already happened elsewhere, essentially over with now.

It was too quiet for Diane. She disappeared and came back with a small silver box. In the meantime she'd put *Sticky Fingers* on.

'Diane, I already asked you not to do that here, please,' said Marcie.

'I heard you, Marcie. I beg to differ. Share the wealth, I say.'

'I don't want to get thrown out of the university. Or deported.'

'You won't be.'

'It's not your future. It doesn't matter to you.'

'There's nobody here but us chickens. Nothing's going to happen.'

'I don't want you to do that.' Marcie's voice broke. 'Can't you understand?'

'Maybe you should go to bed,' Diane said. 'It's been a long day. It's OK, babe – I'll lock up.' She used a razor blade to lay out three lines on a little mirror. 'Anyone join me?'

Dismissed, Marcie gathered her books together and went indoors. Susie – inevitably – went after her.

Coke was still a comparative rarity in most places in those days, so a certain exotic challenge was invested in the ritual of the five-pound note rolled into a tube. Diane bent to her task, then sat back a moment with her eyes closed. 'Join me?' she said. I was going to decline, but before I could speak Jane reached forward, took the fiver and snorted the second line. She paused, blinked, then bent and snorted the third.

'Hang on,' said Alex. 'What about me?'

'Attagirl,' said Diane. 'Help yourself, Alex.'

Jane stood up and began to dance to the slow-burning sidestep of 'Can't You Hear Me Knocking?', turning in a tiny circle, eyes closed, arms raised as if in exhortation, while the guitars built in waves against Charlie's swaggering snare-beat. At the point when the congas and Bobby Keyes's tenor horn replaced the drumkit and the guitars, she spun more widely away and along the edge of the pool, dancing on her toes, arms flung wide, head back, while the whole band gradually insinuated themselves into the groove once again and the pressure built. At the final drop-out she tilted on the edge of the dark water as if she must fall, then righted herself. We applauded. She turned to us and bowed, then dived gracefully into the pool. Alex followed. I realized that Susie had come back and was sitting beside me.

'What a bitch,' Diane said, her smile all teeth. 'Show-boating.'

'Beat that,' I said.

Diane snorted another line.

Jane climbed out and lay on the edge of the pool.

'I think I'm ready for you now, Diane, if you still want to take a picture,' she said. Diane made no reply but mechanically went ahead. When Alex emerged from the water, Jane said, 'I demand to be carried home, like this, dripping wet, like a mermaid from her wedding.' He picked her up as instructed and carried her away through the trees. She waved to us over his shoulder.

Diane went silently indoors. I sat at the table, drinking cider and watching the moths gathering in the halo of the candles. The record had finished.

Susie appeared in the doorway, talking to Marcie, I supposed, then came over. 'All right, Martin. That's enough excitement.'

'If only you knew.'

'I think I can guess. Tell me on the way home.'

She put her arm through mine as we walked slowly down the moonlit road in the perfumed night. I told her what I'd seen. She wasn't surprised.

Sex can be many things, but until Susie climbed urgently on top of me in our bed that night I had not known it as a form of resistance. For the first time I understood what it felt like to be used until I ached. When she finally lay down beside me, I asked, 'What was that about?'

'I don't want them to have it all,' she said, and turned away. We could hear the others laughing in the next-door room.

'We could leave,' I said.

'Yes, but we won't.' After a moment she went on, 'You won't go unless I go and I won't go until I'm sure Jane's safe.'

'How d'you mean safe?'

'No longer in danger.'

'Is she in danger?'

'Don't you feel it all the time?' I certainly felt something. Maybe it was that. 'Something's wrong. A balance has tipped.'

'We could get her to go with us.'

'No, we couldn't. She won't leave Alex until it's finished.'

'Until what's finished?'

'For God's sake, Martin. Until whatever the three of them are about to be up to is finished.'

11

Sunday was overcast and boiling, weather made for head-aches and recriminations. Everyone would have been better off spending time separately, but something was in process, requiring both actors and audience. No one could settle to anything, not even Susie and Jane. Except for Marcie we were in the pub by opening time. I was in the grip of anxious exhaustion, leafing distractedly through Saturday's local paper, when I noticed a double bill of *Don't Look Now* and *The Wicker Man* playing at the Star in Divott. It was a sign, surely. I'd seen both films with Alex on a wintry Cambridge afternoon when they first came out, and now here they were in the last leg of their release, in at the death of provincial cinema chains. In a rational world it might be a portent; in this one it could be nothing else.

We collected the reluctant Marcie from the archive – she was careful not to let anyone in when we came knocking – and drove into Divott for the four o'clock showing. In the days before all-day pub opening and Sunday shopping the town was as quiet as the grave, the marketplace deserted in the flat headachy light I associated with the Sundays of childhood. St Bart's sandstone tower was prominent against the white sky, a manifestation of why this Sabbath imprisonment should still be the case despite the encroaching secular world. Tucked away off the main street, the little cinema looked as if it was closed, but when we tried the door a wizened old man in ancient red livery came forward from the gloom to admit us, smoothing Brylcreemed hair flecked with dandruff. It would cost us fifty pence each to sit in the circle.

In the auditorium it smelt of dust and sweat and the ancient lusts of those now senile or dead. The seating felt as though it was encrusted with a century of farts and inhibited fumbling. When we sat down along the balcony the advertisements were already playing, the familiar bleached, exhausted colours of generic pieces adapted for local use – the Indian restaurant, the local Ford dealership, the hotel with its misspelt funtcion room. It was like being at home.

'This is England, ladies,' said Alex. 'This is the very heart of it. A trip to the moribund flicks of a Sunday teatime. It maketh the heart glad. Just time afterwards for a knee-trembler down the white-tiled alley with the depraved Akela.'

'Jesus, that smell. What is it? Did something die in here?' said Diane.

'That's authenticity, that is,' said Alex.

My choc ice was giving me a headache.

After an age, the ruched red curtains slid slowly apart again and the showing began. They were doing it in the wrong order, it seemed to me, with *Don't Look Now* running first. The print was still quite decent, though. Roeg's presiding rainy blue-ink tone is present both in the early scenes in England leading up to the daughter's death by drowning, and in the main body of the film set in Venice at the end of the season. Doors bang in the draughty hotel and spinsters stare at the heartbroken, achingly beautiful Julie Christie. A cortège goes by on the canal. Donald Sutherland works on the restoration of San Nicolò dei Mendicoli. A murderer is at large among the alleys and canals. The choice of routes narrows steadily. They will converge. The scaffolding slips and Sutherland almost falls. The couple are reconciled in the famous did-they-didn't-they love scene, which provoked a careful holding of the breath among our party that miserable, baking afternoon in Divott. Love should be like this, we thought, or most of us did. Then death arrives in the narrow alleyway.

As soon as the closing credits began, the usherette, based at a counter to the left of the stalls, down near the screen, began to boil a kettle. The steam drifted across the screen. When we started laughing she shouted up to us to be quiet and not disturb the other patrons, though there were none that we could see. Susie and Marcie went downstairs to buy more ice creams. Diane sat quietly, smoking, wearing her sunglasses, fiddling with her ever-present camera. Did she wear shades in bed as well? As the girls spoke to the usherette, we could see the woman's spectacles glinting up at us.

'She asked if we were all on drugs,' said Marcie when they returned. 'She said we should be ashamed of ourselves for mingling . . .'

'Mingling,' Susie repeated in a Peter Sellers voice.

'. . . with a pair of layabouts like you.'

'As far as drugs are concerned, we could do with re-stocking. Has she got any? Don't tell me you forgot to ask,' Alex said.

I think that was the last time I was unambiguously happy, thinking about Julie Christie and Venice, watching the usherette's winged specs squinting suspiciously up through the smoke and dust-motes. This England.

Although *The Wicker Man* has somehow ascended to the status of a neglected classic in recent years, in my view (apparently that of a minority) it remains what it always was, a piece of half-arsed crap full of unintended humour and bungled eroticism – a sort of porno version of *Whisky Galore* with added human sacrifice. Christopher Lee I exempt from criticism: he invests Lord Summerisle not only with his habitual command but with a wit completely lost on the befuddled Sergeant Howie. Edward Woodward, named with horrible aptness, does his best in the role of an upright plank, but Britt Ekland, Diane Cilento, Ingrid Pitt and company were lucky ever to work again. The tone of the thing varied wildly between genial smut, British New Wave realism and a visionary paganism to which the film-makers were simply unequal. The best scene took place in the Summerisles' drawing room, an unequal verbal contest between the laird and Howie, something that would have been for the most part quite at home in a black-and-white 1950s detective B-feature. And, as with many British films, the colour quality was dire. Our climate used to be black and white. Elizabeth's I's fire-ships and the London Blitz had all worked rather well in black and white.

Of course, I know this is not a universal view. How

would there have been a remake otherwise? Alex was amused, as was Marcie. Jane was silent throughout, but Diane couldn't be quiet. There was no pleasure for her in its absurdity. It was an offence against the movies – clearly a very serious charge in her book.

'Jesus, so that's a British film. It's not even as good as the adverts,' she said, when we came out into the sweaty grey evening. 'No wonder your industry's broke.'

The argument started when we got back to the pub in the village.

Jane and Alex were teaching Marcie to sing 'Somer is icumen in' when we entered the bar. The only other customers were the Pritchard brothers. Gareth was teaching Luke to play chess, patiently, with no expectation of any lasting success. He was relieved to be able to abandon his task when we joined them. 'Been to the pictures, I hear,' he said. 'Any good?'

'The second one – what was it, *The Wicker Man*? – that really stank,' said Diane.

'Supposed to be dirty, that,' said Luke.

'I'm sorry to give you the bad news. Dirty was one of all the things it wasn't. You'd be better off with *Deep Throat*.'

'Didn't have that here. They banned it, like.'

'They should have banned *The Wicker* fucking *Man* while they were at it.'

'Perhaps you didn't understand it,' said Jane.

'I'm sorry, Jane?'

'I mean, Diane, as an outsider from a very different, much newer culture, you may have missed certain elements.

Whatever its undoubted faults, *The Wicker Man* is clearly a film with roots.' Her tone was considerate. Alex cackled expectantly.

'Roots my ass.'

'Part of a culture. Not necessarily accessible to out-siders.'

'Who wants to be inside that? It was garbage, Jane. Admit it.'

'You need to watch in a discriminating way. It's not good to let everything go to waste.'

'Somebody help me here. I know we were speaking English a minute ago.'

Diane was looking at Alex, who shrugged and smiled. 'I wouldn't be so foolish as to intervene at this stage. I'm sure both sides have their points. Let me get us all a drink,' he said, turning to the bar, where Shirley was watching the funny foreigner steadily over the pumps.

I thought the matter was done with. I was wrong.

'It depends what you're searching for,' Jane said tolerantly.

'How about entertainment?'

'Entertainment. Entertainment. I wouldn't know about that. Perhaps that's an American preoccupation. Some of us like to investigate a little further.'

'You're kidding. It's just a horror flick.'

'No, it depends what you're capable of seeing.' This sympathetic understanding of limitations that were not their victim's fault was a new one on Diane. 'It's, well, it's a power we've retained in the old world.'

'Power? You can't even heat the water in the bath-room.'

'The world is not made for your convenience. Imagine the tedium if it were. Two hundred years of democracy culminating in the thermostat.'

'So I'm superficial. Is that what you're saying? Hey, at least I'm clean.'

'Do you think so? I'd rather say that perhaps you're not in touch with . . . with the earth in quite the same way as some of us. It can't be easy.'

Marcie and Susie were trying not to laugh. Luke was awestruck. This might turn out to be the gipsy catfight he'd heard about but been too young to see in *From Russia with Love*.

'The earth? What do you know about the fucking earth? You don't even sound like you're *from* the fuck-ing earth!'

'I know its gods must be served and may not be mocked.' This was pure Jane – barmy, eerie and authori-tative at the same time. Diane shook her head and looked around once more for support. No one would meet her eye. Choking with laughter, Marcie excused herself and ran into the ladies'.

'Wait. What are you, Jane – a duchess or something? How did you get the right to speak to me like that? What am I? A peasant? You say you're a poet. Who cares, man? Who reads that stuff? Nobody reads it. Nobody cares. You think it's important but it's really not. You've got to reach people.'

'I certainly don't want to reach you. Not with a ten-foot pole. Anyway, I thought Alex said you were keen. On poetry, I mean.' She looked at Alex, who assumed a mystified expression.

'Listen, OK? Just so you folks back here in fucking Brigadoon are clear, film is the last art,' said Diane, close to shouting. 'It's the culmination of all the others.'

'But how would you know that?' Jane asked unflappably. 'If you don't mind me asking. It just sounds like something people say, the lazy ones who can't be bothered to read, the sort who think Bob Dylan writes poetry.'

'Film is what I do.'

'You're saying you want to make a film?'

'No. I am making a film. That's what I'm saying.'

'That's terribly clever of you. Isn't it, Alex? Is it about anything in particular?'

'I guess you could say it's about how things end.'

'And how do they end, d'you think?'

'They come to places like this, for instance.'

'I see. But why here? We live very quietly here, just getting on with our work. I mean, it's hard to see what would interest you hereabouts.' Jane stroked Alex's arm.

'I'm interested in what happens to energy when it's got no place to go. In disorder.'

'If that's what you're after, you might be better off in Crewe. Do you know Crewe at all?' Jane toyed with the gold pendant.

'I'm interested in how cultures and subcultures decay,' said Diane, doggedly. 'Like the sixties, for instance, how it decays into right now, the energy fading, the creativity fading, the lack of direction. I think I've found the perfect spot to observe it right here among people like yourself, though I dare say it's hard for you to grasp the concept.'

'Oh, is that what's meant by a concept? I suppose people do need a hobby.'

'That's enough,' said Susie, with weary brightness. 'Everyone's tired. It's hot. Let's go out in the garden and just sit and calm down. I thought the other film was much more interesting. And beautiful to look at.'

'I'm calm, Susie,' Diane hissed. 'I'm calm like a green-fringed fucking millpond right here up nowhere's English asshole.' She gestured Susie impatiently aside. 'So what am I, Jane?'

'Never mind. Let's move on,' said Jane, turning away to pick up her bag. 'Susie's right. It'll be a bit cooler outside.'

'Don't walk away from me. Tell me what I am.'

'Don't worry about it.'

'I said tell me. What am I?'

Marcie had reappeared now, pale and straight-faced.

Jane gazed at her, then said, 'I couldn't honestly tell you what you are. I mean, apart from the obvious, that you're loud and coarse and ignorant and selfish, and jealous of talent, and a wrecker. Let's leave it at that, shall we?'

'Now then, ladies, that's enough,' said Shirley, appearing at my side. 'We can't have this. You're upsetting my regulars.' As usual this was not true. The regulars seemed sad at the imminent end of the fun, but no matter. 'This is no way to go on, is it? Either you be friends or take yourselves home. I expected better of you, Jane. This other one' – she indicated Diane – 'probably can't help it. Knows no better, like you say. But that's no excuse.' Jane nodded to Shirley, rose and went out into the garden. At a loss, the rest of us looked on.

Diane stood up and went to the doorway of the garden. She pointed a finger after Jane. 'Your comments are duly noted, you hear me?' Then she left by the street exit. Marcie went after her. The Pritchard brothers exchanged an impressed glance. I resisted the urge to clap. After a baffled pause somewhere between horror and hilarity, the rest of us followed Jane into the garden.

We found her seated demurely at a table in the shade of the mulberry tree. 'I would like a large vodka,' said Jane, 'with plenty of ice and servility.' She smiled. The men all rose like courtiers to satisfy her wishes. Her attention immediately shifted inwards. I think now that she was considering the accuracy of a calculation. I looked at Alex. He had been untypically silent during the argument in the pub. Now his expression was markedly similar to hers. They sat at opposite ends of the table, but we all knew they were the only people there.

'People arguing about a bloody *film*,' said Luke.

'If you say so, lovey,' said Susie, tousling his cockerel crop.

'Shame whatsername wasn't filming just now,' said Alex. 'Very sexy, I thought.'

12

A few days passed uneventfully. Diane did not put in a further appearance. That Thursday Susie went into work at the crack of dawn to beat the heat. I couldn't get back to sleep. No one else was stirring. The walls and the furniture gave off their stored warmth like batteries. In the bathroom the water would not run cold.

I went and sat in the small bedroom I allegedly used for work and read through the thinnish file of poems written in the last year. One reason I hadn't slept was that I had neither drunk nor smoked anything the night before. It felt exposed but not unpleasant. There was the mental itch that sometimes precedes the beginning of a poem. Perhaps today then, beginning before the heat took hold, I would get somewhere. Exton could have a day off.

I lit a cigarette and looked down into the lane. At seven a.m. Luke went past, then returned with a copy of the local paper and a bottle of milk, his head bowed, his wooden soles scuffing against the road. Silence moved in after him. Departed traveller, empty road, dawn (at a stretch), the unresting line of aspens over the wall of the churchyard opposite, gold lichen on the headstones, head-high grass. Perhaps today, if I was careful.

When I had sat for an hour simply looking, a black VW van with smoke-tinted windows rolled into view and stopped quietly below. It must have come downhill with its engine off. The driver's door opened and a man got out. Faint music accompanied him. He was tall and barefoot, with razor-cut fair hair. He wore a sleeveless red T-shirt and a pair of black leather strides that would normally speak of vanity and self-deception but in his case seemed quite apt, if slightly unseasonable. He leaned back on the edge of the seat and studied a map. Perhaps I could help. Perhaps I could have drawn the curtains and minded my own business. I could have lived quietly, somewhere else, as the poet said.

I went down and opened the front door. A young woman had joined the stranger. She, too, was tall and fair and favoured the leather look, including a ferociously tight halter-top. Her tits must be like prunes in that, I thought. He face was drawn and sallow, as though from too much sun.

'Are you lost? Can I help, perhaps?' I noticed I sounded like my father.

'Yes, thank you, I think so maybe. I think we are near our destination but there is a turn somewhere we are missing,' the man said gravely.

'It was back there, Dieter,' said the woman. 'As I told you.' She looked at me with an unimpressed air, as if I was contributing to their failure to arrive. Fair enough.

'*Vielleicht. Aber* – Do you speak German? he asked.

'*Nur ein bisschen.* A little, from school.'

He nodded and came closer, as though to simplify matters for me. The woman sulkily took his place in the door of the van, then turned and brought out a camera and trained it on us both where we stood by the front step. Dieter held out the map. Irrelevantly, the largeness of the chosen scale struck me.

'This place' – he pointed – 'do you know it?'

'That's Moon House. Your friend was right. You will need to go back the way you came. It's easy to miss the turn. I can show you if you like.'

'It seems you were correct, Irmgard,' said Dieter, studying me.

'I know. Smile, please,' said Irmgard in bored voice, and took a photograph. 'Look at this place. Like a Friedhof.'

'We don't get many visitors hereabouts, especially from overseas.' I realized with embarrassment how this must sound. 'Are you students?' I asked. The camera clicked again.

'Eternally,' said Dieter, after a moment, with a wolfish grin. 'We are Germans, after all. The search for wisdom is everything. The quest for enlightenment is eternal, yes? There is nowhere we are not prepared to go in its pursuit. Even here is not too far.' It was hard to tell if the joke was on you or with you.

'Nah, this is a step too far,' said Irmgard, turning her lens on the cottage. 'This is nowhere.'

'Some people find that an attraction,' I said, but she appeared to ignore me.

Dieter gave his grin again, like a formality, then took a

packet of cigarettes seemingly from his armpit and offered one to me. The brand was new to me: Roth-Handle. The taste was fierce and acrid.

'Wisdom is what we seek,' he said, stretching and looking around up the empty street, 'plus a fuck and a smoke and the death of *Kapitalismus*. And not forgetting music, well-tempered and otherwise.' I recognized the song playing on the van's stereo now. Steppenwolf, 'The Pusher', sounding very odd in the village street at that time of day, like a shofar blown on the far side of an innocent hill.

'Moon House is a study centre,' I said. 'Part of the university.'

'Is that so?' He seemed amused. 'There is a university here?'

'Well, nearby.'

'It is small, then.'

'It's very new.'

'We're here though for the party, *ja*?' said Irmgard, impatient with distraction.

'The party?'

'What's the matter?' She raised her eyebrows. 'You are not invited? Oh dear.' She sniggered and put a hand to her mouth.

Dieter smiled again as if to excuse her, then turned to his companion and frowned. Irmgard shrugged.

'Diane's party? On Midsummer Eve?' he said, turning back. 'You know Diane Eckhart? American? Big dark hair?'

'Yes, I've met her but she doesn't live at Moon House. She's just staying, for a short while. She's a visitor.'

'That is no problem,' said Irmgard. 'This thing will occupy one evening only. One evening in the evening of the West.' She laughed. It turned into a dry, racking Roth-Handle-fired cough. She reminded me of Nico without the human warmth.

'It may not be that simple. The person who lives there, Marcie—'

'Diane told us of her,' said Irmgard. 'She is – what is the word? – the caretaker.'

'No. She's not the caretaker.' That must be Diane's joke, if you could call it such.

'Well, whatever this Marcie thinks she is or is not, can you direct us, please, to Moon House?' asked Dieter, climbing back into the van. 'There is not much time to prepare.'

I thought about sending them off to Bishop's Castle where, with luck, the locals would greet them with pitch-forks and blazing tar.

'It may not be possible to have a party there,' I said feebly. 'It is the property of the university. It is a place of study. There are valuable papers there.'

'If necessary we will worry about all these matters later– the protocols and regulations concerning the party. At that time we will make suitable arrangements,' said Dieter, patiently, an anarchist and a German. 'If you will tell us, please, how to get there?'

'Go back up the hill past the pub. Go on for another

two hundred yards, then take the left turn. There's a set of tall iron gates on a bend near the top of the hill. They're hard to miss.'

Dieter nodded and climbed into the driver's seat. 'That's what they said about Coventry,' he said, starting the engine. 'Anyway—'

'Martin—'

'Come to the party, Martin. There. Now you are invited. *Alles klar.*' He reversed the van ferociously along the street and did a U-turn at the entrance to the church-yard before disappearing uphill among the trees. Shirley's dog started up his flinty bark in the pub yard, which seemed to prove that the encounter had actually taken place.

There would be no poems for me today, I sensed. As for the party, who could say?

The party – Marcie's party, the do at Moon House, Diane's party according to some – took on what might nowadays be called cultural dominance in the village over the next few days. No announcement had been made, no official invitations issued, but everyone, from Shirley in the pub ('Think of all those flies') to the two elderly Pacey sisters in the shop and Raymond the sexton in the churchyard over the road, was aware of it. More, by the end of Wednesday afternoon the party seemed to have changed instantane-ously from being news to a phenomenon requiring a weary grin or grimace of acknowledgement. No good would come of it, but a bit of income might result, and in the aimlessness of the never-ending heatwave, the party on

Midsummer Eve represented an aiming point, an outcome of sorts, even for those who would never have dreamed of going anywhere near it. There were suddenly more young people in the vicinity than one had imagined, not to mention ageing groovers in the hidden valleys, sniffing action from their tepees, and in dank Nissen huts once used as PoW camps. Leo and Sophie, skeletal twin junkie children of the absentee gentry, were suddenly to be found in the pub with Diane's name on their lips, like a guarantee of access to all areas. Word gets around. Impressions form and become the case. I found myself feeling a bit proprietorial – I mean, who *were* these people?

It seemed to me that for Marcie, in contrast, the whole expanding, ramifying thing was like the confirmation of her worst fears. There was no escape from Diane. The way to stop it happening would be to rouse the torpid authorities at the Marches, but apparently Marcie felt that she was somehow to blame for Diane's ungovernable presence and that she would also be sent packing in disgrace if the thing got out. At the same time, being a well brought-up citizen with a sense of the obligations of hospitality, she threw herself into such preparations as she could control, and insisted that for reasons of practicality the party should take place in the grounds rather than inside Moon House.

Seeing Marcie accept the inevitable, Susie began going over to Moon House to help. If nothing else, there would be proper food for the guests to throw at each other. The monstrous and long-neglected iron range in the kitchen was blackleaded, tested with fascination and made ready for much baking. A copy of Mrs Beeton was unearthed from a cupboard and agreed to be somehow apt to the setting, if not the occasion. Food was the index of civilization. It might encourage the barbarians to adopt the manners of the bourgeois.

For Luke the party was something to look forward to in the eventless desert of the unemployable. For a while he could loiter near the epicentre. He seemed to imagine nurses in uniform being bussed in from all points of the compass. He was conscripted for errands and heavy lifting. On his tea-breaks he sat at the kitchen table sampling gradually more successful loaves and increasingly ambitious proto-pies. The two women would stand with folded arms assessing his reactions. As far as Luke was concerned, it was simply food and meant for eating, but to be the object of female solicitude – a pat on the arm, his hair ruffled, a pie to go home with – was such a novelty that he could not believe his good fortune. All his life he had waited for this.

And Gwyther had been waiting for me, without being so impolitely pressing as actually to mention it. I had given him a copy of the introductory chapter I'd been trying to pull together, arranging to meet him in the Green Man for a supervision.

' "Say not the struggle naught availeth," he said, when I looked anxiously round the door of the snug at five past eleven. 'Will you take some refreshment?'

'It's a bit early for me.'

'If you say so. Ginger beer for my young friend, please, Sal.' He drank the top off his pint, picked up the folder

containing my work, then put it down again. 'According
to the accepted wisdom, which in this case is quite correct,
I'm supposed to tell you to write something every day,
even if it's only a few sentences on an index card. The
point is to be *doing*, steadily, by rote if necessary. But I can
see I don't have to tell you that.'

This was news to me. Activity had been conspicuously
absent much of the time. I felt as if I had spent at least as
much time worrying as working. 'Do you think so?' I said.

'I do, Martin. Your draft chapter here shows the signs
of daily struggle to a degree that is at some points agoniz-
ing to read and which in turn makes it hard to contemplate
what it might be costing you to go on from one paragraph
to the next. You are having a horrible time.' After this he
drank half the pint and looked at me.

My turn. 'I'm not sure I'd go as far as that. It has been
a bit difficult, now and then,' I said, unwillingly.

'Believe me, Martin, I can recognize the signs – for
example, you leave no sentence unmurdered by qualification, no shining notion without its mirror of doubt.'

'Well, you know, I'm trying to be exact about things.
To focus.'

'It reads as if you are trying to drive yourself mad.'

'I don't have to try,' I said, with a laugh.

Gwyther didn't join in. He fiddled with his pipe. 'May
I ask if you're a believer?' he asked, squinting at the bowl
as he dug at it with a penknife.

'Is that relevant?'

'You're studying a religious poet. It was of the greatest
relevance to him, of course.'

'William Empson's an atheist. He studies Milton.'

'Indeed he does, in his inimitable way. And my question?' Gwyther lit the pipe, then rested it on the table.

'I don't know. I doubt it. Hard to say.'

'And there's a "but" waiting to be added, I should imagine.'

'Professor Gwyther, I don't mean to be rude, but is this some sort of test? Other than an academic one, I mean.'

'Not of my devising, Martin. The subject simply presents itself in a rather insistent way when I read this.' He picked up the file and put it down again. It was the first time I had seen him uncomfortable. 'As it happens, I have a faith, and I feel fortunate in it, and for what it's worth I think it preserves me from the worst of myself.' He indicated the glass in front of him. 'But I certainly wouldn't try to force it on to others or even especially to recommend it to them. It's just that I see you struggling.'

'I'm sorry – I don't follow.'

'Don't you?' He smiled at me enquiringly. I didn't take up the invitation.

'As far as it goes, this is not a bad piece of work at all,' he said eventually. 'A very promising start.'

'Well, then – I mean, thank you.'

He hadn't given up altogether. 'I like the fact that it seems more the product of love, of a sort, than of duty. But there is more of disquiet here than either. Are you punishing yourself?'

'What for?'

'That I couldn't say. But it feels as if you might be.'

'I don't like wasting time. I've wasted quite a lot before

now, before coming here, as I suspect you know, and now I don't want to waste any more. I think, I hope, that's progress.' I was beginning to feel very young beneath Gwyther's crinkly gaze. He smiled and swallowed what remained in his glass. Sal appeared at the hatch with a fresh pint.

'Your friend Mr Farren is an exacting companion, I would think.' I said nothing to this. 'Very certain of where he stands, according to Dr Pyne.' *That fucking prat Pyne*, as Alex referred to his supervisor after their occasional encounters. *Wouldn't know a poem if it bit him on the arse. As for his so-called poems, couldn't write fuck on a bog door.* Alex didn't like homosexuals, which Pyne was (*fucking international faggot conspiracy, man*) and he didn't much like people disagreeing with him. Pyne must be wondering what he had done to deserve Alex.

'Alex knows his own mind,' I said.

'His "unconquerable mind", I dare say. And you are part of a nest of singing birds, of the modern sort, with your young ladies and all the comforts of home, no doubt. Sure you won't join me?' Gwyther handed back the heavily annotated pages. 'But you're not happy in yourself.'

'Show me someone who is.'

'Bad faith, Martin. You can't give in to these things. Mustn't, I mean. Can't do the devil's work for him.'

'I've never had a supervision quite like this before. I'm beginning to feel as if I'm on trial.'

'I'm not the problem. I mean you no ill, I assure you.' He smiled in his more familiar avuncular way and leant forward. 'I'm sorry. I'm not being very helpful. And, despite myself, I'm intruding. Something in your work worries me. It seems like the work of someone very troubled.'

'Exton wasn't exactly frivolous.'

'You're not Exton.'

'Eh? Of course not.'

'Keep the distinction in mind, yes?' He smiled at me sadly. 'People assume that their sophistication will preserve them from error. Sometimes they're mistaken.' I had no reply to this. 'Anyway, enough. Shall we start on page three?' Gwyther's courtesy always felt like a compliment. Now I felt I had insulted him by putting on a brave face.

We moved on to matters of detail – a normal super-vision, in other words – and arranged to meet at the end of the summer when Gwyther and his wife returned from Greece. Eventually I left him settled in the pub with his paper and went to get the bus back to Summer Street.

I missed the stop by going over the conversation in my head. By the time I noticed, we were arriving in Church Green, on the far south-western side of May Hill. Rather than wait for the return bus, I set off to walk.

The afternoon was grey and hot. Exton did not refer to this kind of weather in his journals, but it would surely have suited him to sweat his way over the hills in clerical black with his notebook and a copy of scripture, damned to burn but keenly and lovingly observant in the mean-time.

I had lied to Gwyther. That he had seen the extent of my identification with Exton had made it seem necessary. To have told the truth would have granted the world at large admission to something whose ambiguous relation to fact retained a mildly comforting status while kept in the privacy of my mind. It was as bald as that. He thought I was on the brink of going nuts. He feared for my spiritual welfare, which meant he believed there was spiritual welfare for me to *have*, whereas I seemed to think that all I could do was fall off the edge of the world. Failure was to be a form of exoneration, proof that I couldn't live up to my own demands and the expectations of others. Which others? Susie? My parents? Perhaps all they wanted me to do was live, even if only to tell the tale of my failure. After the hot, headachy bus, it all seemed horribly obvious, as though I had been caught out believing in a lie of my own devising. The insult of illumination. He was right: I was punishing myself. I wanted to fail. As usual Exton had something to say on the matter:

> Man may not make an end of his estate.
> The keys are with the angel at the gate.

Damned if you do, damned if you don't.

The fallow, thistled ground rose slowly towards a group of abandoned farm buildings. I approached along a hedgerow and stopped when a movement caught my eye. The rounded roof of a black van was drawing away down the lane, as someone stepped out of sight behind the old wooden barn. I knew Jane liked this place and came here on her walks, but for once I didn't want to meet her. It was particularly annoying not to have the landscape for the exclusive use of my gloom and mortification that afternoon, and I paused, crouching behind the screen of hawthorns, hoping it would not be necessary to talk to anyone.

It was Diane who re-emerged, movie camera in hand. She moved backwards away from the barn to frame and film it. The place was an obvious gift to her sense of an ending. I could easily have called out to her. We were, after all, acquaintances. I supposed we got along well enough socially, since, like Susie, I was of no interest to her, but she was certainly not someone I wished to meet there, especially not then. I was walking the ground but she was trespassing on one of Jane's places. Worse, Irmgard appeared from the other end of the barn, pointing back at something out of view. Diane went over to join her and they rounded the corner out of sight.

I struck off into the dead ground of the field, still masked by the hedgerow, wondering as I went if I, too, was observed, and if so by whom, and to what effect. Exton sensed the displeasure of the angels; I was hot and tired now, and longing for a drink. Nothing was settled by my meeting with Gwyther, or by my glum and bitty reflections. I had not been changed. Nothing was clear, or finished, and neither was the end in sight.

The temple in the woods was undergoing some temporary refurbishment. Having taken on the role of Diane's cultural lieutenants, Dieter and Irmgard appeared, their van stuffed with dusty glass-and-velvet hangings and heavy dark rugs. Apparently they'd picked the stuff up for next to nothing from a bankrupt headshop in Hereford. Where did all the rest of it go, by the way, the vats of patchouli and the forests of joss sticks and the entire works of Hermann Hesse? Into the aspic of warehouses, awaiting the emergence of retro and a new generation of sentimental mug punters?

Luke, uncomplaining, hauled this frowsty trove up the back steps of the temple, then arranged it according to Irmgard's meticulous and exacting instructions – she could easily be heard at a distance through the trees – while she continued to photograph everything that moved. The temple gradually began to look like a hitherto unseen interior from Böcklin's *The Isle of the Dead*, opulent and portentous, its dark, decaying velvets giving off the wholly practical odour of decay.

Alex watched, and kept his counsel, while *Beggars Banquet* became the most frequently played record at the cottage. He had let it be known that the party would also mark the publication of the first issue of the *Summer Hill Review*, though it was hard to see who among those attending would notice or think it was important. He said he would be inviting 'a few people' and that the band would re-form to provide some rough and ready musical entertainment for the occasion. After all, there'd be no show without Punch.

Since the argument in the pub, Jane had stayed mostly in her room, working more intently than ever. Diane had commandeered Marcie's car and was away a good deal during the day, as was Alex. Nobody said anything.

The heat never wavered. Although I pleaded pressures of study, I was enlisted for the odd afternoon to move furniture suitable for outside use, and to hang lamps around the pool and along the paths into the woods. When I was helping at Moon House, every couple of hours I went and lay in the pool, though often there was no sun, only the white sky of an English childhood. I hung in the water, half dozing, as if in the silent interval before a thundercrack. Events were taking their own course. All these absurdly detailed preparations were being carried out in the service of something whose name had not yet been spoken.

Late one afternoon I had sat down on a bench in the woods to smoke a joint when Susie appeared. She sat down, too, and kissed me. 'Are you frightened?' she asked. 'You look a bit bothered.'

'Not about this, not specially. But I've been busy out here. It makes a change.'

'I am.'

'What about?'

She shrugged. 'I don't know why we're doing this.'

'It's a party.'

'Parties aren't compulsory.'

'I mean, *it's just a party*. It'll be a laugh.'

She shook her head. 'It's more like – well, more like some kind of *project*. Not like a laugh. It's not just a bit of fun, is it? I mean, it's hard work. It's like being in a documentary, what with bloody Irmgard and Diane and their cameras.'

'Well, you seem to have volunteered yourself.'

'That's to help Marcie.'

'And Marcie's been railroaded.'

'In a way that's my point.'

'She could have put her foot down. If she really wanted to.'

Susie's expression indicated that she was not surprised by how little I knew. 'You're wrong.'

'Am I? Why?'

'Martin, Martin. You really haven't noticed. She's in love with Diane.'

'Eh? She told me they're not a couple.'

'They're not. Diane doesn't live like that. But Marcie's besotted with her.'

'But she seems a bit scared of her.'

'Yes.'

'She doesn't even like her.'

'Yes again.'

'Blimey. And Diane's playing her for all she's worth.' Susie nodded and took the joint from my hand. She rarely smoked. 'Well, what can we do?'

'Keep an eye on Marcie. Be around. Be her friends. And watch out for those bloody Germans.' Susie coughed and handed back the joint. 'Come on, let's go for a walk.'

'To be honest,' I said, 'I'm never entirely happy in these woods. Too much Exton and Bromsgrove. Too much smoke and jism.'

'All the more reason to beat the bounds. I'll hold your hand.'

After a time we came out at the spot where Jane had emerged from the woods a few days previously. We followed a path along the edge of the dry pool, then climbed a few steps to the broad forecourt of the temple. Now it looked like a not terribly good film set, and I thought of the girls in *The Wicker Man* apparently leaping through the flame. For the moment the place was deserted. Upright chairs with padded wooden arms had been fetched in and roughly hung with heavy fabrics in red and blue. Gauzes were draped between some of the pillars, with heavier hangings pinned up at the back wall and spread over the altar where now a bust of Dionysos stood. The stone floor was covered with rugs. An urn held the ashes of incense.

'Very Dennis Wheatley,' said Susie.

'If you would just care to disrobe and lie on the altar, miss, this won't take long.'

'Tell me something I don't know.'

The altar was hollow, open at the back with shelves where decanters of oil and bowls of petals were stored.

'Shit, have you seen this lot?' I said.

'Actually, it is a bit creepy,' said Susie.

'Is that in a sexy way?' I asked.

'What are you doing here?' said Irmgard's voice, from close behind us. She came and positioned herself between us and the altar.

'Having a look,' said Susie. 'What's your excuse?' Irmgard took a photograph. 'D'you mind not doing that?'

'It is only a documentary record,' said Irmgard. 'This area – ' she gestured ' – is for the moment forbidden.'

'Says who?'

'Diane.'

'This place is nothing to do with Diane,' said Susie, holding her ground. 'She doesn't own it, does she? It belongs to the university.'

'And it does not then belong to you also.' Irmgard gave a steely smile. 'Best if you go now and ask Diane. I have my orders.' She took another photograph.

'I bet you do.'

'Orders for the party, for preparations. Look, no problem, is simply taboo for a little time, OK?'

'You're joking. What are you doing down here? Beheading chickens?'

'The . . . event, the situation . . . is until Saturday only. You don't want to spoil the party, after all.'

'No, flower, I imagine that's your job,' said Susie. 'Anyway, I hope you're going to clean all this tat somehow. It smells awful. Feel that,' she said to me. 'The velvet's all matted. It's like Velcro.'

'It is not meant for you to lie down on it.'

'Come on, Martin. Let's leave Miss Riefenstahl to her work.' We heard the camera clicking again as we walked away.

'Where do you suppose she sprang from?' I asked.

'Maybe there's a secret door at the back of the temple. In this place it would hardly be surprising.'

'It's like Enid Blyton with dirty bits. Enid was a xenophobe as well.'

'I'm not a xenophobe, Martin. How dare you?' She was laughing now.

'Well, I couldn't help noticing you're not terribly keen on Irmgard.'

'She acts up to the expectation, doesn't she? I bet she wears leather knickers. I mean, for God's sake, we've already got Diane to cope with. One wrecker's enough, d'you not think? Let's go home. Where is Diane, anyway?' We walked through the woods like a real couple, which we were, more or less.

13

Another crisis had presented itself when we got back to May Cottage. Alex stood in the kitchen, staring into the sink, shaking his head.

'Where's Jane?' asked Susie.

'Wrong question, I'm afraid.'

'I'm sorry, Alex. You're upset. What is it?'

'I'm not "upset",' he said tightly, without turning round. 'Whatever I am, it's not that, all right?'

'All right,' said Susie. 'So where is Jane?'

'The pub. We've got things the wrong way round today.'

'I'd better go and see her.'

'Would you mind staying here, Susie?' Alex said, still facing away. Susie looked at me. 'Let Martin go.' I shrugged.

'Of course,' she said. 'Go on, Martin. I'll sit with Alex for a bit. You keep Jane company.'

Jane was sitting in the garden under the mulberry tree, a cardigan over her bikini top. A nearly empty glass and an opened letter lay on the table. She was smoking a roll-up.

'Susie was going to come, but you've got me instead. Do you want another of those?'

'You'll have to do, I suppose. Yes, get me another, but

give us a hug first.' When I put my arms round her, her grip was almost fierce. I could tell she'd been crying, which I'd never seen her do before. 'Get me a large one.'

In the bar Shirley looked up from reading a Georgette Heyer. She marked her place and indicated the optics. I nodded, gesturing for doubles. I live here, I thought, looking round the dim brown interior. I don't want to lose this.

She poured the drinks, then leaned over confidentially. 'Gone wrong indoors with that Alex, has it? I thought so. She's too much for him, mebbe.' I couldn't help grinning at this. 'Well, she *is*. Full of beans, her. Ask me, it's obvious. Only – she's a lovely girl, not like that American article, but can you get her to cover up when she comes in the bar? That skimpy stuff's all right for the seaside, or the back garden even, but it makes some of my regulars nervous, whatsits nearly showing and that.'

Under the oiled, brazen enticement of the calendar pin-up from the local garage, the half-dozen septuagenarian regulars seemed as phlegmatically attentive to their pints and racing pages as usual. However, I assured Shirley that I would try and went back out to Jane.

'Bad news?' I asked as I put the drinks on the table.

'Awful.' She handed me a letter.

'Shirley asked me to ask you to cover up when you're in the bar.'

'That's a pity. I was thinking of painting my arse blue and jumping down the chimney. But would anyone notice?'

'What's the row about?'

'It's not a row. Though there will be one, probably.'

'So what will it be about if it happens?'

'The Jerome.'

I could guess what this meant but she wanted to say it aloud. The Jerome was the Jerome Award, given annually to a handful of poets under thirty, and viewed as a strong indication of future prospects. People were very cool about the Jerome. They spoke of it in tics and small shifts of conversational weight, as though it were a preoccupation for other people that they were dutifully observing. I did the same myself. 'What about it?'

'Alex didn't get one.'

'Oh dear. I see.' I suppressed a deafening interior cheer. 'Well, it's early days.'

'That's what I told him. He was playing it down.'

'And that was no good. Sympathizing.'

'It made things worse. Early days are his thing. He wants to be in there first. Obviously. A pioneering spirit, you might say.'

'Difficult for him. And for you.'

'Did you enter?'

'No. I didn't think I was ready.' We both laughed. 'I tend to go in a bit later on, with the colonial administration.'

'Anyway, he wants to be alone for a bit.'

'He's with Susie.'

'He wants to not be with me.' Jane emptied her glass and sipped from the fresh one, shivering a little at the vodka hit. 'There's something else, Martin. I hadn't told him I'd applied for the Jerome as well.'

'Why not?' I hoped the smirk I was experiencing didn't show on my face.

'Because something like this latest row would simply have happened sooner.'

'He could have worked it out.'

'It was all right while he didn't officially know, a bit like me not knowing about his floozies.'

'His what?'

'His bits of skirt, Martin. His fancy pieces. Need I go on?'

'The news came out.'

'I'm afraid so. Another postal catastrophe. Have a look at this.' She passed me the letter.

The Jerome committee had awarded her five thousand pounds. A lot of money in those days. A fortune for a poet. 'Oh, fuck,' I said. 'I mean, that's brilliant, Jane. Oh, fuck. Anyway, I didn't know you'd been interviewed.'

'I suppose not. Anyway, he thinks I've betrayed him.'

'I don't follow. What's one got to do with the other?'

'Well, you can see what he means, can't you? How it must feel. I've betrayed him with knowledge, haven't I? With something previously unstated.' I'd never quite got used to her matter-of-factness. 'He feels as if he knows that for me it wasn't enough just to apply – even though to apply and fail would probably have been acceptable in his terms. But, no, I had to go and be successful. Very difficult for Alex, poor love. And I mean, it's not as if I need the money.'

'I'm sure it will come in handy.'

'Of course I offered it to him immediately.'

'Oh, Jane, that was a bad idea. That was really daft.'

'Evidently it was. I'm not good at things like that. I just wanted to show it didn't matter.'

'Oh, Janey, anyone could tell you've got money! It matters like mad. You can't unhave your money. And, really, Alex must be as skint as I am.'

'Do you want it, then?' I laughed and stared at her. Imagine what that would do in the current climate. 'I can give you it. I don't mind.' She was right: not good at that sort of thing. Because she never doubted anyone's dignity she couldn't imagine the doubts they suffered about it themselves. It looked like superiority, but it was more a fatal kind of honesty, as though she'd missed some key part of the social curriculum.

'What kind of boy do you think I am?'

As was her way, she didn't laugh or even blink, but reached out and stroked my hand. 'Have I managed to offend you as well?' she asked.

'No, Janey, my standards are much lower altogether. It's a very kind offer and Susie would kill me if I accepted it.'

'I could talk to her.'

'I'm sure you could. But I hope you won't.' She took a large sip of her drink and looked at me as if expecting to be told off. 'Did it ever occur to you – not that I'm saying it should have – but did it ever occur to you not to apply, to leave the field free for Alex?' I asked.

'For a moment, yes, it crossed my mind that I might do that. But it was like a thought someone else was vaguely entertaining. You know – a long way off in a language I didn't properly understand. And why would I do such a thing, anyway? Am I supposed to handicap myself?'

'You're better than he is. You have more talent.'

'I repeat my question.'

'You don't want to hurt him, but you go ahead and hurt him anyway.'

'That's the way it goes, it seems.'

'You're right. You have to be – be the steward of your talents.'

'Sort of like a doorkeeper in a brothel.'

I shook my head at the analogy. 'You can support each other, but the work has to stand by itself.'

'Obviously. But you don't sound convinced.' She stroked my hand again then drained her glass. 'Will you get me another drink? I'll pay.'

'No, you won't. I shall spend my last halfpenny getting you drunk to help you recover from the injury you have inflicted on my best friend.'

'Very well.' She moved her hand to my cheek. 'You should have gone in for the award, Martin. You know you're better than he is. *I* could be your best friend.'

I could have done it then, kissed her, pulled her down on to the grass. I think she was waiting to see if I would. I gathered the glasses and stood up. 'When did you ever read my work?'

'I wonder.' She smiled now and killed me all over again. 'But I must have, mustn't I?'

The bar was filling up. As I waited to be served, I considered the date of interview mentioned in the award letter. To the best of my knowledge Jane had been in

Aberystwyth visiting her sister then. But what did I know about anything, when it seemed Jane could read my poems telepathically?

We got drunk in the slow twilight, then supported each other on the short walk to the cottage. Susie was reading in the kitchen.

'I've brought your man back, darling. Thank you for the lend,' said Jane.

'I trust he was satisfactory, flower.' Susie went on reading.

'Oh, he was a perfect gent. Weren't you, Martin? As always.' Jane kissed me chastely on the cheek. 'Where's Alex?'

'Out. He must have left an hour or so ago. I thought he was going to the pub.'

'Oh, well. We must have missed him. I need my sleep.' Jane gave a little wave and disappeared upstairs.

'I'm knackered, too,' I said.

'Sit down a minute,' Susie said quietly, indicating the chair across from her.

'What's wrong? Is it Alex? What's happened now?' I asked.

'Alex reckons you're fucking Jane. Is that right?'

'What?'

'Is he right?'

'What do you think?'

'Is it true?'

'No, Susie, it's not. I love you.'

'That's not what I'm talking about. Love is all very well.'

'I've never been unfaithful.' I reached for her hand.

'You're free, you know,' she said, 'to do what you want. Otherwise what's the point? But you have to be straight. And if there was anything between you and her, then you'd have to go. I can't have you sleeping with my best friend. You know that, don't you?' Her voice thickened. 'Do you want to fuck her? I wouldn't be surprised if you did. People generally do.'

'That's not fair.' She made no reply. 'There's nothing going on, Susie. I don't know why Alex said what he said. To cause trouble, I suppose. Anyway, he can talk. What a cunt. I'm surprised he can remember who all the ones he fucks actually are.'

Susie looked at me for a while without speaking. I poured a glass of wine.

'His floozies,' she said eventually. We both laughed at this, though her eyes were full of tears.

'He says stupid things when he's upset,' I said. 'He lashes out if he thinks he's not in control.'

'And now he looks like being left behind. Everyone had better watch it. Oh dear.'

'What did he say about the Jerome?'

'That she hadn't told him. That every time he did something she's been there before him. By that reckoning she's had Diane go down on her.' Susie cackled.

I got Jane's vodka from the fridge and we went and sat outside on the bench for a bit without talking. Susie put her arm through mine and rested her head on my shoulder. The night showed no signs of cooling down. There were lights still burning at Moon House.

'He thinks it's a competition,' I said.

'Yes, but he can't understand why she's taking part. He can't see what it's got to do with her. She's supposed to be with him, isn't she? No matter if she's got more talent. Though he couldn't admit it in those terms.' Susie gestured up towards Moon House. 'This party business isn't helping.'

'If there had been something between me and Jane,' I said, 'what would you have done about her?'

Susie straightened and lit a cigarette. 'I'm not sure. I'm not sure there'd be anything *to* be done.'

'So you could still be friends?'

'Probably. I think so. You'd have to go, but Jane and I have always been friends. You and Alex aren't the first boys to attract our attention.'

'Yes, you do go back.' I imagined them as schoolgirls in straw boaters, plotting.

'That wouldn't be enough in itself, though. I suppose it's just that some people have the power to command. Jane's one of them. The way she sees things is the big picture the rest of us have to populate. It's not even egotism, really. She's just how things are.' At times Susie's matter-of-factness was as alarming as Jane's.

I wanted to tell her then that I had been tempted, repeatedly, for years, most recently that very evening, and that I had gone on resisting temptation, though the temptation showed no signs of diminishing. But I was neither brave nor stupid enough to try to say any of it that night.

Eventually Susie stood up and stretched. 'It always

seems to be the middle of the night round here,' she said, yawning. 'And boiling hot. Make it rain.'

'I'd better go and have a look for Alex,' I said. 'He'll probably be in a state.'

'You're not going to hit him or anything, are you?'

'Probably not.'

'Don't be too long. I'm getting sleepy. All this strife is quite rousing in a weird way.' She grinned and kissed me and went indoors. It struck me that I rather liked to make love to her when she was half asleep. I could have been anybody. So could she.

I took a guess and made my way round the field paths up to Moon House. By this time the building was in darkness. The sky had cleared and the moon was approaching the half. The heat had barely slackened. More confident of the ground now after my work on the party preparations, I took a route through the woods to bring me out near the station. The pale lanterns seemed faintly luminous in the scented blue dark. As I came along the platform I could see a light flickering in the signal box. The last thing I wanted was to find Alex at it again with Diane or someone. I found a bit of mortar and tossed it up at the door.

After a few moments the door opened. 'Yeah? Who's that?' said Alex.

'It's me.'

He turned back inside, leaving the door open. I went up the stairs. When I entered the box he was sitting on the low wooden revolving chair in the light of the paraffin lamp, rolling a joint on a copy of *Men Only*.

'You know the big advantage of the girls in these mags?'
he said. 'Compared to the rest? They don't *do* anything.
They don't act, they don't talk, they don't have abilities,
they don't . . . conspire. They just fucking lie there like
they're supposed to.'

'Don't be daft.'

'I'm daft, am I?' He lit the joint.

'They're not real, are they?'

'Oddly enough, I recognized one of the models in a
wank mag once. She was a friend of a friend of my sister's.
She went to do modern languages at Reading. Must have
been supplementing her grant. Nice girl. And good to know
she was actually blonde. Never managed to find that out
in the real world. My sister kept her well away from me.
Cow.'

'Give us the joint.' It didn't seem to be drawing very
well. 'What's wrong with this?'

'The dope's a bit damp, that's all.'

'Damp?'

'It's been marinated.'

'Eh? What in?'

'An opiate, apparently. New one on me.'

'Where'd you get it? Diane?'

'She's very generous.'

'So I've noticed.'

'Fuck off, man. Fuck right off. You're so pure in heart,
aren't you?'

I took a drink from the wine bottle that stood on the
floor. 'I'm not with you, Alex,' I said.

'No, you're not, are you? Not any more.'

'What are you talking about?' I felt slightly sick. I refused the joint this time.

'Talking about Jane.'

'I've never touched Jane. You know that.'

'Do I, though?'

'Well, I haven't.'

'But you'd like to. Go on. Admit it.'

'I don't like the way you treat her.'

'And you'd do a better job.'

'If you've got her, why on earth do you want anyone else?'

'You'd be fidelity itself, right?' He nodded sagely, raising his eyebrows. 'I sometimes wonder if you've actually got a cock, man.'

'She's worth it.'

'Minted, in fact.'

'I don't mean that.'

'Of course not. Nothing so fucking vulgar. Mr fucking Honour Bright. Why have you come here, by the way? Have you no home to go to? No one to snuggle up to?'

'You told Susie I'd fucked Jane.'

'Did I? And she believed it?'

'She was upset.'

'I can well imagine. Them being such old pals. Shame.'

'Why did you do that?'

He drank from the bottle. His eyes had become unfocused. 'You know what? Badness, Martin. I did it for fucking badness, pure and simple.'

'We're not to blame, me and Susie.'

'I never said you were. Anyway, blame for what?'

'Because Jane seems to be leaving you behind a bit.'

'I must say, I like "a bit". Very nicely measured utterance.'

'With getting published, and getting the Jerome. I know it's hard, but you can't begrudge her success. You mustn't.'

'You think so?'

'It's destructive.'

'And that's bad, yeah?'

'You can't go on like this. You'll ruin everything.'

'Who says I can't? Who says? You? F. R. Leavis? Beatrix cuntface Potter? On the contrary, Martin, I think I can go on, just to see what happens. After all, it's a long night.' He saluted me with the empty bottle.

'You can't live like that.'

'We'll have to see. I have confidence, whereas you've never fucking had any to speak of.'

'It's not confidence that makes you so jealous of Jane.'

'Jealous of what?'

'Of what she's achieving.'

'You can call it an achievement if you like.'

'Then what is it?'

He rolled his eyes ceilingward. 'It's a *hobby*, man. You can't tell, because you've got the same fucking hobby, only you're not so "accomplished". You haven't got the "talent" and you haven't got the chick either. So fuck off, right?'

I blinked. 'You really hate her.'

He was rolling another joint now. 'I hate the illusion. I hate the pretence.'

'You're afraid, Alex. You don't understand why you can't own her like you seemed to once.'

Sean O'Brien

'But you wouldn't mind, right? Exercising a bit of possession.'

'You have to let her be herself. Otherwise you'll lose her. Stop being afraid. Be happy for her.'

'Are you *advising* me? When did you get your promotion?'

'Where does all this anger come from, Alex?'

'I don't know, man. I think it was here all the time and I just found it again. It's like Johnny Angelo's magic jar – it never stops being replenished.'

'I'm not sure we can continue as friends if you keep going on like this, Alex.'

'You pompous cunt. Now I think of it, you've always been a pompous cunt.'

'It's true, though. I'm sorry, man. You're making things impossible.'

'I'll tell you another true thing from the great repository of terrible true things, shall I? I've fucked Susie, okay? And she liked it.'

'You're fucking mad.'

'Very likely. But I'm telling the truth.'

'Enough, Alex. That's enough of you and your shit.'

We were on our feet now. Alex wagged a finger at me, grinning, the bottle still in his other hand. 'Go on, then, Martin. Have a go. I fucking had her. I did. A screamer and a scratcher, don't you find? And grateful with it. Desperate for seconds. We're belly-cousins, you and me.' I moved towards him. 'Go on – try and plant one, you silly cunt.'

He spread his arms wide and took up the slack-kneed

braggart's posture I had seen so often on stage with the band. He swung with the bottle. I leaned inside, parrying his arm with my shoulder, then, to my surprise, punched him in the stomach, as though I'd been practising for years. He fell forward on to the floor, gasping, winded, then was violently sick. I hadn't struck anyone since I was nine years old. It felt great. I kicked him in the ribs. He groaned. I grabbed the bottle where it had fallen. I held it by the neck and raised it over my head. The crown of Alex's was exposed, the hair thinned with sweat. My chest seemed full of adrenalin. I put the bottle down on the windowsill and turned to go. I was faint and sweating, with checkerboard flashes sliding across my vision. I looked at Alex where he lay retching.

'She's fucking killing me, man,' he gasped. 'Jane's killing me.' He was weeping now. 'There's nowhere for me to be any more, nowhere to stand. What can I fucking do? I can't have it, man. It can't stay like this.'

'I'll let you know when I think of something.' After a while I went down the stairs and back along the platform into the woods. When I reached the house, there were people in the pool. Diane and Irmgard were swimming lengths, while Dieter sat on the diving board with yet another camera.

'Nice night for it,' I said. He nodded slowly and photographed me.

In the bedroom at the cottage I could tell that Susie was awake. But she said nothing, and neither did I. She didn't scratch. Afterwards, sleepless again, I rolled a joint and studied my night-self in the moon-silvered mirror. In the open door of the other bedroom, I could see Jane sitting naked, her feet drawn up. She too was looking. Neither of us gave any sign.

14

On Saturday morning I pleaded exhaustion when Susie roused me to go with her to help Marcie finish preparations at Moon House. Jane and Alex, separately or together, were nowhere to be seen, so I had the kitchen to myself. I began reading over some of my Exton notes, sitting at the table with a mug of tea and a bacon sandwich, feeling remarkably sober and intact – a state I was keen to encourage in myself, though also inured to its fragility.

About eleven o'clock there was a noise in the distance to the south. It grew louder. For some reason I went upstairs for a look. The street was completely empty – as though the doors had just that second closed behind everyone.

Then the first of the bikes glided past. The lead rider wore a German helmet with smoked goggles over his eyes and had a handlebar moustache. His leathers carried a set of ragged colours featuring a psychedelic skull-and-roses with the lettering *Bewdley Huns*. I recalled that the Grateful Dead, to whom we had all more or less stopped listening by that time, had always enjoyed good relations with the Angels. Most middle-class English people, however, were inclined to shit themselves with fear at the faintest suggestion that the Angels were in the vicinity, never mind thinking of popping in across teatime.

The outrider cruised to a halt, looked expressionlessly about him, then spat richly and greenly into the road. Satisfied, he raised a hand to signal for his as yet invisible companions to proceed. As he slid away, a dozen or so other bikes followed, all loyal works of British engineering – Triumphs and BSAs and Nortons, all soon to be extinct. Their riders wore the same Bewdley colours and various headgear including Viking horns and in one case a hoplite's helmet, which must have been intolerably hot – but then perhaps that was the sort of effect the Angels appreciated, as being likely to promote the righteous fury they valued so highly. Some of them carried their equally feral-looking and underdressed womenfolk on the pillions of their bikes.

The company moved away steadily until the road was lost in the trees. A surly roar, like a plague of hung-over flies, extended in its wake. This, I supposed, was Diane's doing, or Dieter and Irmgard's. It wouldn't be enough to have a party, it had to be 'a situation'. There had to be action, an outcome.

Sunk deep in cow parsley at this time of year, a little way down the road and set back into the hedge, stood the bus shelter. From behind it Luke now emerged, glanced back at the village, then clattered after the riders at a trot. No need to to spread the news to the blind and deaf residents, none of whom would have missed a thing or been daft enough to show their faces when the bikers arrived. He saw me, grinned widely and gave a double thumbs-up. All this and nurses too. I thought about Susie and Marcie up at Moon House and hurriedly put my shoes on.

When I arrived there was no sign of the visitors. Bare-chested, some local lads were erecting a stage made of pallets, watched by a pale Marcie.

'Bewdley Vandals? Are they lending a hand too?' I asked.

'They stopped at the gates for a little while,' she said. 'They had a look. Actually it was more of a stare.'

'Did you speak to them?'

'God, no. I was peeking through the bedroom window wondering what to do.'

'So what happened?'

'They took off.'

'Proves nothing, Marcie. They probably just wanted to make sure of the location. They'll go for a run over the border and have a few bevvies in the principality, sacrifice the odd sheep, and then they'll probably look in on the way back, when the, ah, celebrations are in full swing.'

'Yeah. I guess they might.'

'Did Diane invite them?'

'Search me. She didn't say.'

'Who else would?'

'Alex, maybe. Or both of them.'

'Where is she?'

'Like I say, search me. Off in Hereford sleeping with a soldier?' Marcie gave a tired smile. 'I'm not privy to her plans, Martin.'

'There's bound to be trouble if you let the bikers in. They can't help it.'

'I know. But it's too late now. Anyway, how could I stop them?'

'You could call the police.'

'You mean Constable Jenkins? What would he do? Breathe on them?'

'Well, there's more police in Hereford.'

'And then we'd all get busted, wouldn't we? And that would be the end. Schoolteaching for me, like my mom and dad, if I'm lucky. I think we just have to hope for the best. Can I have one of your cigarettes?'

In the boiling kitchen I found Susie in a bikini top and shorts taking a cake out of the oven.

'It's not cake that lot'll be after, you know,' I said.

She extended a floury cheek for me to kiss. Heat thrummed from the cake tin as she put it on the table. 'I suppose not. Shame to waste it, though.'

'We should just leave, Susie. Get in the car and bugger off for the day. Go and have something to eat somewhere. Find a B and B.'

'We've got food here. As you can see, I'm cooking it. You're meant to be impressed by the cake.'

'You know what I mean. Anyway, we could take some with us.'

'We can't just desert Marcie, can we?'

'Well, we could take her too.'

'She wouldn't abandon her post. Which means you can't either, or you renounce all claims to be the keeper of Exton's extremely bloody inconvenient flame. And we'd need to take Jane as well, and we don't know where she is.

So we just have to get on with it, as my auntie would say when faced with some new catastrophe.'

'Aren't you frightened? Something horrible might happen. Probably will happen.'

Susie sighed and lit a cigarette. 'Yes, of course I'm frightened. All the time. But you have to get on with things. Otherwise I'd just sit here screaming. And there's quite enough nutters about without me joining in. And it wouldn't be fair to leave. And I don't know what else to do except stay occupied.'

'Where's Diane? Where are Dieter and Irmgard?'

'God knows. I haven't seen them at all today. Off in the woods, maybe, mucking about in that stupid bloody temple. Why don't you go and have a look? A walk might calm your nerves.'

'Am I sounding a bit that way on?'

'A bit.' She kissed me again.

'What the hell are they all up to?'

'You can ask them if you see them – supposing they actually know, that is. I think they're just putting the mixture together to see what happens.'

'Very radical. Fucking burned-out hippies – I hate them.'

'So what are you, then?'

'Me? I'm a freak, darling.'

'A hippie without the vague general affection.'

'In it for the drugs and water-skiing.'

'But German freaks are quite political, aren't they?'

'Supposedly. I don't see much affection there, by the way. But what about Jane and Alex? Where are they?'

'No idea.' She came and stood in front of me, holding another large tin. 'Look, Martin, you can see I'm busy. Why don't you just go and find out? Stop fretting. Keep yourself occupied.' She turned the tin upside down and a loaf slid smoothly on to the table-top.

'Anyone would think you were domesticated at heart,' I said.

'Watch it. Anyway, at least girls are taught to *do* things.'

'Some girls. I don't think Diane's grasped the joy of cooking.'

'Yes. Now go away, Martin.'

I went back to the doorway and looked out at Luke and his friends stacking the pallets. Luke seemed jittery with excitement at being so close to the music. I realized I should take responsibility for some of this – like the senior British officer in a PoW film, I remember thinking, like the calm, saturnine Eric Portman. Fat chance.

There was the sound of a vehicle in the driveway. I went through the house to see who it was. The old white Transit van was disgorging the Rakes, a bunch of middle-class college graduates disguised as oily ne'er-do-wells. Only Mickey Shane, the lead guitarist, was a professional musician, beginning to make his way as a session player in London. The other three were there for wish-fulfilment, fresh from their teacher-training and social-work courses. The prematurely balding drummer was already skinning up on the bonnet.

'Now then, lads.' I shook Mickey's hand.

'Where's his nibs, then? Lost his nerve?'

'Lost something, certainly. I imagine he'll be here.'

'I hope so. None of us can fucking sing.'

'And he can?'

'Approximately. Where do we take the gear?'

'Round the back. I'll show you. Watch out for the Germans.'

'I thought my dad exterminated them.'

'And mind the Angels.'

'I take it you've hidden the billiard cues.'

In the later afternoon people began to show up in dribs and drabs, gathering around the big trestle tables outside the kitchen door, eating their way through stacks of sandwiches and cakes. Among the arrivals were a few couples with young children, and the innocent relaxation they brought to the place made me think that with a bit of luck it might be OK. Somebody put some music on through the onstage speakers – Van Morrison, I remember, and I remember Luke dancing with a girl of nine or ten, like the happy drunken harmless uncle he might – with some more of that luck – become.

Unable to settle, deciding not to drink or smoke as yet, I went for a turn in the woods. The sound of the music faded quite suddenly. None of the guests seemed to have penetrated the grounds yet, but after a minute I nearly walked straight past Gareth. He was sitting in the shade of a cavernous laurel bush at the meeting of two paths, patiently prodding at his pipe with a penknife. Even in this heat, he kept his leather overcoat on.

'Why don't you take your coat off, Gareth? You look as if you're not stopping.'

'No, thanks, if you don't mind, Martin. I know where I am with me coat on.' He looked at me consideringly. 'Bit of a tinder-box you've got here. Worth keeping an eye out.'

'Let's hope we don't need to.'

'You get a ruck of them town boys in later on, or them Angels, or both, might get very messy.'

'So what do you advise?'

'Carry a big bloody stick, boy. That'd be my recommendation.' He reached out and took up a walking-stick which rested behind the bench. He weighed it in his hands and winked. 'Takes me back. I was a Ted, right at the tail end of all that, when I was at the art college. Bet you never would have guessed it, looking at me. We were always behind the times here, I suppose. Not that it matters. Used to have some fun and games in Hereford of a weekend when the squaddies were on the town.' I was impressed by a vision of flailing bike chains and razor-work in the streets around the sleeping cathedral. 'You go on now, Martin. Have a look about. Mind you stay sober, though. And keep an eye on the womenfolk, all right? I'll stay handy.' He paused for a moment. 'If you see Luke, ask him to bring me a beer in a little while. I'll be hereabouts for a bit.' He repositioned the walking-stick and sat down on the bench to stare into space, apparently satisfied that the pipe was drawing properly now.

Dismissed and somehow at a loss, I made my way to the signal box. It was empty but there was dried sick on the floor. No other sign of Alex. Surely he wouldn't miss the great occasion he had done so much to instigate. I wandered up the railway line to the mouth of the tunnel. It was sealed with planks and a door where a padlock hung loose. In the interests of thoroughness I ought to take a look in there, but I had neither torch nor inclination. Moving on through the western edge of the woods, I followed the high stone boundary wall, where a couple of pigeons walked carefully along the loose coping-stones. After a while I reached another gate, this one bricked up. I followed the gravelled dry-rutted track that ran away from it, while the green gloom of the woods fell away on the right, with the cuckoos shouting at nothing as prescribed. In a few minutes the track itself descended to pass behind the rear of the temple. Now that I was nearly completing a circuit I was slightly disappointed to find how small this private world appeared to be, though equally I wondered why I should care. It wasn't mine, was it?

The black VW van was parked next to a gardener's open-fronted hut, which contained a heavy roller and some scattered tools that the brambles were steadily consuming. There was a sweet smell of burning nearby. I climbed the steps flanking the brick back wall of the temple. On the wooden stage, Irmgard sat at a low table, drinking wine. She raised her camera languidly but thought better of it. On a tripod next to her the smoke of heavy incense rose from an urn. The trees across the pond already had a vesperal blue tint. In the dry pool before the temple a tepee of firewood had been assembled. Dieter had his back to me but turned and greeted me with a smile. The pair of them seemed slightly out of it.

15

'Would you like to hear a poem?' asked Dieter, indicating the book he was holding. 'We were just discussing it.'

The idea that Dieter really read anything, as distinct from going to various universities and showing them his elaborate contempt, was arresting. I sat down in one of the scroll-armed chairs, feeling the tacky velvet under my bare forearms. There was the incense, but also the discredited reek of patchouli. 'Go ahead.'

He began to read:

'They shut the road through the woods
Seventy years ago.
Weather and rain have undone it again,
And now you would never know
There was once a road through the woods
Before they planted the trees.
It is underneath the coppice and heath,
And the thin anemones.
Only the keeper sees
That, where the ring-dove broods,
And the badgers roll at ease,
There was once a road through the woods.

Yet, if you enter the woods
Of a summer evening late,
When the night-air cools on the trout-ringed pools
Where the otter whistles his mate.
(They fear not men in the woods,
Because they see so few)
You will hear the beat of a horse's feet,
And the swish of a skirt in the dew,
Steadily cantering through
The misty solitudes,
As though they perfectly knew
The old lost road through the woods . . .
But there is no road through the woods.'

In a studied way Dieter made rather a good job of it, like a distinguished old actor indicating his pedigree to an audience of provincials.

'Do you know this poem, Martin?' he said.

'Of course.'

'And what is your judgement?'

'Well, it's an anthology piece. Quite popular.'

'*Scheisse*,' croaked Irmgard. '*Imperialismus*.'

'You could say that about a lot of things.'

Dieter looked on, nodding, his eyes bright.

'*Ja*. So?' said Irmgard.

'Well, it won't get you very far,' I replied.

'Neither will this fucking road that is not there,' she spat.

'I don't particularly want to defend the poem.'

'You are not committed to it.'

'How could anyone be committed to it?'

'That is the question. This Kipling, he speaks for England, yes?'

'He may have spoken for some of it at one time.'

'You are neither hot nor cold. You will be vomited out.'

'If you say so, Irmgard.' She turned towards me and I saw the works set out neatly on the table. 'I thought you were supposed to be political.'

'What is this' – she indicated the syringe – 'if not political? This is where it leads. This is the end.'

'If you'll forgive me saying so, fuck off out of it.'

'It is not my forgiveness you need.'

'Do you put money in her, or what?' I asked Dieter.

'She is a free subject. She may do as she wishes.'

'And you film each other getting fucked up? And Diane films the pair of you? I suppose this is leading the life of the imagination, is it?'

'What are you doing here, Martin?' asked Dieter, amiable and unconcerned.

'Beating the bounds, I suppose.'

'Looking for a way through the woods,' said Irmgard. 'Maybe this will help.' She gestured with the syringe. I shook my head 'No?' She raised her bare foot and injected herself between the toes. Dieter and I watched as though she was attempting an athletic feat. The hit came, her body slackened and she lay back in the chair.

'What are *you* doing here, Dieter?' I asked.

'Trying to understand. This England of yours.' He came and sat down, resting his arms on the table. 'Set in a silver sea. As a moat defensive to a house, *und so weiter*. The speech of a dying man. Decadence was shortly to piss on his grave and be pissed on in turn. This England of yours.'

'It's not my England. I just live in some of it.'

'Like Mariana in her moated grange. This nostalgic mythology is one of the things that absorb me. This dying-away, your melancholy long withdrawing roar, *und so weiter*. When in fact you've barely got started. How long did the empire endure in effect? A fortnight? A month?' He lit a joint.

'I don't care about that. And as I say, it's hard to generalize.'

'History generalizes. That is its purpose,' said Irmgard, tightly.

'Obviously I haven't got your certainty.'

'Are you cool with this?' Dieter indicated Irmgard, as he passed me the joint.

'It's your funeral. What can I do? Call the police? Obviously not, for Marcie's sake.'

'Yes, then there is the cult of personal relations. Rather betray your country than a friend.'

'You seem to be leaping ahead somewhat.'

'Am I? Then let us at any rate have a drink.' Dieter poured red wine from a jug and handed me a glass. *The Oxford Book of Nineteenth-Century English Verse* lay between us on the table. I noticed the catalogue number on the spine. It was from the book store in the basement at Moon House.

'How did you get this?'

'From the cellar.'

'You would need a key.'

'Yes, I would.' He produced it from his pocket.

'How did you get that?'

'I asked for it.'

'You asked Marcie?'

Dieter smiled. 'Drink, Martin. Or do you want to fight me for the key?' Irmgard sniggered at this.

'You should give it back as soon as possible. Diane had no business to take it from Marcie or give it to you.'

He shrugged. 'That's politics, I suppose. Diane understands what is taking place.'

'You mean here?'

'Here will do. You can enter the stage from any point.' I wondered if he too had been injecting, and if that was the source of his pitying benevolence. 'Help me a little, Martin, with the poem. I do not understand what is in it that appeals. I am not making a joke.'

'It is a form of consolation.'

'What, though, is consoling in it?'

I had known the poem since schooldays, Monday afternoons with Mr Nash in the old junior wing, when the class acquired the whole carious confection of Georgianism which the kindly master had carried with him through the trenches of the Great War and on to the year of his retirement, when we met him for poetry. You would never have heard of Wilfred Owen, still less Isaac Rosenberg, from Mr Nash. 'The Way Through the Woods' had been there, along with 'The Listeners' and 'The Railway Junction'. At the age of nine or ten, this was what we supposed poetry to be. It was much later on, in my mid-teens, that

'Prufrock' and 'Mauberley' and Yeats began to change everything I read. But I had never denounced, or wanted or attempted to despise the first poems I encountered. They were like an ancestral flaw – a cast in the eye, a webbed toe, a tendency to melancholy-madness – something that seemed to lie beyond the reach of judgement, or at any rate to make it feel excessive in proportion to the matter under consideration. The matter being foggy woods, damp, neglected houses glimpsed at the end of rutted lanes, quietly insistent absences – the matter of England, or one of the Englands, at any rate, something as ineradicable as the sound of blood in your ears. Though it seemed I had never lived there until these last months: I had looked over the wall or through the railings at the forbidden interior. Only now was I a resident. I realized I did not intend to leave. These were not matters I wanted, or would have felt able, to convey to Dieter.

I had drunk very little so far that day, but momentarily my eyes pricked with tears as I looked out across the dry pond at the tongue of rock and the heavy woods. If Dieter noticed he did not reveal it. We sat for a few minutes in silence.

'You were – what is it? – miles away there,' he said eventually. 'Can you enlighten me?' Though he could not be trusted, his interest was evidently genuine, part of the search for ammunition in whatever war he was waging.

I took a sip of the heavy red wine. Now Irmgard was listening expectantly too.

'I suppose the poem is consoling because its idea of the past does two things. On the one hand, it contradicts the wisdom of the present by proposing a kind of elsewhere, or maybe *elsewhen*. But on the other hand it also suggests that, for the dead, the war, as it were, is over – the war that has yet to happen – and that for the dead the writ of time does not run.'

'Is that a point worth making? Is that it?' asked Irmgard, stirring in her chair.

'For the living, perhaps.'

'Not much to call life, then,' she said.

She made me want to speak in defence of being half in love with easeful death.

'Surely you understand. You have romanticism in Germany too.'

'It is more robust there, I think,' said Dieter.

'Naturally. And as the evidence indicates.'

'And you had an empire. And we had Nietzsche – so what is hard for me, for us, is this idea of yours—'

'Not mine, especially—'

'This English idea, this desire almost to be gone even before knowing the ecstasy of death.'

I prevented myself laughing out loud. 'It's a terribly respectable kind of death wish, I agree. But call no man happy while he lives.'

Dieter refilled our glasses. 'To Dionysos,' he said. 'Down the hatch. Is that correct?'

'To Dionysos,' I replied. My tongue felt thick.

'A belated god,' said Imgard, raising a glass, 'late but necessary. Half mortal but nevertheless divine. A vital addition to the pantheon. Dionysos!'

I imagined Dionysos appearing from the woods, riding side-saddle on his panther, and what he might do to this silly creature, this metaphysical groupie who made so free with his name. At the same time, her capacity to provoke desire was not to be denied. I finished my drink too quickly.

'And this Thomas Exton?' Dieter said. 'What is the nature of your interest in him?'

'Our English friend is a dabbler in the work of another dabbler,' said Irmgard.

'It's hard to define my interest exactly, just at the moment. It's early days.' Something was prompting me to leave, but the warmth and the wine pinned me to the chair. I hated the stickiness of my hands. The grey, damp weight of the evening pressed in. Occasionally I could hear snatches of music in the distance, slightly out of phase.

'Exton was a damned soul,' said Irmgard, nodding pantomimically. 'He anticipated the judgement of the Almighty – one more sign that his was a religion of slaves. Where was his defiance? Where is yours, Martin?' She turned to Dieter. 'It's more efficient maybe as Martin says for these people to get on to death without delaying over the living part.'

'Have you actually read Exton?'

'I have informed myself.'

'You've been in the archive.'

She nodded. 'And I have the notes kept by Marcie which we requested from Diane. The project is a futile one, I think. It is more nostalgia. Nostalgia for a spiritual conflict which is in fact none of her concern or yours. And yet you dabble. People will have to learn, one way or another, sooner or later.'

'Learn what?'

'How things are, Martin. They will learn that, however painfully.'

'I'm listening to the table-talk of a junkie who lives in a van. Why am I not convinced, Irmgard?'

'Wait and see. Now, don't you want to go to your party?'

'I'm going, but tell me what all this fucking tat's for – all this incense and velvet.'

'To see what follows. To provoke whatever will happen to the revellers. This is a temple used by Crowley and Mathers. Did you know that?'

'Yes, but so are half the follies in England. So what?'

'Who knows? Who knows what will emerge?' She looked at Dieter and gave a racked Roth-Handle laugh.

I was already getting to my feet, but she, too, like Gareth, had managed to dismiss me.

16

I have a copious memory – more than I need, perhaps, certainly more than I want. Yet on the occasion of the party at Moon House, an event I have always wished and needed, and feared, to recall in every detail, my memory is selective, fragmentary and in places apparently detached from the actual sequence of events. In a sense I have spent the last thirty years trying to reclaim the lost passages of that evening, when several streams flowed together to such destructive effect.

I estimate that it must have been about eight o'clock when I left the temple. I walked back along a path through the woods towards the music, aware of a few figures wandering about in the trees. What I most clearly recall is the sheer effort. The air was like glue and it was hard to get my breath or raise my anvil-heavy feet to take a step.

When I came out behind the swimming-pool into the full roar of the music, the first thing that struck me was that the children had gone. That was a relief. The stacks of food, too, seemed to have vanished, but there was plenty of drink – beer in chocked-up barrels, wine, spirits, punch in a huge old mixing bowl. Someone must have been paying for it. The lights rigged among the trees had come on now, drawing in the thickening dusk.

Though I knew the band were playing I didn't really hear the music properly until I walked into the middle of it. The area in front of the low stage was filled with dancers. There was scarcely a face I recognized, but there was that peculiar, familiar (to me, anyway) sense that on the other hand they must all know each other intimately. The band were locked into a spiralling groove where the silvery drone of a twelve-string rode a Bo Diddley beat. There at last was Alex, stooped over his guitar, churning out chords, while the rest of the band worked around him, slowly raising tempo and volume. Finally I spotted Jane in the crowd, dancing with Susie, and Luke apparently rooted to the spot, staring at the stage, his arms outstretched as though at a religious occasion.

Just as it threatened to ascend towards the heaven of fixed stars, the riff locked down on to a single hammering block chord from Alex, repeated and repeated until the drums dropped out, before the whole band slammed back in and Alex, impassive behind his daft blue-tinted NHS spectacles, took up the vocal. I couldn't help laughing when he sang, though I knew part of him was in deadly earnest.

When the song ended there was uproarious delight. Was it a melodrama or a threat, that song? I looked again for Jane and Susie. They were supporting each other, shouting with the rest of the crowd. Perhaps the evening could be redeemed. Perhaps it would simply be a noisy good time and all gone by the morning except for a bit of clearing up. Perhaps Irmgard and Dieter, Diane and the Bewdley Huns were simply inconvenient figments of my imagination. But as Susie turned towards me, smiling, beckoning, there was a tremor like heavy wings, beating but earthbound, on the edge of my sight, and then thick reds and blues swarmed across Susie's face and closed it away before beginning to colonize the ground underfoot and the crowd's raised hands, flying up into the air from the ends of their fingers. They seemed to have been applauding for hours. I felt positioned oddly low to the ground, and looked down, expecting to be on my knees, but I was still upright. My breathing took on a deep bass note, while a shuddering stack of energy rushed upwards from my chest to take off the roof of my skull. Then it began all over again, as though inside the previous instalment but each time larger, putting physics to flight. To bird-cries from the crowd, new dark chords struck up, passing through the wooden stage relentlessly, like saws, and I heard the opening lines of 'I Put a Spell on You'.

When at last I looked up again from the heaving flagstones, I knew without having to ask that I wasn't the only one who'd been spiked. I remembered the recession of reflected mirrors curving away to infinity in the changing booth at the school outfitters. It was like falling, slowly. Next time I opened my eyes, Susie leaned blankly with her back on the edge of the stage. I set off towards her, trying to get round the immobile Luke, but Jane loomed out of the surging air, grabbed my arm and pulled me aside so I lost the sense of direction for a moment.

'Hold on to me,' she said. 'I'm frightened.' She wriggled

her way into my embrace like a child. Her white skin was luminous, her hair scarlet fire. For a moment I could see Susie staring at us now, pale and lost and hurt and horribly further away, but by the time I somehow shifted myself and Jane over to the stage she had disappeared. I looked round, feeling sick.

'I'm frightened,' Jane said again.

'Me too.' Slowly I led her towards the kitchen door. I could see no sign of Susie now.

'Has someone done this to me?'

'Not just to you, Janey. The thing is to keep calm. It will pass.'

'I'm frightened.'

'No need, love. It's only for a bit.'

I had expected to find Marcie in the kitchen but she wasn't there, and neither was Susie. A large kettle screamed on the hob. I steered Jane to the table and pulled out a chair, then removed the kettle. The music crowded in after us.

'Just sit here for a minute,' I said.

'No – where are you going?'

'I'm just getting us a drink.'

'Don't go, Martin.'

'I'm just here. Look: here I am.' It was like speaking through an anaesthetist's mask. Jane stared at me. God knows what she could see. The lines of tension on the iron range suggested it might burst asunder in a rain of red-hot blackleading. Refusing this distraction, I discovered and opened the fridge and took out a jug of orange juice, then managed to identify a couple of glasses on the molten draining-board.

'I'm not here, am I?' she said. 'Do you know what I mean, Martin?'

'Yes, but you are here. Don't worry. Look, drink this.'

'Like Alice.'

'Not quite.'

I gave her the glass, looking about for a bag of sugar but not finding one. Jane took it and said nothing, but raised it to her lips and drank. How like a child she looked now, a child overtired and teary at the end of the day. I struggled to drink my own glass of juice.

'Is it going to stay like this?' she asked.

'Of course not.' Not unless we're dead unlucky, I thought, in large letters. I blinked at the idea of a corridor of locked doors and gave Jane's shoulder a squeeze. She rested her cheek on my hand. Her face was smudged with tears.

On the table I noticed an open cardboard box. It contained copies of issue one of the *Summer Hill Review*. The plain, sober typeface on the off-white cover; the plain, sober boasts about who we'd managed to persuade to contribute; the modest cover price. We were Men of Letters. I picked up a copy, flicked through and watched the print fly past like a science-fiction countdown, the letters flaking off over my hands. The very idea of it seemed hilarious and otherworldly. But this had been the *raison d'être* for Alex and me. It was far too complicated to think about. When I tried to say the word 'literature', it sounded like someone striking the steel hull of a ship with a giant hammer.

'It should feel a little better in a bit,' I remember saying.

Jane finished her drink, looked at me reproachfully, put the glass on the table. 'No, it won't,' she said. 'I can tell. This is what it's going to be like. This was what was arranged.' Then she knelt down, crawled under the table and curled herself in a foetal position, placing her hands over her face. She was crying.

'Jane. Don't do that.' No reply. She had turned her back and shrunk away. 'We can sort it out.'

'You can't,' she said, her voice muffled with weeping. 'No one can.'

I remember saying, 'I'm just going to find Susie,' and thinking how like fire the music was, fire sustained by what it consumed, and how I needed to start running, anywhere away from here before my face fell off and the fire got inside. So I left Jane behind.

There were some people in the pool, carefully cross-hatched like illustrations. They were sawn off somehow by the water, like the traitors at the ice-locked bottom of the *Inferno*, their cries drowned out by the Stones' 'Live With Me'.

If Susie wasn't out here within reach of the kitchen, I couldn't imagine where she'd gone. Diane passed in front of me in a red dress, brandishing her Super-8 camera. She gave a cruel, glittery, Goneril-ish smile that seemed directed to someone else entirely, though she was looking straight at me. She might know where Susie had gone, but now I found myself unable to speak. I stood and watched her as she swayed to the music. Her body began to replicate itself, like the slowed frames of a cartoon, the discarded images folding gracefully on to the flagstones and disappearing only to reappear as I looked back up at her and once again she shed the deck of fleeting selves. Around her the other dancers' faces were blanking out like snuffed candles. The air itself must be burning.

I had ceased to be able to understand the music now. The problem as I laboriously saw it was to get away somewhere quieter before the part of myself that was still capable of observing and separating me from the hallucinations was in turn swallowed up, made over into fiction and placed at the service of the developing nightmare. 'That would be something to avoid, clearly,' I heard myself say, my voice echoing, as I struggled through the crowd, feeling myself becoming invisible. The last part of me to go would be my fingertips. After an age, I managed to skirt the pool and its intimate screaming faces, and passed through the fringe of the woods. There I went blundering on through fern-beds and elder trees, waiting for instructions, as though a nurse or a teacher might come to collect me. I kept forgetting the fear and then remembering it, looking for signs of it but unable to separate it from my breathing and the language that ran like a broken thesaurus through my head. Every botanical detail was equally and intolerably interesting, but it was clear that this – here, now, permanently – was where I belonged, arriving continually at the brink. After a time I could no longer remember why I had set out on this journey. The dark flowed under the bushes and over my feet. *Perduta gente* repeated itself endlessly in my head without my volition, iron tongues abrading great scorched bells.

At last I came to the crossing of the paths where I recognized Gareth's bench and sat down on it to wait, without knowing what for. Everyone was gone. The woods, the world, seemed to have emptied themselves, leaving behind only the great laurel bush and the bench. The fear was steady and implacable. My throat, I now knew, was a vortex down which my spinning head would shortly be sucked, until in the end my body would excrete itself in eviscerated form. I tried to cling to the rim of the maelstrom by sitting very quietly and digging my finger-nails into the wood of the bench. An enemy had done this.

After an interval, I registered that the music had stopped. Then, some time later, I could hear a commotion approaching. I stood and moved further back into the dark interior of the bush. Luke came past, shirtless and smeared with paint, pushing a trolley on which stood Irmgard, shouting into a loud-hailer. The corvine scraking noise that came out seemed to be an exhortation to the crowd of dancers who followed, many of them half naked and likewise painted, dazed with hilarity. Soon they disappeared round the bend in the near-dark. I went back to the bench and carried on sitting. The heat was almost past bearing.

'I thought I told you to stay sober,' said Gareth, materializing at my side. It was night now.

'I'm not drunk,' I said, my voice loud and far-off like that of an irascible prompter. 'The drinks have been spiked.'

'Cunt's trick. Fuck people up good and proper like that.

Seen it before.' His equanimity amazed me.

'Believe me, I know. But I don't want to think about it now, if you don't mind, though of course I can't bloody *stop* thinking about it.' Gareth nodded at me consideringly, as though conducting triage. 'Did you see the procession just now?' I asked.

'No, I could hear something, though. Sounded like a Victorian madhouse. That was a while back, mind you.'

'Luke was with them.'

'Might have known. He can't help himself. Brains of a tree-stump, poor bugger.'

'He was pushing Irmgard's triumphal chariot. He looked a bit out of it.'

'I shouldn't be in the least surprised. What's that one up to, that Irmgard?'

'Search me.' The fear came again. 'Have you seen Susie?'

'Not for hours. What a fucking mess.'

'I have to go back to the house and see if she's there.'

'Can you manage that?'

'It's peaked, I think. Better do something.'

'I'll go and see what's going on with the strayed revellers, then. You got a watch? Can you still tell the time with it? Let's meet up here in an hour.' Then he was lost among the trees.

Some time later I found myself back at the pool. The waters were still and no one seemed to be about. The equipment was gone from the stage. I crossed the flagstones to the kitchen, switched on the light by the door and stood blinking in the flat yellow ordinariness of it all. Unwashed crockery, empty bottles, half-eaten sandwiches. There was no sign of Jane. The box of magazines had gone as well.

'Susie?' There was no reply. The place seemed full of waiting emptiness. 'Jane?'

17

There was a gap, hard to say how long or what occupied it. I heard a van driving away and came to myself again. I was still alone.

I opened the kitchen door and went along the dim brown passageway until I came to the foot of the stairs. Someone higher up seemed to be laughing. There was a crash like falling cutlery. Gingerly I began to climb, feeling I might sink through the stairs. The newel-posts, I noticed, were in the shape of urns. Must look them up in something. At the first landing I paused and listened, peering along the unused corridor. Nothing. Then, from further up, I heard the same laughter. I closed my eyes – which didn't help – and held on to the banisters until I reached the second storey. Here there was water on the polished oak, lapping slowly towards the top of the stairs from a half-open door. Steam was leaking out as well.

When I peered round the door, the room was bleary with vapour. Stepping inside, I saw that the mirror over the wash-basin had been smashed, the bowl left full of eager, glinting fragments. I opened the window to clear the steam, then turned and saw a female figure in the bath. She wore a shower-cap, and had her hands over her eyes. I struggled to make her out as her body melted and re-formed in the overflowing water. To my relief there didn't appear to be any blood or razor blades, which I now discovered I had been expecting.

'Marcie? Is that you? Are you all right?' I cursed my stupid question.

'Who's that?' She was petrified. 'Please, who is it? What's happening?'

'It's Martin. Let me turn the taps off and I'll get you a towel.'

'Don't look. Please don't look at me.'

'I'm not looking, Marcie. I'm trying to find you a towel.' The old bathtaps were stiff but I managed to turn off the water. Under the window there was a cupboard containing ancient towels, and at the bottom of the pile a large, greying bathsheet, threadbare but still more or less service-able. 'Okay, I've got one.'

'It was the only thing I could think of,' Marcie said, her hands still clamped to her eyes. 'Have a bath and relax. My grandmother told me that, and to drink valerian tea before, or after, I forget which. It always worked before – usually, I mean.' Her voice was reasonable to the point of madness. 'When I had an essay crisis, for example. Or a difficult boy on my mind.' She laughed again. 'But this is different, I guess. Yeah.'

'There's no need to fret. It's okay. If you reach out to your left, I'll hand you a towel.'

'What happened? Why is it like this?'

'I think someone spiked the drinks.'

'What about the mirror?'

Good question, I thought. 'Was there an accident?' I asked.

'Is it gone?'

'It's broken. Did you smash it accidentally?' As the steam cleared I saw an old white enamel jug lying on the floor under the basin.

'Not accidentally. But it wasn't planned.'

'Have the towel. Here. I'm not looking.'

I heard her stand up in the water. She took the towel from my hand.

'I'll be in the corridor.'

'Don't go, please.'

'I'll only be outside.' The stair-carpet was stained darkly by the water now. Maybe it wouldn't show in the morning.

Pale and grey and shivering, Marcie came out wrapped in the towel and scurried along the corridor without looking at me. I wished she'd take off the ridiculous shower cap.

'Do you want me to come in?' I asked. 'Or shall I wait while you get dressed?' I observed myself behaving as if I had a plan of action. She shook her head as I went hesitantly after her.

'I'm not getting dressed, Martin. I have to go to bed now and get my sleep. I want it to be tomorrow. I feel kind of sick.'

'Okay.' There seemed to be no point in arguing with her. If I could have gone to sleep myself in a hole somewhere I would have done, but the energy kept jolting through me.

'Can you look in my bedroom with me?'

'Was somebody there?'

'Just need to make sure. I had to break that mirror in the bathroom, Martin.'

'I dare say it couldn't be helped.'

'What about Administration?' she wailed. 'What can I tell them?'

'We'll fix it so they don't find out.' I opened the door of Marcie's room. 'We can always bribe the cleaners,' I said breezily.

'Umm.' She peered at me. 'Can you go in first, please?'

Apart from sharing the building's general tendency to seethe and shift, the pale blue room seemed undisturbed. It required me to notice it in some detail, however. There was a sink in one corner with a mirror over it. The neat desk by the window was decorated only with a jar of pencils and a framed photograph of a smiling, appallingly healthy-looking middle-aged couple standing on a snowy lawn outside a frame house. Marcie's parents. The wardrobe was closed and a ghastly yellow candlewick bedspread was drawn neatly over the single pillow. Books were arranged along the windowsill. It was not really a student's room, more that of a keenly conformist boarding-school pupil, a cheerful early riser intent on reaching the state finals of the spelling bee and being the uncomplaining reserve for the swimming team.

There was silence outside now, I noticed.

'It seems all right, Marcie. There's nobody here.'

'I didn't think there was, really.'

'Well, then. Can I get you anything?'

'A glass of water, please. I can't see properly. Everything's too close. Is that the drug? There should be a glass by the sink. Don't look while I get into bed.'

'I promise.' But I glimpsed her in the mirror over the wash-basin, slipping under the covers, pale as the pillowcase. She turned to the wall. The tap spat breathily.

I put the glass of water down beside her. 'I need to find Susie. Have you seen her?'

'She went away.'

'Where did she go?'

'I don't know. She just wasn't there any more. I didn't like that. She shouldn't have left me. Diane was there too. She was laughing at me and taking pictures. Then she went.'

'Where was this?'

'We were in the kitchen, there was the music, and then I don't remember, only little flashes.'

'Can you try to think back?'

'I *can't* fucking think!' she screamed. 'I can't see, so I can't think. Don't you understand that?'

'I'm sorry, Marcie. I'm confused as well.' I sat down on the bedside chair. 'I'm just trying to work out what's been going on. Jane's vanished too.'

Marcie snorted through her tears at this. 'Jane, Jane – she's what we've got to pay for.'

'Why?'

'Why? Because she's – she's too much, too clever, too gifted. It's like there's just too much of her. She's too wonderful all over. She's your friend. You know her. Lady

Jane. What did you expect? Oh, God, what am I going to do about the bathroom mirror? I can't go home. I can't fail. Not now.'

'I said I'd sort it out. How did it get broken?'

'I think Exton was in there.'

'In the mirror?'

'That's what I said.' Marcie's voice cracked. 'I know what it sounds like, Martin.'

'No, look, it's okay. Do you still think he was there?' By reflex I checked in the mirror over the wash-basin. For the moment, there was no one there but me. Maybe Exton only liked bathrooms. It seemed a little unfair that he should have appeared to Marcie rather than me. Surely I had the prior claim.

'I don't know what I think,' she replied. 'I said I can't think any more. I'm sick of thinking. It's all I ever do. All my life. Think. Make notes. Aspire. Think. Look where it got me – in the booby-hatch.'

'Welcome to the club.'

'When Exton was in the mirror he was about to speak. I could see that.'

'But he didn't actually say anything?'

'I broke the mirror to prevent him. If he'd spoken it would have been, well, irrevocable.'

A pity, I thought. She rolled over and looked at me in appeal.

'I think I take your point, Marcie. What did he look like?'

'Like the van Houten picture.'

I found myself laughing.

'Don't be cruel,' Marcie said.

'I'm not. It just seems a bit of a coincidence.'

'What? Am I making it up?'

'Well – not exactly. It's too complicated to go into at the moment.'

'The floor in the hall will be ruined. It's solid oak. It's really old.'

'Nothing we can't fix,' I lied. 'We'll deal with it tomorrow.'

'I hope so. When did you get so practical? You can't even drive.'

I was laughing again. 'Now you've cut me to the quick,' I said, but the joke was lost on her.

'I'm cold.'

'I'll get you a blanket.' I looked in the wardrobe. On the top shelf there was some extra bedding. Wrapped in it was an archive box I recognized. I laid a blanket over Marcie. 'What are the journals doing there?'

'Journals?'

'Exton's.'

'Oh.'

'Look at me.' She moved closer to the wall and put her hands over her ears. 'No, look at me, Marcie. This is important. Tell me why you've got the journals. You've no business to take them out of the archive. You of all people know that, surely.'

She turned over again and sat up, still wearing the shower cap, her expression fierce. The bedclothes fell away. Until now I hadn't seen the word 'Diane' tattooed on her left breast. It looked like a classroom biro job.

'I took them yesterday because someone has to look after that stuff,' she said. 'What do you think is going on out there? Anything could happen. You can't be relied on, clearly, can you? You're just playing at scholarship, Martin. So I'm looking after them until the party's over. Otherwise God knows what could happen.'

She gathered the bedclothes around herself and glared at me.

'You think the barbarian hordes or whatever you're expecting are less likely to pillage a nice young lady's bedroom than a locked library?' I shouted. 'You're nuts.'

Tears ran down Marcie's face. 'I didn't know what else to do. I tried my best.'

'But you gave Diane your keys, didn't you? Do you think that might be why you saw Exton in the mirror?' I asked. 'Naughty naughty, Marcie. You're as mad as she is.' My sudden anger frightened me, banging along my bloodstream like a heart-attack. Marcie shrugged and turned to the wall once more. I straightened the blanket and stood up to leave. 'Where are the keys now? Has Diane still got them?'

'I got them back.'

'How?'

'I had to steal them,' Marcie said.

I snorted at this. 'You're full of surprises, aren't you? Where are they now?'

'In my purse.'

I upended her bag on the desk. The house keys were unmistakable, large mortices on a ring.

'Don't go,' I heard her say. 'What are you going to do?'

'Put the bloody journals back, of course.'

I found the change of activity newly disorienting, nego-
tiating the damp stairs with difficulty as they bucked and
slid. Already I felt guilty about locking Marcie in, but
something told me it was also for the best. On the ground
floor I tested the door of the archive. Locked but, given the
presence of Dieter in the vicinity, that didn't prove anything. I opened the door and entered the large room, feeling
the fireplace and the dark walls giving out cold. The
journals' cabinet was undisturbed, still locked. Far off,
there was a faint crash. I ignored it. When I opened the
cabinet and inspected the shelves I could identify nothing
missing except the journals, which I now put back,
abstractedly enjoying the pressure of key in lock, the
leathery cool of the room. I turned to go and saw the paler
rectangle over the fireplace.

I locked up again and ran upstairs. Now I could hear
weeping from behind the door of Marcie's room. When I
went in she was crouching in front of the basin. That
mirror was broken too.

'Where's the painting, Marcie?'

'He came back.'

'What? Who did?'

'Exton, of course.'

'Did he remember what he'd been about to say?'

'What?' She gave me a pained look and shook her head.

'Where have you put the painting?'

'I haven't touched it.'

'It's missing.'

'I don't know anything about that.'

I heard voices and footsteps outside the house. 'How can I believe you? You took the journals, remember? Are you sure you haven't got the painting under the mattress?'

'Why don't you look? I swear it isn't, though. Anyway, I'm Marcie,' she said in a trembling voice, 'and I'm not someone who tells lies.'

'The journals.'

'That wasn't a lie. That was different.' But she didn't really believe this. 'Anyway, the painting's a copy.'

'What?'

'The real one's in Utrecht. You should know that, shouldn't you, Martin?'

The voices were inside the building now. I bit down on my anger. If I left her now she might harm herself.

'Get dressed, Marcie.'

'I need to go back to bed. I'm really tired now. It needs to be tomorrow.'

'We have to move. It's not safe. Get fucking dressed.'

'I don't want to meet those people.'

'Neither do I. Come on, for Christ's sake.'

'I need to pee.'

'Use the sink.'

'That's not nice. And it's too high up.'

'Use a chair. Come on. I mean it.'

Downstairs the noise intensified. There was the crash of something heavy falling over, and a ragged cheer of approval that carried on into a sort of wordless chanting. The last time I'd heard such atonal baying and screeching was in my second year, when the college rugby team had won a trophy and gone on the rampage, emptying fire

extinguishers into the rooms of supposed lefties and breaking the fingers of a student journalist who'd taken the
mickey out of them. This lot sounded as if they might be
more committed to whatever their cause proved to be.

Listlessly, Marcie peed in the sink, then pulled on jeans
and a T-shirt. While she did so, the noise downstairs
peaked and faded: a party on the move. It was tempting to
stay in the room as she wanted. *I should like a cave with
two exits. I wish I weren't so silly.* Better to have room to
manoeuvre and a chance to run. I would sort out the why
and the who later on, if we ever got there.

The racket stopped as suddenly as it had begun. I took
Marcie by the hand and led her to the second staircase.
When I looked through the window at the top I saw a
couple of figures running into the trees.

Downstairs the lights glared wintry yellow. There
seemed to be no one around. I checked the archive – still
locked – then led Marcie down to the reference collection.
This door was standing open and the lights were on, giving
the slightly medical atmosphere that goes with windowless
illumination.

'Oh, God,' she said. 'Let me see the keys.' She snatched
them out of my hand. 'Diane must have taken it off the ring.'

The room was dark-panelled, the smell of beeswax not
concealing a genteel air of virtual disuse. One of the heavy
wooden stacks that ran down the middle of the room had
been turned over. A few books were scattered on the floor,
loose pages lying among them. An entire section seemed
to have been emptied and taken away. Longfellow and
Whittier, Lascelles Abercrombie and Harold Monro had

been left behind, I noticed. As above, so below. Posterity is cruel.

'Oh, Lord,' said Marcie. 'Why would anyone do this? It's ruined. They'll send me away.'

'Hey, baby.' Diane appeared round the end of the stack. 'It's just a shot away, shot away, shot away, right?' She aimed the camera. 'That's good. Keep the shocked look, okay? Yeah. It's the event of the season. Think of me as Cecil Beaton.' More like Harrison Marks, I thought.

'What have you done?' said Marcie.

'I've been a witness. You can tell them it was thieves, vandals, wanton destroyers of your literary heritage. There's no reason why they shouldn't believe you. And, anyway, that's what actually happened.'

'You're the fucking vandal,' I said. 'It was nothing to do with you. You don't care about books or poetry or language. Why couldn't you leave the place alone, you stupid cunt?'

'What? This crap?' Diane laughed. 'Even I, pig-fucking-ignorant politics major like you suppose I am, you snob – even I can tell all this is nothing. This is just old shit. Not even valuable old shit. This is just stuff. This is the fucking extras, man. This is bulk. They could put this in the holds of old wooden battleships instead of sand.'

'You shouldn't have done this, whatever you imagine you believe. You don't know what the books in here represent. It's more complicated than you think. They all count. Even if no one opens them, they're part of the whole.' My voice sounded reedy and resigned. It was a waste of time. I hardly believed it myself. Who was I meant to be? Funes the Memorious? And it was clearly mad to be standing among the wreckage arguing the case like some Roman branch librarian as the Goths rode up to the issue desk. Let me be not mad. Not again.

'I think I do understand, Martin. The dead books represent dead people, dead people, dead like you're dead. Your time isn't simply gone. You were never in it. You were dead before you started. You never even got here.'

The blood thudded in my head. I didn't know whether to kill Diane or burst into tears. 'Never mind me,' I said. 'What's wrong with the past?'

'Everything. But it doesn't matter. We don't have to be there any more.'

'Year zero culture.'

'Sure. Why not?'

'Where have they taken the books? What have they done with them?'

'We needed them over at the temple.'

'Needed them? What for?' I already knew, but until Diane spoke the words I would be able to go on disbelieving it.

Marcie interrupted: 'Diane, what about the painting?'

'Oh, well, you'll have to ask Dieter about that, I'm afraid.'

Diane lowered the camera and came forward. I wanted to punch her in the mouth. She placed a hand on Marcie's cheek; Marcie did not resist. Diane put her arms round her and Marcie began to weep once again. 'Hey, Marcie, it's okay,' Diane crooned. 'Don't worry, baby. Diane's here. We're gonna put you to bed. Make it all better.'

'I'm looking after her,' I said. Marcie clung to her more tightly.

'Sure,' said Diane, gently rocking Marcie where they stood among the fallen books. 'Obviously you've been doing a good job.'

'How can you treat her like this?' I asked. 'You destroy what matters to her.'

'Marcie understands, don't you, baby?' whispered Diane. 'It's painful. There's a new world not yet born.'

'Make him go away, Diane,' said Marcie. 'He scares me. I had to pee in the wash-basin. Make him go.'

'Well, that wasn't very nice, was it, Martin? You call that looking after her? That's no way to treat a lady. Marcie, Marcie, it's okay, baby.'

'You're fucking mad. Or evil,' I said.

She shrugged. 'Look, there's nothing for you here now, Martin. Why don't you go find the picture? Let me take care of Marcie.'

'Where is the picture, Diane?' Marcie asked, her voice muffled. 'I just need to know.'

'We've all got to make sacrifices,' Diane said, kissing Marcie's lank hair. 'It's a picture of some nobody. And it's old. So what? We're living now, not then. You'll see. You're not responsible for any of that. Let the dead bury the dead. Let Martin worry about it now, if he's got nothing better to do. I'll just take you upstairs and put you to sleep, baby.' Diane looked up at me delightedly. 'Better run, Martin. You don't want to be late for the show. Maybe Susie's there. And Jane. Remember them?'

18

As I blundered through the woods I could smell smoke. After a while I managed to find the slope overlooking the pond again. As I struggled up across the dry, rooty soil I could feel that I had become a thin, rather papery medium, someone probably invisible if encountered side-on, immune to life as well as insult. I also seemed to be dying of a sudden immense thirst, in the same way as the enclosed model landscape of Moon House itself was suddenly magnified to an epic scale. The heat of the night was choking. By the time I reached the top I had forgotten why I'd come. I lay on my back for a while, rehearsing my name to myself, as though requiring the assent of some invisible authority. The back of my head began to dissolve into the ground, but that seemed to be all right, even a relief, since when my head was gone, the thirst and the thinness would be gone too.

A short coughing laugh from the pond below brought me round. I rolled on to my front and peered down over the crumbling edge. In the heavy dusk the bonfire was burning strongly, though the smoke was tending to linger in the depression, which made it hard to see anybody clearly and impossible to estimate how many of them there were. The fire roared eagerly, but otherwise it was oddly quiet. Figures were coming and going intently, as though undertaking serious labour, which I suppose was what they were doing after a fashion, having been enlisted in an employment scheme for a Third Republic of demons. They scurried sweatily out of the shadows with armloads of books, braving the glowing rim of ash to add them to the blaze, before stepping backwards away from the fire, as if to honour it, vanishing into the dark, then anonymously re-emerging next time around. For some reason they reminded me of schoolboys testing and extending a slide in a frozen playground before lessons, where the bravado of the individual is subordinated to the collective effort. By breaktime a caretaker would have put down salt and the slide would have melted and might as well never have been there. These servants were not equal to the fire they were trying to tend. They could not impress it.

The flames intermittently illuminated the front of the stage, where two figures I knew must be Dieter and Irmgard stood crouched with their movie cameras. Now I remembered the painting. I skated and slid back down to the wood's floor level and slipped round through a patch of laurels into the area behind the pond. On a pathway a couple of trolleys stood piled with books. None of the blackened firemen was taking any notice of me as they came and went.

The burning was not a celebration, more like some kind of appeasement or penance. The book-burners had to prove themselves worthy of their own destructiveness. But after a while they simply ran out of material. A couple of them tried shoving a trolley over the edge of the pond and into the flames, but it didn't seem to be in keeping and wouldn't catch fire properly, managing only the miserable smoulder of a vinyl-padded bar or slashed settee on the green space behind the council estate near where I grew up. Eventually they stopped and gathered in silence in a loose semi-circle in front of the fire, watching, as if weary of the business now but not yet free to go. It seemed I had survived the massacre and missed the orgy.

There were far fewer participants than I had imagined, though some might already have slipped away, waking, as the poet has it, in the fogs of deflated mirth. I was certain that news would not leak out from that quarter. It would be a long time before anyone found a joke or a boast in this night's merrymaking.

I counted six or seven still there, all male, predictably enough, lads from the village, filthy with smoke and sweat, most of their clothes gone, one or two of them bollock-naked, their glistening skins slashed with paint. Their grubby faces were exhausted and drawn now, as they began to pass cigarettes and bottles of home-brewed cider between them.

After a little while I found myself next to Luke. His cockscomb was blackened. He looked incuriously my way and didn't seem to recognize me. After a few moments he sat down on the concrete rim of the pond, still staring as the fire began to collapse on itself with a series of ashy roars that hurled sparks at the stars above the flickering roof of the temple. No one might talk but surely someone must see the smoke. Someone would come. There would be terrible trouble. I began to imagine working as a schoolteacher, standing up for Blake and Wordsworth in some hellish unpunctuated outpost of Birmingham, forgotten by Rome and beyond saving, like Ovid in Tomis, with spears raining over the walls in the evenings. It would be all I was fit for. I found myself laughing.

I took the bottle from Luke's hand and drank, hoping the contents hadn't been interfered with. 'Luke.'

'Fuck off, okay? I've had enough now. Not doing any more now. Just let me sit here for a bit, okay?'

'Luke, it's Martin. Here, look at me.' He didn't turn his head. 'Can you tell me where Susie and Jane are?' I reached for his arm and he shrugged me away. I gave him back the bottle.

He emptied it and let it roll down into the ashes. 'I want to go home now,' he said, putting his head in hands.

'Yes, I imagine we all do,' I said.

'Never any bloody nurses either. Not a sniff of 'em. Bloody rip-off. All think I'm daft.'

'Of course they don't,' I lied.

'Where's our Gareth?' he asked. Good question. 'Tell him I want him, will you? Tell him Luke said.' He lowered his head towards his knees.

'Wait there.' I went round the pond and climbed the steps on to the stage. Unlike the book-burners, who seemed depressed and uncertain now, as though their efforts had been in vain – I could feel the energy leaking out of the dying event, as if the god had abandoned the building, leaving his barbarians wearied by their umpteenth invasion – Dieter and Irmgard were serene. They had finished their filming and sat smoking contemplatively on their crusty velvet thrones. Dieter raised his glass.

'You spiked the drink,' I said.

'I drank what you drank, Martin. We were comrades in temporary psychosis. We have been through this experience together, to the end of the night, or almost.'

'You had no right to do that.'

'I did not, if you say so.'

He poured wine into an empty glass and pushed it across the table toward me. Despite myself I drank it. Red and heavy, it simply magnified my thirst, but I seemed unable to ask for water here.

'What have you done with the painting?'

'What do you think?' croaked Irmgard. 'Up in smoke – *ffffffft* – on the everlasting bonfire. It's a pity it wasn't bigger.'

'There was no reason to burn it.'

'Correct,' said Irmgard. 'Therefore ... oh, therefore fuck you, you cowardly little clerk.'

'It was something of value.'

'It was a work of art in the age of mechanical reproduction. It had no aura. It was a fetish commodity. And it was a lousy painting.'

'You've made things impossible for Marcie,' I said. Neither of them replied. 'I ought to call the police.'

'Then you would be an informer as well as a coward.' Irmgard smirked and nodded. 'The Tambov wolf must be your comrade now.'

'But I don't think you're going to do that, are you, Martin?' asked Dieter. 'Everyone is implicated here. You would bring trouble on them all. It would not help. They would not thank you.'

Irmgard picked up the megaphone from beside her chair. She stood and addressed those standing below: 'You may dismiss now, comrades, thank you. Thank you for your zeal and your selfless participation in this purgative festival. Our activities are at an end for the time being.' The group looked hesitantly at one another, not understanding a word of it. Irmgard shook her head with exasperated amusement. 'Comrades, the party is over. Our revels now are ended. Have you no home to go to? Good night.' The Caliban-groundlings considered. Then a bottle arced half-heartedly on to the stage and rolled away. I searched for the thrower and realized that Luke was no longer there. I looked at the huddled, disconsolate group around the fire but I couldn't tell them apart. They were beginning to disperse into the woods when another anonymous figure came running swiftly out of the dark with a fresh armful of something – papers, apparently – which he flung on to the glaring embers. The others stared at him uncertainly – not one of theirs, it seemed – and without a word they melted away.

'Excelsior,' the figure said, quietly but perfectly clearly, looking directly at me, before stepping back into the trees after the others.

I jumped down off the stage and tried to snatch the papers from the fire, but most of them were already half burned, and I only managed to rescue a handful of sheets. Irmgard had followed me. She threw a heavy log on to the stack of pages. Sparks flew up as the fire collapsed entirely into its white core, taking the rest of the paper with it.

'Are you mad? Why did you do that?'

'Housekeeping. *Kinder, Kirche, Kuchen.* You know?'

'I should throw you in after it, you stupid cunt.'

'Yes? You would hit a defenceless woman?' She put a finger to her lips in coquettish alarm.

'If that's what you are. What's *wrong* with you?' I tilted the papers to try to catch a little of the stage light. Irmgard came closer. 'I'm warning you,' I said.

'Maybe what you need is a fuck, hmm? Expend some of that fine fury. What do you think?' She was laughing as usual as I turned away and set off through the woods. 'Take note that we are not finished yet.'

I stopped beneath a lantern at a crossways and peered at the pages. They were drafts of poems, annotated in Jane's small exact handwriting.

The signal box was lit, dimly. I called from the bottom of the stairs. There was no reply, but I could sense waiting. I went gingerly up and opened the door.

'About bloody time, Martin,' hissed Susie. She was slumped in the chair. Jane sat with her head on Susie's knee, her face turned aside. Susie stroked Jane's hair as she talked. 'Where have you been?'

'All over, looking for you. Where did you get to?'

'I was by the stage. Then you went away. You fucked off.'

I thought of explaining in detail, but it was too exhausting. Besides, I could barely make sense of it. 'I was coming over, then there was Jane. Then you seemed to vanish, I thought.'

'I do that, don't I?' Susie paused, then continued stroking Jane's hair.

'Then there was Jane—'

'And you left her behind as well, by the look of it.' She looked down at the hunched figure and contemptuously back at me.

'There was Marcie, too. Oh, fuck.'

'Were you going for the set?'

'It's not my fault.'

'For Christ's sake, Martin. You're just *not there*.'

'We'd been spiked. It wasn't in my control.'

'No, Martin, I see that.' Tumblers were aligning, locks about to seal themselves. In some way that stood beyond the scope of reason or mitigation, I had failed, simply by being in the orbit of this evening's events, these 'incidents', as the dean would have called them. They bore my stamp: they were the sort of scrape I got into over and over again by being magnetized to the nearest scene of disorder and waste. Susie didn't need to say any of this. It had never ceased to be true; it had simply been in abeyance. The blood in my chest felt black and ragged. I held out the scorched pages as if they were evidence of good intent, or even of sacrifice

'What's that you've got?' Susie asked, with weary incredulity. 'Are you having a read, or something? Got to keep occupied? Fucking hell, Mart.' She shook her head.

Jane sat up, suddenly alert. Her face was smeary from weeping, pale from the comedown. They'd both been drinking. 'Are those my papers?' she asked. 'My manuscript?'

'I'm not sure.' Uncertainly, I held them out to her, but it was Susie who took them. After glancing at them, she stared at me in desperation and shook her head once more.

'Let me see,' said Jane, reaching for them.

'Better wait, lovey,' said Susie. 'Wait till morning. Then we'll—'

'Give me them,' Jane said harshly. Susie handed them over. We were all standing now.

Jane held up the damaged pages. Then she crumpled them and threw them onto the pile of magazines. Then she picked them up again.

'I'm very sorry, Jane. I tried to save them but Irmgard— There was a bonfire at the temple—'

'Never mind. It doesn't matter,' she said. Tears ran down her face but she gave off an odd, glassy confidence. 'That doesn't matter now. It was Alex who did this, I take it.'

'He was out of it, Jane.'

'I dare say he was.'

'Let's just go,' said Susie. 'It seems to have more or less worn off. What d'you think, Janey? I need a cup of tea and a bath and some aspirin, and, for some reason, a bacon sandwich. You can do that, can't you, Martin?'

I picked up a bottle of wine from the floor. Jane was looking out of the window towards the tunnel gate. It was open now.

'What's that?' she said. 'That noise.'

They came gliding through the open gate in close file like stunt riders leaving the back of a lorry. The guy in the German helmet was at the front. A scouting party, it seemed. They drew up below and dismounted. Perhaps we could distract them by finding a dog for them to cook. Irmgard, for example, I thought unkindly.

'Where's the party?' Squarehead called, in a cut-glass Dudley accent. He raised a hand to his iron ear. 'Yoo-hoo.' The others laughed. They were inching quite casually towards the foot of the stairs, clinking with bladed regalia.

I could smell them from where I stood. I went to the doorway. 'All finished now, lads, I'm sorry to say.'

'Fookin' will be,' muttered one of the group.

'Finished? That won't do, will it?' said Squarehead. 'We've come all this way. Where's the tart that invited us – the Yank?'

'Everyone's gone.' I shrugged. What could you do? 'No staying power.'

'Except you, eh?' said Squarehead, reasonably. I couldn't help glancing back into the signal box. The girls were sitting in the far corner.

'I'm the last. I'm just off, actually.'

'You seem a bit nervous.'

'Fuckin' brickin' himself,' said the second voice. Laughter.

'I'm just knackered, mate,' I said.

'Yeah. Anyway,' Squarehead went on, 'as you are no doubt aware, the laws of hospitality mean that you cannot send your guests away empty-handed. That would be discourteous. And, in fact, unforgivable.' Laughter.

Irmgard appeared from the trees. 'A pity you are so late,' she said.

'There was a holdup,' said Squarehead, affably. 'Had to be dealt with. Anyway, we're here now. So what can you give us to take home?'

'What are your appetites?' said Irmgard.

'We're very versatile,' Squarehead replied.

'I've got a bottle of wine,' I said. 'That's all, really.'

'Let's have that, then.' He stretched out a hand. 'I think you'd better come down here.' I did as he asked and offered him the bottle.

'Much obliged.' He took it with one hand and punched me in the stomach with the other. 'Posh coont,' he said, mildly, moving away, sipping approvingly. I lay on the ground, winded. It was all as my reading in this field had suggested. The other Angels began kicking me, speculatively as first, like athletes doing a warm-up. Between the swinging, booted legs I saw Irmgard moving in closely, camera in hand, her face lit with excitement. Maybe Susie was on to something with the Riefenstahl joke.

A voice from above said, 'The lying coont. He's only got some females put away in the shed.' There were growls of approval.

'He's been less than frank, hasn't he? Finish him, then form a queue,' said Squarehead. 'Remember party discipline.' A boot caught me on the ear, then one found the base of my spine. I wanted to get into a ball but I couldn't make my body work. Things grew dark. Then the kicking stopped.

'All right,' said Gareth. I peered through the crowd. He stood on the edge of the trees, side on so everyone could see the muzzle of a shotgun jammed under the back of Squarehead's helmet. 'Time you lads went home.'

'He'll not do anything,' said one. 'Fookin' sheep-shagger, innee?'

'You wanna find out?' said Gareth, cocking the weapon. 'Go on, then, boy.' No one moved. ''Cos I don't care what I do to your guv'nor here. Brains in, brains out, all the same to me. And there's another one up the spout for any clever cunt who fancies it. That includes you, Irmgard. Put that fucking camera away or I'll shove it up your arse. Just get down them stairs and back on your bikes and fuck off home. Eh?'

Squarehead nodded slightly. The bikers climbed wordlessly on to their machines and started up. I tried to stand. Irmgard gave me a coquettish little wave as she mounted a spare pillion.

'The guv'nor comes with us,' someone said.

'In a minute. Mebbe. And tell the rest of your pals out there on the other end to fuck off an' all.'

The group moved off and slid back slowly into the tunnel. Susie was helping me up.

After a minute, Gareth said, 'Right, Adolf, off you go.'

Squarehead climbed on to his bike and kicked it into life.'Be sorry you did this, Bab. Promise you that.'

'I shouldn't think so. Good evening to you now.'

As he disappeared, Squarehead flashed a V-sign back. Gareth trotted gently to the tunnel mouth and fired the shotgun after him into the dark. The roar bounced about in the tunnel. Far off, Irmgard squealed with delight.

When the noise had died away, Gareth said, 'That's no

way to have fun, is it?' He put down the rifle, pushed the gate to and hauled a couple of bags of cement to rest against it. We stood and watched, oddly interested. Eventually he added, 'Mind you, I was aiming high, of course.' It was starting to get light.

19

The bacon sandwiches were made but left uneaten. A bath was run but no one got into it. For several hours we sat in the kitchen, staring at the floor like accident victims or witnesses to a bombing. What had happened was bad enough – it scarcely bore thinking about. And all the rest, all the things that might have happened, that nearly did happen, had, for a time, the same weight as the real. Rape and pillage, book-burning and collective madness: hard to extract the precisely actual from all that.

At some point that Sunday evening the three of us gave up and went to bed, but I don't think anyone slept. It was as though we had been holding our breath for so long that we'd forgotten how to release it. The heat was no help. It was torture, having nothing else to think about, the mind having no suburbs to go home to. Despite the drought I got up in the night and ran a shower simply to stand in its relative cool. The water seemed to slide off me as though my skin were veneered.

In the days that followed the sense of fracture persisted. It became part of the baking climate of every day. There were comings and goings – Susie went to help Marcie clear up – and we got on with ordinary tasks, but the atmosphere was of exhaustion and inaction. Alex and Diane were apparently staying with the local junkies in the big house beyond the church. We glimpsed them in a new car – a red MG, presumably requisitioned from their hosts – but we didn't approach each other. Jane avoided everyone. To all intents and purposes she was no longer there. The longer she stayed away, the more anxious I became.

The indecision was not ours alone. It manifested itself vaguely after the party. The authorities must surely have been well aware that something had gone awry at Moon House, but these were the years following strife at a good many centres of higher education, and there appeared to be no further appetite for recrimination. A day or two after Marcie and I had reshelved the depleted reserve collection as well as we could while barely exchanging a word, we found the locks had been changed, access silently forbidden to us. And that was all. In the archive the blank space where the painting had been was filled with a picture of Izaak Walton, which it transpired was a copy, like its predecessor. The Exton papers remained available – after all, they were the subject of our labours. The hand of Gwyther could be inferred from this absolute tact. In the meantime the wet first-floor passageway and staircase began to dry out. Susie told me later that Marcie had replaced the mirrors out of her own pocket – naturally I had no reason to go upstairs again.

Like the weather, time seemed to have come to a grinding standstill. There was sand in the engine. There were events but no development, actions but no progress, and there was a generalized sense of impersonation that alarmed me whenever I found myself considering it. I seemed to keep leaking from my own outline. Within a day or two it already seemed too late to discuss what had happened, supposing discussion was what was needed. It felt like the aftermath of a crash or a beating. In my case the latter was literally true, but the damage was slight and the bruises faded.

Things were not meant to be like this, but here we were, with no visible way out, down in the *Carceri d'invenzione* of relative privilege. I wished there was someone who could have intervened, with the immaculate, implacable sense of timing that parents are supposed to have – mother approaching quietly over the lawn in a summer dress with her cardigan over her shoulders for the evening chill, suddenly in charge, talking to one of the other mothers, leaving us, me, idling within easy reach, awaiting instructions, free of the cares of office. Misery is sentimental. Misery was out of luck that summer. Gwyther might have helped if I had asked, but it would never have occurred to me to turn to him. We went on, starved of resources, the three of us at the cottage knowing – I see now – that a reckoning of some sort had merely been postponed and was awaiting its hour. My anxiety was such that my teeth ached from clenching, as if I'd been speeding for a fortnight.

Most of the strangers were gone as quickly as they had arrived, leaving the disrupted expectation, the sense of having been robbed of a promised outcome, that tends to characterize dreams. At the same time, it was as if something had been decisively concluded on the basis of overwhelming evidence – though I couldn't imagine what the something might have been. There was no presiding narrative we could follow or argue with. There was just what there happened to be, and no way out, round or down.

Most strikingly, Irmgard and Dieter simply weren't there any more. How quickly they had come to seem like a structural necessity! Perhaps they felt they had succeeded in hastening the collapse of late capitalism by means of exposing and exploiting its internal contradictions and so on, but from our admittedly bucolic perspective the iniquitous structures still seemed to be in place when we began to surface from the comedown. Perhaps they might have claimed, not wholly without justification, that they had at least exposed the walls of the prison of false consciousness and sentimentality in which they had found us. But no doubt they would also have found our nervy derangement half-hearted and historically insignificant.

I remember it was criminally *boring* too, in that aftertime. We seemed to wake up while already awake, slumped in the kitchen. It was six a.m., then it was noon or teatime and a day had gone by very slowly and without leaving a trace, though a threat still resounded in the baking air. All three of us worked hard, but I found the texture of the experience oddly thin.

When eventually I made myself go to the pub in search of Gareth, I learned from Shirley that he and Luke had gone to Wales – Machynlleth, maybe – to visit an auntie or something for a bit. No one was quite sure. Luke had had a bit of a turn, they said. Always a bit daft, and now he'd gone and overdone it. Needed a bit of peace and quiet for a while. Those Germans hadn't helped. For the first time, I saw Shirley worried by something beyond her experience and power to control. The rest of the local lads looked sheepish at the dartboard, while their girls had never really been in the picture and as a matter of policy the old men knew and saw nothing. After all, it had got them this far, what with Hitler and so forth.

Though she didn't quite meet my gaze, Shirley poured me a pint unbidden, as if nothing had changed, but I found I couldn't get more than half of it down. I slipped out through the pub garden and set off for a walk round the grounds of Moon House: the job of bottle-collecting had been assigned to me by Susie, as though I were responsible for them being there. There was remarkably little visibly amiss. The statues were intact, the satyrs grimacing at the action they had missed out on, yet the woods continued to hold an atmosphere of unspecified damage and injury, a smokiness not actually to be seen but rather felt in the texture of the air and shade.

The temple had been completely stripped of its temporary decorations and fittings, presumably by Dieter and Irmgard. There was a low mound of bonfire ash in the dry pond below it, but the rain, when at last it came, would disperse it.

The scattering of bottles in the bushes and pathways I put in a bag to take back to Moon House. As I was placing it in the dustbin I glimpsed Marcie behind the kitchen window washing up, but she was careful not to notice me.

After the awkward co-operation with which we'd handled the damage, we'd reversed into a state of formality that she seemed to think befitted a decent young lady and the interloper who had seen her with no clothes on. Guilt and hostility can assume very similar manifestations. I wanted to tell her it wasn't really her fault, but I wasn't someone she'd consider qualified to say it. I didn't press the matter. All this was of course only a crisis for a few young bourgeois, but I could imagine that I was not the only one for whom it felt like the end of the world. *At World's End All shall be judged, but All shall find Justice solitary.*

As I pondered and rejected the idea of talking to Marcie, the pool sat smugly on its darkness, as though cataloguing and admiring its own shadows. It was tempting to swim, just to assert something – the bravado of the acid casualty, confined to the shallow end. Something in me quailed, but I slid into the water and hung suspended in the darkness for as long as my breath lasted. There was no sign of Geryon, loathly worms or other malevolent dwellers in the depths, which were empty, just as Exton's poems had now become innocuous and over-familiar when I sat to work on them. They had closed and died on me, and I found it both hard to care and terrifying to face up to.

When I surfaced I seemed to hear the click of a camera nearby in the woods. I trod water for a time, staring into the shade, but no one emerged.

Afterwards I made myself walk back through the woods. I sat for a while on the steps of the signal box. Even allowing for the chemical murk of the evening in question, there was really no doubting that 'certain events' had taken place. I had the memory of bruises to prove it.

No harm done, I told myself, for a joke. Time stood still, and yet it escaped me effortlessly. After a while I went and moved the bags of cement from the tunnel gateway and peered into the darkness under the hill. Perhaps it smelt of cordite, or only of damp stone and extreme age. I walked a few paces in and listened. Nothing. The sound of dust doing extremely long division. The tunnel led nowhere. There was nothing coming now but fear and sorrow.

As I keep saying – because I still don't understand it – those were two-headed days. In one lay imprisoning idleness, in the other – and I can't account for the simultaneity – a frenzy of compensatory labour. The only course available seemed to be a practical one: tidy up, get back to work or be seen to appear to do so. Jane spent most of her time in her room, working, I supposed. Susie went to the art college, Marcie to the archive, I to the university library, blissfully deserted outside term-time, not to mention cool, like a cave using time in lieu to get on with the stalactites. The heat simply continued under a headachy overcast. The weather seemed out of sympathy with our common-sense resolutions, evoking the hangover we were all trying to ignore and outlive.

Everyone must have been expecting a confrontation – a part of the ritual that remained incomplete, a wholly impersonal dramatic necessity. Alex and Diane vs. The Rest: unfinished business. It was like living under a wave just about to break. Expecting it, and facing it, were two different matters. It stayed quiet.

Though I imagine none of us thought of much else, we

tried to avoid looking back together, across the strange break in the continuum of time. *Then* could no longer be grasped or imagined while *now* was short of conviction and substance, like an austerity version of a world whose rich original we could no longer describe properly, however much we might miss it.

So the summer was still not over, not by a long chalk, and everything was wrong. I recognized the depression and anxiety of old, and for the most part I managed to keep them at bay with the help of work, and by carefully not pursuing analogies between Exton's agonized spirit and my own. *I fear I shall be fetched away before due Time*, he wrote. *The Maw might open in the Meddow's or the Greenwood's Earth itself.* But it wouldn't, would it? Not for me. Don't let other people get your kicks for you.

Susie and I were like actors lost in a very long run of a play whose meaning and basic story they could scarcely be bothered to recall. We did the moves, avoided the furniture, and somehow the words came out of our mouths. There were silent, palely polite meals in the kitchen, just the two of us, since Jane avoided contact as much as possible. Conversation was thin and practical, a matter of bread, milk, putting out the rubbish, feeding a stray cat that came to the door horribly burdened with sentimental associations of no practical use whatever. The animal, a scrawny tabby probably driven off a farm by its peers, turned up much too late in the day, exposing us to what we had not quite admitted in so many words. We were done for as a couple. We couldn't bear to drive the cat away, although it whined and was never satisfied with what it got, despite its good fortune. It never acquired a name, and one day it wasn't there.

Eventually one evening Susie put down her fork and said, 'I'm worried about Jane. She's not right.'

'I'm not sure she ever has been.'

Susie was about to get irritated with me, then thought better of it. 'She's worse, though. I think what happened at the party has really damaged her. I think she's losing her way. Do you feel that?'

'It's hard to know what to do. Should she see a doctor?'

'I don't think she'd agree to that. She must know she's not well. But you know what she's like – in charge, even when she isn't, because her intelligence tells her she should be. She wouldn't want to end up being sectioned or something.'

'Who would? Would it come to that?' There was a silence. 'Well, then.' The cat had got in. It rubbed against my legs.

'Maybe you could talk to her.'

'Me?' It was the last thing I wanted, though I wanted her to come and talk to me.

'I mean about her work. You can do that. She hasn't said anything to me, but she might be willing to talk if you raised the subject. Don't let the cat on the table, Martin.'

'What? You think the work's important?' The cat tensed in my lap. I hadn't meant to sound bitter.

'It's important to her,' Susie said patiently.

I found it hard to imagine how I'd ever ended up in this

room talking to her. The idea that we'd ever met seemed implausible. 'She's your friend,' I said.

'Don't be such a fucking wanker.'

'I didn't mean I was trying to get out of it.'

'Then do something, just for once. Please, Martin. Just do what I'm asking you to do.'

'Fair enough. But I don't know why you can't do it. You'd be better at it.'

'I don't know either, do I? I feel fucking helpless.'

Nothing had been said about the burning of the manuscript since the party. The scorched pages had come back with Jane from the signal box and she had presumably taken them up to her room. My mind flinched at the idea of someone's work being deliberately destroyed. It seemed a crime against nature, and somehow it managed to be meaningless and at the same time grotesquely, blaringly symbolic – which was presumably Alex's intention. I found it hard to think of him without wanting to kill him. I wanted to meet him in the village street and kick his face in. What could I offer Jane except outraged sympathy? And, equally, how could I conceal the fascinating horror of the act? It was like evil – something for which no motive but the awful improvising energy of the deed itself could be adequate.

Was everything gone? All her work? It could be. It might. We had no word processors or disks or flashdrives then. In that day before yesterday, before the numberless digital infinities were laid open or inflicted on us, the world was made of paper. Even among those who hated them and were willing or eager to destroy them, books, the written language, had a sacred status that has now almost vanished from the Western world. The integrity of the object has failed. You might say that it was only a few poems, but in that case it seems unlikely you'd be reading this. Then again, in a sense you'd be right: *Vanity, all is vanity*. It might have been only a sheaf of early work, but it seemed to be all Jane had.

Susie was still looking at me. I went upstairs and knocked on Jane's door. There was a faint reply. Inside it seemed very bare now. All the posters had been taken down. She had packed up Alex's stuff in a few boxes. She was sitting on the window-seat with her knees drawn up, looking out into the parched evening garden. Despite the heat she wore a long blue skirt and a graying T-shirt with the sleeves pulled down over her hands. Her hair was tied back with a rubber band.

When she looked up, I saw that the light had gone from her face. Her presence, to be honest, seemed purely notional. She had been here, Jane, alive, strange, imperious, lovable, but all that remained was the rumour of that sweet impossible girl. In the arse-backwards way of these things, I felt embarrassed by my lack of desire for this small, pale creature. She studied me as if the coming conversation were something she would have to endure for the sake of manners, or completeness. She gestured me to sit down beside her. The desk was deep in papers covered with her neat but swarming black handwriting.

'You've been at work, then?' I asked. She smiled and shrugged. 'I mean, it looks as if you've been busy.'

'I suppose so, but it's all shit.'

'I doubt it.'

'You don't know, do you, Martin? How would you know?'

I rode the punch. 'Give yourself a chance,' I said. 'You've had a hell of a shock.'

'I'm not asking for reassurance.'

'No, but I'm your friend. Unworthy as I am, at least let me sympathize.' The joke died on the air.

'Anyway,' she said, 'now I know why I never took it before.'

'Personally I wish I'd never bloody heard of it. It doesn't suit some people. It doesn't suit me.'

'Took you a while to find out, though. You seem to have had a period of instructive grace before the demons started to infiltrate. I had no such luck, it seems.'

Demons? 'The comedown can be upsetting,' I said. 'It happens to lots of people. Sort of the price you pay.'

'But it's voluntary pleasures you're supposed to pay for, isn't it? Conscripts get in free.'

'It was cruel and irresponsible, whoever did it.'

'There's not much doubt about who did it, is there?'

'You mean Alex?'

'Yes. Him and his friends.'

'I suppose it could have been worse,' I offered, like a moron, 'what with the bikers turning up.' She gave no sign that this had registered.

'I think I might be getting a bit schitzy,' she said, with a smile. I felt a chill.

'It can seem like that.'

She nodded slowly. 'I've just been reading this,' she said. She handed me an old copy of *Encounter*, open at an essay on writers and drugs by Kenneth Allsop. 'When in doubt, what do our sort of people do? They find something to read. Tell me what you think.'

Reading an essay was not what I'd had in mind when I came up to Jane's room, but clearly I was required to do so immediately. The sense of the ridiculous and the pulse of alarm in my chest would have to be set aside. I sat and went through the piece, aware of her complete stillness and attention. Allsop argued that the pursuit of *le paradis artificiel* offered by opiates and psychedelic drugs was futile and self-defeating. Ho-hum. In the effort to escape the confines of the unaltered mind, the seeker merely intro- duced himself to a further cage, from which return might prove impossible. Tick. Allsop referred to Piranesi's *Carceri d'invenzione* to illustrate his contention. Tick. There was nothing very original there, and De Quincey had put the matter more memorably. Not very long before, I'd have discarded the piece as reactionary and timid, but just at the moment it was one of the most alarming things I'd ever read, as though someone had put a page fizzing with poisons into my hand.

'Interesting.' I stood up and put the magazine down carefully on the bed. 'Are you sure you should be reading this kind of thing just at the moment?'

'What? Now that I'm mad? I can't catch anything from it, can I? Anything I haven't already got. It's too late.'

'Jane, you're not mad.'

'Well something's amiss, petal. Being polite about what name you give it won't help.'

'I just mean that reading stuff like this, although you find it very interesting, doesn't help when you're upset and suggestible and when you need to take time to relax and recover.' I could see for myself the pull of the imagery, driven to its grim conclusion. Private hell and damnation. Language itself could terrify, as I knew from experience. It could produce what it proposed, if you were open to suggestion. It might be a blessing, but you might be dead unlucky. I wouldn't be saying this to Jane, though.

'There's no cure for knowledge, is there? Do you find that?'

I could think of one but I wasn't stupid enough to mention it. Now I was at a loss. Allsop was probably right.

'So has Susie sent you?' Jane asked, after a while.

'We were a bit worried about you.'

'Your schitzy pal.'

'Don't say that, Jane.' I sounded faintly desperate.

'All right. What shall I say instead?'

'It's been a difficult time for everyone, you know.'

'But the school's going to rally round and we'll show them all at the regatta.'

'What have you been working on? Some new stuff?'

'Best approach via the poetry? That would be Susie's idea, then.'

'It looks as if you've been hard at it.'

'I don't know. Marks on paper and noises on the air.'

'Business as usual.' I nodded at the table.

'I'm afraid not, Martin. Far from it. Have a look if you like.'

I went over to the table. What I saw made me cold. It made me want to leave the room, the building, the county. Like the legendary exam paper of someone experiencing amphetamine psychosis, endlessly rehearsing the same sentence, the pages of manuscript were covered with the same two lines of verse:

> Within the Stygian Mines of doubt,
> Mine is the Soule, I fear, cast out.

I'd had similar experiences with speed, getting locked into a single stanza all night until it wore off. That was the point, though: it did wear off. Jane's table was invisible under the waves of paper, all meticulously timed and dated.

'I didn't know you were interested in Exton.'

'Well, I've read him, of course.'

'You never said.'

'No.'

And why would you bother to tell me? I thought. I would have nothing to offer on the subject, clearly. 'So why come back to him now?'

'I thought it might be the way into something, a stepping-off point. An invocation.'

'I don't know if I'd start from there,' I said, with clumsy lightness. 'Exton was a very worried man.'

'With reason,' she said. 'As it were. Mad as a snake, clearly.' She stared at me as though unsure whether I was actually there. 'But, then, language chooses you, of course, as you know, not the other way round.' She stood up, took the magazine from where I'd put it and placed it beside the papers on the table. 'Anyway, it wasn't what I hoped. More like a cage than a door. No matter. No harm done. Actually that last part's not true – as you can see.' She gestured at the reams of urgent, mobile handwriting. 'The language is peeling off the objects.'

'Language is conventional. It's not really attached to its objects, is it?

'No poet has ever really believed that,' she said, in a forlorn voice. 'You couldn't write if it were true, or if you thought it was. I assumed that you knew that. And now it's peeling off. You should be glad you're not seeing it everywhere too.'

Nowadays I occasionally notice people making jokes about the madness of poor Syd Barrett, but there's no laughter to be had if you look squarely at his gaze in that famous photograph – the million-mile stare from nowhere into nowhere with no hope of coming back and no here to come back to anyway. I was frightened then, looking at Jane, glimpsing the steadily growing distance between her and the safety of the mundane. It was difficult even to stay in the room, but I needed at least to try to be of comfort.

'So this experience, you think, has inhibited your writing in some way.' I sounded like a social worker.

'Being spiked with acid's fucked my mind up, Martin, if that's what you're trying to say. It's like moving into a house next door and not being able to get home. Things that aren't – that aren't real keep leaking into the wrong area. Terrifying nonsense.' She didn't sound terrified, just exhausted. 'And I don't seem to be able to hear the language any more. My language, I mean. Other people's, though, other people's won't bloody shut up from morning to bloody night. And I can't sleep. Can't. Can't fucking sleep.'

'You'll get over it, Jane. I mean, I managed to.'

'No, I don't think I will.'

'You're a lot tougher than I am – that's obvious.'

'I'm afraid I'm one of the unlucky ones. "Her existing but dormant disposition towards going barmy was fatally exacerbated by traumatic stimulus."' She laughed. It had a peculiarly formal sound. 'Sorry – that's a bit previous of me, to suppose I'll merit an obituary.'

'I'm sure you will, eventually. But as to being barmy, there's no point in looking at it like that.'

'I quite agree. But there we are. That's how it is, or how it seems, not that I can tell the difference any more. Never mind, Martin, I can be Blow-Your-Mind-Pete's girlfriend, frolicking round the loos in Cambridge market, flashing my knickers and depressing the visitors.'

'Janey, please don't talk like this. You just need to rest and calm down. Maybe you should go and see your sister, get away for a break.' I'm glad I didn't have to listen to myself while I was saying this rubbish. I hadn't saved her. I would never have been able to do so. The mere fact of it passed judgement on me. Of course, it was me I was most worried about: logic aside, I might catch something. A millisecond of the Medusa's gaze.

I realized that Jane was being very patient. There was nothing for her in this conversation if I didn't instantly follow where she led. Whatever had linked us was gone, and now she was simply doing her decent best to keep her end up. I made to go. She touched my arm. 'Have you ever been lost, Martin? Really lost?' The question meant: You're not serious enough for me now, if you ever were. 'I mean completely unmoored – all detail and no context, like "The Domain of Arnheim".'

'Well, as you know, I had a bad time a while back. So I kind of know a bit about it. But here I am, more or less.'

She didn't believe me. I hardly believed myself. Even my madness – the great shaping event of my life so far, I now saw, something I could actually claim as my own! – seemed tiny and inadequate in comparison with Jane's affliction. She gathered the pages on the table and formed them into a neat cone, which she placed in the wastepaper basket. We both watched as the sheaf unfolded to fit the basket's contours.

Susie came in with a cup of tea. She raised an eyebrow at me. I shook my head.

'This is a bit parental, don't you think?' said Jane, taking the mug of tea and putting it on the table. 'Coming for a talk in my bedroom.'

'We're just worried about you, love,' said Susie, sitting on the edge of the bed.

Jane sat down beside her and took her hand. 'There's nothing you can do, believe me. You should just get on with your own stuff. I'm happy enough in here.'

'Well, you can't go on like this for ever. Perhaps you could see someone.'

'Such as an alienist, Mama?'

'Someone who could help. Please, Jane.'

'If I encounter such a person when I'm out for a walk I'll let you know.'

'Have you spoken to Alex?' Susie asked.

'Strangely enough, now that you ask, I haven't. He hasn't come anywhere near me.'

'It's only that I wondered how things stand.'

'I know you want to talk about him burning my poems, but there's nothing to be said about it, is there?'

'Shall I talk to him? Or maybe Martin could.'

'About what? I know why he did it.'

'Well, can you tell us?'

'It doesn't show him in a very good light.' There was a glimpse of the old Jane here, travelling by a different map.

'Does that matter now?' I asked.

She shook her head, as though bemused by someone else's problem. 'He didn't want me to send out a manuscript to publishers. He said I wasn't ready.'

'He wasn't ready, more like.'

'Reeves and Reeves had already asked to see something – after the Jerome. That's quite usual. Doesn't mean anything necessarily. Doesn't seem very important now, anyway.' She paused. 'And I told him about it because it seemed only fair that he should know. So he said he didn't want me to send the stuff. Then there was the party, and you know what happened there.'

'Bastard,' I said.

'Didn't matter,' she said.

'Oh, Jane. That's awful.' Susie put her arms round her. Jane hugged Susie, then stood up and stepped away.

'No, I mean it didn't matter. I had a spare copy. Of course I did – wouldn't you? I mean, seriously, wouldn't you? And he didn't know about that and he was so off his head making mad gestures and taking revenge by shagging that Diane person he just didn't think of it. I sent the poems off anyway. And now I've lost him.'

'You're much better of rid of him,' said Susie. 'I never liked him.'

'I know you didn't. I don't like him much either. Liking's not in it. We're meant for each other, stuck with each other, nailed together like the bits of a bloody teapot stand or something. I would never leave him, even now. He has to leave me. I don't know whether he can do that or not.'

'Well, he's made a beginning,' said Susie, 'with that tart Diane.'

'It must be beyond saving.' I said. 'Too much has happened.'

'It hasn't finished happening,' Jane replied. 'I got a letter.' She took an envelope from a drawer and handed it to Susie. I read the letter over her shoulder. Reeves and Reeves wanted to publish a collection.

'Bloody hell,' I said. 'I mean, I'm not surprised. But this is wonderful.'

'I ought to be very pleased,' said Jane, 'and it seems ungrateful not to be, but at present I just feel very flat somehow, as though this publishing business had happened somewhere else or, I don't know, too late. I don't suppose that makes sense.'

'You need to let it sink in,' Susie suggested.

'But you are going to accept the offer, aren't you?' I asked. 'I mean . . .' Susie glanced sharply at me.

Jane shrugged.'I dare say, yes.'

'You must. We ought to have a drink,' I said.

'I'm feeling worn out,' Jane replied. 'I think I want to go to bed. Not that I can sleep. But I want to turn the light off and close my eyes.'

'Perhaps you'll feel more like it tomorrow,' said Susie.

'Things can't just be left as they are, can they?' I said.

'I haven't the energy for recriminations and all that. I need to use what I've got in order to work, or at any rate try to. I know you'll understand, Susie. You've been a good friend, haven't you?'

'Oh, Jane,' said Susie, 'what are we going to do? Are you going to tell Alex? How are you going to do that?'

'You don't need to do anything, lovey, just please leave it.' Jane's thin, glassy self-assurance was heartbreaking. 'I'm going to try to sleep now. Goodnight.' She climbed into the bed, still dressed, and turned away.

Susie and I looked at her for a few moments, trying to absorb the terrible good news, I think, then went downstairs. I decided to go to the pub, and Susie said she had somewhere to be, but I didn't ask where.

That evening there was still time enough before closing to get very drunk at a leisurely pace. The pub remained very quiet. Blue fag in hand and *Cosmo* at the ready, Shirley kept a discreet eye on me while I sat at the other end of the bar and read the paper until I couldn't see straight. It was great news, wasn't it? I asked Shirley for the phone book.

'Yeah? Who's that?' It was Alex. He, too, was clearly drunk.

'Evening, cunt. You'll never guess what's happened now,' I said.

It seemed like a good idea at the time.

20

On the other side of Summer Hill there was that view far into the west, beyond the domesticity of hopfields and orchards, over the hills. It stretched away to the Black Mountains, which sometimes moved tantalizingly to the edge of definition. It was abroad, out there, elsewhere. Its pull was quiet and constant. You wanted to be sure it was still in place, waiting. Even at my laziest and most stoned I made the effort to go up Summer Hill sometimes to have a look. It had something to do with the future. It was also connected with another of those poems that would have infuriated Irmgard by the very mildness of its aspirations – a piece of something and nothing, outgunned even by Edward Thomas's conspicuously unassertive 'Adlestrop'. I mean Walter de la Mare's 'The Railway Junction':

> From here through tunnelled gloom the track
> Forks into two; and one of these
> Wheels onwards into darkening hills
> And one towards distant seas.

The tail-end of romanticism empties itself of consequence here. It's the kind of poem that Alex's hero Ezra Pound was born to try to stamp out. I can quite understand why, but it's stuck with me for more than forty years and I still read it from time to time. Victorian travellers on a lonely rural platform – 'the bow-legged groom, / The parson in black, the widow and son, / The sailor with his cage, the gaunt / Gamekeeper with his gun, // That fair one, too, discreetly veiled' – are all joined by Larkin's 'frail travelling coincidence' to an end so far beyond divination as to be inconsequential. For me to dislike this poem would be like hating the colour blue. The emptiness is the consolation.

Jane, needless to say, liked the view from the hill – she seemed to claim it as her own, as people sometimes claim pieces of music. Of all of us she had explored the area most thoroughly, so it was her territory in a way that it could never be ours. As I said, she was attached to the old farm buildings on the far slope, masked from the top by a line of huge ash trees. This was where she would take herself off for a day at a time with a bottle and a notebook. I think she spent the hours looking and sleeping rather than writing.

Separately rather than together, Susie and I would happen along now and then, but Jane knew what we were doing so it was an awkward business, a falsehood committed against our friend, and we hated it. So I suppose we let that slide a bit. Jane seemed content enough, not frightened or irrational, though we knew this was only an interval. We were glad enough to cling to some kind of routine for now.

It was a Saturday lunchtime. Susie had gone into college to work while I stayed at home. There'd been no sound at all from Jane that morning, so after a while I made a cup of tea and took it up to her room. When I knocked there was no answer. I hadn't heard her go out, so I opened the door. The bed hadn't been slept in and the desk was bare of paper. For a moment I thought she must have left and gone to Wales or something. But her clothes were still there. I went round to the pub but she hadn't been in. She was perfectly at liberty to stay out all night if she wanted to, but her absence nagged at me and after while I set out up the hill, taking the left fork before Moon House, then beginning to make my way down the gentle slope of unused grazing towards the line of ash trees that hid what I thought of as Jane's barn, where she had made herself a sort of nest on the upper half-floor, with pillows and blankets, and liked to lie looking out. Only when I got quite close did I notice the smoke rising above the trees, and even then I didn't immediately connect it with Jane. This was the country: people burned things whenever they felt like it.

I climbed the fence and made my way down behind the farm cottage, coming out in the yard. It was then that I saw the thicker smoke flooding from the open door of the old plank barn. One side of the barn was alight. I began to run. 'Jane! Are you in there?'

No answer. The fire crackled and began to roar, sensing its strength. I went to the open doors. It was hard to see anything. If I went inside I might not get out again, let alone find Jane, even supposing she was there. Next I ran to the back of the barn. It rested against an old stone wall. I scrambled on top and edged my way along to the window. There was a louder roar and a crash from inside.

I tried to remember what the barn contained – no fodder, really, just odds and ends of tack and old tools. I didn't think there'd been petrol or any other flammable spirit. I hoped to God there hadn't.

Smoke was whispering out of the window now as I leaned in. I called for Jane again but couldn't hear anything. It was no good. I'd have to get inside. I hauled myself over the sill on to the half-floor and into immediate choking darkness. The noise and the sense of intense heat close at hand were terrifying. Above me for a moment I saw a line of flame running down the planking to the window frame, then another. I screamed Jane's name and couldn't breathe.

Under my hands were blankets, a pillow, then someone else's hand. I took hold of it, then found I could just make out Jane's form. I shook her and shouted her name again but she was already unconscious. The knees of my jeans were starting to scorch, as though the floor would go up at any moment, so I grabbed Jane under the arms and hauled her out through the window. Then I lost my footing on the top of the wall and slipped backwards with her still in my arms. That was what I must have done.

It wasn't a long drop, but the weight and the impact on the ground winded me and I lost consciousness for a few seconds. When I came to, the wall of the barn above us was thick with dark grey tongues of smoke, and little bolts of flame kept bursting through the window-space. Jane lay beside me, her face black with smoke, still not moving, not breathing. I dragged her away from the barn, round the end of the outbuildings to an old enamel bath half full of treacly water dark with leaves. I splashed some on to her face. Nothing. I shook her and shouted at her and pleaded with her to wake up. I tried to remember artificial respiration. But it was, of course, perfectly clear even as I began that nothing would happen even if I suddenly became an expert in first aid. Nowadays I would have had a phone. But then there was no help nearer than a mile. I struggled to get her into a fireman's lift, then began to stagger back over the hill towards the village and the pub.

Afterwards people kept asking me questions I couldn't answer. How long had Jane been at the barn? Why did she go there? To say that she liked it didn't mean much to the police. And what was I doing there? Looking for Jane. Why? This other young lady's your girlfriend, or that's what you've been telling us. Do you want to tell us something else now? This is very serious, you realize. Where was she, this Susan, at the time? At college? What was she doing there? On a Saturday? Was your dead friend on drugs at all? Are you? Because you look as if you are – doesn't he? They searched and found nothing, but they could tell that the facts were not proof. Facts were susceptible to change. Facts could be flushed down the lavatory or stuffed into a hedgerow. It wasn't the truth they were after, either, not exactly. Truth was too complicated, involved too many competing factors. It required three dimensions – not that the policemen would have put it that way – and there was no time. What they needed was a story that made sense, and in my clever-clever way I knew

I couldn't offer them that, even supposing I could get them to listen long enough so that I could try to explain.

What you are reading now is as close as I can get, and of course it's incomplete, and of course it's vitiated by love and prejudice to such an extent, and in such a variety of ways, as to exceed my power to grasp or suggest. You might say these pages are something on account, a gesture at a debt of guilt when I'm not even sure who the creditor would be. All this is by the way: Jane was dead, and that was a thing beyond all comprehension. Nowadays people we know are dying all the time, but this was the first death for all of us. It created winter in July and August, and there was nothing to be said or done. Had it not been for me, it might not have happened.

Susie and I waited for the inquest and the burial to be over before we split up. She moved into Willeford. Although I'd no idea it would happen, it came as no real surprise when she got together with Gareth Pritchard around Christmas time, or that quite soon they went abroad – to Canada, where they apparently took teaching work. Luke, it was said, remained in Machynlleth. At any rate, he has never returned.

I remember the coroner's court, its bare wooden-benched sobriety, and I remember Jane's sister, Jessica, a near-identical twin with gripped dark hair and a hat, in a middle-aged black woollen suit, sitting in silence throughout the proceedings, usually looking upwards through the windows at the roofs around the marketplace. She accepted our condolences without a glimmer of either gratitude or hostility. We might as well not have existed, it seemed, given that her sister no longer did. In all these proceedings Alex was nowhere to be seen: he and Diane had gone to the United States.

I was called and gave my account of events, and the inescapable impression generated itself that Jane and I had been lovers – we had to have been, surely. Otherwise, as the police could have told you, it made no sense. There was no room for half-measures or the unspoken, for the climate, the times or the pharmacological disposition of the moon and planets. The conclusion was accidental death. The suggestion – it didn't need to be made explicit – was that the balance of Jane's mind had been disturbed. The belief – I could feel it unspoken around the town – was that this was somehow partly my fault. Although I could hardly disagree, I would have liked to share out the aspersions more equitably.

I may not feel I ever knew Jane, but only one thing emerged at the inquest about which I had had no previous idea at all. She was married. She had married Alex in the Easter vacation before finals. I looked at Susie when this was announced and clearly she had been as much in the dark as I had, though within a moment her expression changed to indicate that she suspected I must have known. She was with the majority there. If, Mr Stone, you were as close to Mrs Farren as you claim – which I hadn't claimed, of course – then surely you must have known this and, *ergo*, you were up to no good. No one said it, but again everyone thought it.

I wondered for a while what hold Alex had over Jane,

sufficient to make her marry him; but in time I came to think it was equally likely that Jane had felt she needed to be married – it was exactly the kind of counter-intuitive thing she might do – and had got Alex to agree. It would have meant very little to him, I thought, except as a token of an outmoded form of ownership he might feel like exercising, from time to time, as a joke.

So he would have said, though I see now that in fact he had no sense of humour and his hilarity was rage and hatred. He did not come to his late wife's funeral, held on a grey, humid afternoon in Aberystwyth. It was thinly attended, an occasion of extreme blankness. I cannot remember anything that was said, only the silent drive there and back with Susie. She had acquired a black suit from somewhere.

When in doubt I usually give in to inertia. After Susie left there were still some months remaining on the lease at May Cottage, so I stayed. I allowed the post to accumulate on the windowsill by the front door. After a while I made myself go through it. Bills, a couple of magazines, material for what I took to be the now defunct *Summer Hill Review*. I'd opened the last envelope before I realized it was something for Jane. It was a contract from Reeves and Reeves for her book of poems. I burst out laughing. Then I went to the pub at eleven o'clock in the morning and set about getting mortal drunk. When I'd made a decent start I rang Susie at college. 'There's something here you've got to read.'

'Not unless it's to do with Jane.'

At teatime we sat in the kitchen like visitors while Susie

read the letter. 'She managed to do it again,' she said eventually. 'Poor cow. She's won.' Her eyes glittered and she squeezed them shut.

'What shall we do?'

'Well, the book exists so it can be published. I'd better ring Jessica. No need for you to come too.'

After a while she came back. 'According to the will – yes, she did make one, and Jessica has a copy – control of Jane's literary estate passes to Alex,' she said, sitting down once more at the kitchen table.

I should have moved away, but I didn't. Routine was all I had. Marcie gave up suddenly and went home – for a couple of weeks I didn't realize she'd gone. The field was clear for me. Time passed. I finished the thesis and began working at Divott, *pro tem*. Years passed. I edited Exton's poems. I began to edit the journals.

The world in which we had come of age began to disappear, at first unnoticeably and then with a rapidity too great for me to take in, supposing I'd wanted or been able to at the time. Those five or six years ending in that summer have no status as a period, it seems to me. I imagine many people would vehemently disagree, but I'm too old to care, and with certain reservations my memory is clear. Those years were afterwards, they were before, but they were nothing much on their own account. We inherited and spent our dream-capital and created very little in the way of signature material. We were exhausted without knowing it, waiting to be transformed or abolished.

The most notable thing is that in the last generation those times have become an established repository for the contempt of people who came after, those whose world properly begins in 1976, when ours, or at any rate mine, was ending. A lot of things changed, most obviously the elements with which young people identify most strongly – music, fashion, drugs to some extent – but also the more embedded conditions of life, including what in this country passes for politics. There is more than time between now and then: adapt or die, as they say, learn to breathe the air of another planet. So I did, successfully, albeit with a certain chestiness.

Yet I ought really to have begun by saying that after a while I met Molly, since that was surely the most important development in the intervening years. She came along after a long period of relative solitude, when I was in my mid-forties and had long since decided, or accepted, that the single life was the thing, refreshed by occasional brief intervals of indulgence at conferences and the like. Quite often I hated this *modus vivendi* but it was how matters had turned out, and I was used to it. I had work, the pub, the large first-floor study of my house behind the market-place in Divott, and as much dreamless sleep as possible.

Molly and I met when she attended a summer school at which I was teaching. The overall subject was the literature of the Marches, so naturally I was talking about Exton. By this point my interest had shifted predominantly to the journals and I offered a guided walk over some of Exton's landscape away to the south of Summer Hill, along the wooded banks of the river Dawney, where he had nosed

around among the old settlements and tried his hand
(without much success) at fishing. There had been eels in
the river then, which perturbed him.

The day of the walk was hot and muggy and the party
were glad to pause for lunch at the pub in Dawney Bridge.
In the way of these things Molly and I fell into conversation. She was an attractive, self-possessed woman of
forty, neither anxious nor impressed by my presence.
Unlike some of the people who come on these outings,
she'd actually read Exton, including my selections from the
journals. She had questions, real ones. Although her
interest did not extend to the religious matters that still
preoccupied me, to encounter her was like coming upon
water in a desert. She understood that Exton was in a sense
one of the earliest, and certainly among the most important
explorers of the diverse and secretive landscape where
he had sought sanctuary. There was a kind of steady,
unsurprised curiosity to her questioning, and she had a
mind of her own, in which Exton was a significant but
not dominant figure.

In those days she was a librarian at Birmingham University, but she was thinking of using the proceeds of the sale
of her late parents' house to start up a bookshop somewhere in the Marches. You wouldn't advise your worst
enemy to open a bookshop, but for her the idea had the
status of a vision. She'd been looking round Divott, among
other places, for suitable premises. She held my attention
with her unfussy prettiness, the directness of her enthusiasm and, though it will make it sound as if I were assessing
a book, her seriousness.

At the end of the course we ended up sharing a drink in town. Molly's own especial literary enthusiasm was the novels of Eleanor Gray, another local writer, a forgotten early rival of Daphne du Maurier. She had been devoted to Gray's (I still feel, if anything more strongly) rather wordy and worthy border-Gothic romances since her schooldays in Edgbaston. Gray's books had shaped her idea of the Marches, and numerous visits had neither disappointed her nor weakened the novels' hold on her imagination. There was an unrecognized need, she proposed, for a popular biography of Eleanor Gray, a free spirit who had had a markedly rackety, indeed scandalous life, to draw new readers to the work, especially given the expansion of interest in neglected women novelists, and the search for a female canon. I admired Molly's commitment, and she understood mine.

She had not long ended a relationship and was not particularly in search of another. Once we had explored the landscape on foot together for a few weekends, and she had begun to stay with me on her visits, it made sense to move in together, or it simply happened that we did, or something. She went ahead and found her shop and started up in business and did well, and her work on Eleanor Gray progressed slowly.

I was surprised to discover something resembling happiness. Our habits were compatible. Molly made few demands, and she listened when I tried for the umpteenth time to formulate what it was Exton meant to me. In turn I helped her with the accumulation and assembly of material for her life of Eleanor Gray. What has it been like to live with

Molly? Like a calm afternoon that has never threatened to end, made up of long walks, crosswords, quotations and the ability, almost always, to know when to leave each other alone. I've been far luckier than I deserve. She deserves much better, of course. And here we are, in deepest middle age, a scholar of sorts and his bookshop-owning lady-friend, making the best of things, deep in the still-green Marches.

But for all this it must be said that life since Jane's death has been to a great extent a matter of trying and failing to recover from that nightmare of carelessness fastened on by malice, and of managing to live with the subsequent deformity of spirit. My contentment with Molly has been real and substantial, but it does not have a supernatural power to transform. What I have done is to adapt, not to forget, never to escape.

Who do I blame? Myself, lavishly, with all the ingenuity I can muster, to the point of exhaustion and beyond. People say casually that guilt is a prison, as if they know what guilt is and what the prison walls are made of. Guilt is a *carcere* of perpetual *invenzione*: the inmate is always arriving at the same place of torment by a different, unsuspected route. All roads lead home to the place of perpetual unrest.

And, of course, there was Alex. He had had the privilege of Jane's affection and her bed, and had decided that it was not enough, that Jane was only one choice among many, and that things would be better or more encouraging if Jane were somehow reduced, changed from the marvellous creature she was into something more biddable.

It seemed she had gone part of the way to meet him. Marriage, wills, property. It was hard to avoid occasional news of him in the years that followed her death: I knew, and didn't know, what he was up to. Oddly enough, at intervals I also received postcards from Dieter and Irmgard, recording their presence at various festivals and interventions and riots in Europe and beyond.

Would I have been any better than Alex? I had lacked the courage to try, to find out – in which case, no? I had obligations – not the less so because they were also excuses, not the less so because they sustained me into the afterlife of adulthood.

Professor Gwyther is long dead, but I sit at the same end of the bench in the snug where he used to hold forth, and I feel at times that I am growing into the part, though of course I will never be the scholar he was. Some years back I began to teach writing on the strength of the few collections of poetry I'd published. The professor would have understood, I think. I cannot match his drinking either, though I try, but I like to sit with a book and a crossword through the dimming afternoons, pretending I'm not there, being simply an aperture through which language travels for storage. The brown hours! The other impending dotards sit remembering their dead friends and their beery exploits, their own leg-overs on Summer Hill with long-since respectably married women.

To paraphrase a poet: I have learned to pretend I live like this, at least for the benefit of others. But Jane in her careless half-undress is often here beside me, wondering why I don't make the move, and my slovenly cock stirs for a moment in its long coma. Molly understands, or thinks she does. She thinks I am slowly awakening from a long and troubled sleep, though I don't feel as if I've ever woken since the day of the death. Anyway, Molly and I offer each other great kindness. I have drink and she has the shop.

It is very difficult to be ignorant unless you're born into it. So, yes, I have been aware of Jane's posthumous career – the publication of her first collection, *Night Watch*, its quietly respectful reviews in the press, the reference to a life cut short before the fulfilment of her gifts, and the slowly growing impact as readers found their way to the book and made it their own and found their own meanings there. I have simply not participated in the creation of the myth. I have given no interviews, not that anyone's asked for one. I have not tried to keep my place in the narrative, not sought to become more than an 'early acquaintance' glimpsed in passing in one of Alex's memoirs. Tried not to be the bitter, disappointed bastard I partly am.

Even the second book did not goad me into action. This, as you know, was *Into the West*, and it was a great boon to the publishers. They do their best with very little but they need *something* to work with, if only to help refocus attention on the original product when it's time for repackaging. Even *Into the West* didn't stir me. In any case, what could I have done that would not have brought fresh pain, which for my own sake I was trying to avoid?

But *Into the West* was a fake. It contained a few early poems that Jane would not have bothered to republish, plus a handful of (in some cases admittedly very good) poems that must have been written in the last few months of her life, before the party. In addition there were a dozen or so pieces purporting to mark a new, late stage in her work – fragmentary, enigmatic things, formally very free, in which 'early Jane' was intermittently recognizable, juxtaposed with something cruder and more insistent, like a knowingly imperfect parody of the original. Not content with burning her poems, Alex, as I could see, had now begun to invent Jane's work for himself. And there wasn't much I could do about it.

I know there is starvation and poverty, torture and disease, but such intimate unkindness as this carries a particular horror, perhaps because its hatred is so closely interwoven with its object as to be hard to separate from love. This was Alex's version of the desire and pursuit of the whole. Alex had the talents of the leech and the impersonator. When he had made that tiny alteration in Jane's poem thirty years before, he had known what he was doing. He had no gift of his own, but he could make use of hers, so that she would never escape him, in life or afterwards. He would consume her, slowly.

Into the West was Alex's doing, but how was I to prove it? I could argue in print, but then my life would be utterly taken up, as Jane's had been – except that it would happen in the dry death-house of scholarly journals. People would take sides. They would believe they understood and knew, that they alone could separate the personal from the literary, the fact from its accumulated crust of interpretations, the greater good from the personal spat. Is this bad faith towards my presumed vocation? And then it would get into the literary press, and the combination of the public's excruciating ignorance and the journalists' empty knowing-ness would be a torment all of its own. Everyone wants to think they know; nobody wants to take the trouble to understand. There is no longer anything common sense will not impatiently tell you. In Divott I had quiet, anonymity and Molly's immense discretion. I had the Divott Poetry Festival – I had it how I wanted it: serious, unspectacular, sober. I drank and kept quiet. Then, of course, the idiots came up with the reinterment, which would mean Alex all over the place, the press and the rest of it. His struggle to make a life following the early tragedy. His meticulous care for the work. His new book.

I never wanted to hate anybody, but I have proved to be extremely good at it. Some people lack stamina and lapse into indifference: not me. It's exhausting to spend your life pretending otherwise, and finding you enjoy the pretence – the ordinary, beer and language, routine, all that you have lost and yet somehow keep hold of. It feels like hell, believe me, but I manage.

21

During the festival, on the day before my Exton lecture, Molly and I had had one of our very occasional, very quiet rows. It was my fault. It was always my fault. This time, of course, it was because I was wound up about the idea of Alex being there, with his talk and his film and his *In Conversation*. It would not have been possible to tell Molly all that I knew, because some of it was only knowledge, not fact, and she would quite reasonably have asked questions in order to assess the matter for herself, and I couldn't stand the idea of having to justify what I simply *knew*. She knew a lot – I'd told her a lot – but I *knew*. There should be a scientific instrument that measures pain as an index of authenticity. So, since I couldn't tell the whole tale, I found a pretext for anger instead. Molly doesn't rise to provocation. A one-sided row is especially maddening, I find. It dragged on overnight, and the following afternoon I went glumly down to the parish hall to do my stuff. Molly wasn't missing much. Someone else would be minding the bookstall.

My talk, 'Thomas Exton: Infernal Retirement', turned out to be well attended. The audience were in shirtsleeves and blouses for the oppressive grey heat that had settled over the place again that summer, as it seemed to do every other year. I raised my voice to allow for the sound of an electric fan flailing vainly away by the stage. The listeners inclined their heads the better to hear. These were older people, versed in patience. They thought knowledge was good, however grey the delivery. The bookstall at the entrance was stacked with copies of Exton's poems and journals, guarded by Molly's teenage assistant.

I've given more lectures than I would care to count, and I've developed the ability to think about something else entirely while addressing an audience. This can be useful: for example, it lets you assess the response and make pre-emptive adjustments to later parts of the material if necessary. But today I should have been all attention to my words: I was standing up for a principle, even if the audience had no way of knowing it. By doing my stuff I was protesting, on behalf of seriousness, maan. But in the event even I couldn't be bothered to listen.

Instead, while I ventriloquized, I fretted, thinking my way briskly towards the nearest catastrophe. There had to be something of Exton in the festival: he was its original underpinning, the local made flesh, the claim to fame. But very soon, I knew, this was bound to change. What had been essential would become an option, like history or modern languages in schools, and soon after that people would begin to find the matter of Exton not only unnecessary but disagreeable and in need of removal. It would not occur to them that this was the process, but that was how it would work. Morning assembly ceases to be compulsory: next week religion is proscribed. Do I exaggerate? Very well: one day the students say that *Ulysses* is too long; *Dubliners* replaces it; a little while later they wonder if they have to read all these stories. And so on. It is only a matter of time until language and value themselves fall under the same vexed, incurious and suddenly orthodox scrutiny. So this might be Exton's swan-song. I ought to do my journeyman best for him.

But that was not yet. For the moment the vicar, stronger on silvery courtesy than substance, probably found Exton a bit hard going theologically, while his fellow committee members, the Tunnocks, used words like 'gloomy' and 'morbid', though in such a way as to show that they understood Exton mattered to *me*. They were conflating me and English literature, but I forbore to mention it. They had also wondered if we ought not to do something about Edward Thomas. I pointed out that there was another festival not far away that looked after him so it might be wiser to stick to our Unique Selling Point. This was language they could more or less understand. In any case, I added, Thomas was hardly frivolous himself. Look at 'Midnight Rain', look at 'The Long Small Room'. Look at 'Lights Out' – it's a poem with a death wish, isn't it? And what about Jane's work? It wasn't Ogden fucking Nash, was it? I wondered if the cunts had ever actually *read* anything.

Facts notwithstanding, my colleagues on the committee didn't believe me: they got *nice feelings* from Edward Thomas. But I managed to stare them down for another year – God, it was exhausting – and my talk went ahead, and Exton was unavoidably prominent in the festival as a whole, given that a fellow poet and fellow troubled spirit was shortly to join him in the churchyard. It was intended that I should be mollified by giving a lecture at the festival. Everyone had been very insistent that I should. Divott would not be Divott without me, they said. The mere statement changed everything, for now I was part of the problem, which left the Tunnocks and their like as the solution. I should have refused, but what would have been the point? And then the festival was upon us, bunting in the streets, the car parks and shops full, the visitors with their bags of hopeful books. It would pass, I told myself, while in the sweaty hall my pedagogue's voice droned on towards what must have seemed to the listeners its extremely remote conclusion.

The fact that the media were taking an interest – that was the apotheosis, the evidence that we were real! – was more problematic. There were arts correspondents on hand from the papers, radio presenters, a crew from an alleged BBC Television arts programme. None of them showed up for my talk, naturally, but they were sniffing around, and I knew they would think we needed taking in hand, improving, making relevant, because that was how it had to be. Forgive me. I just find it irritating.

Clearly, though, I was quite mad, I thought, living with the nightmare prospect of Alex's appearance as if it were simply one more daily obstruction to be negotiated, pretending I had other matters that could really command my attention. The Tunnocks were honest idiots, I must admit: they also asked – because they really wanted to know – why I devoted so much time to a poet whose beliefs it seemed I didn't share. I didn't go to church, did I? At least, they had never seen me there. That was sort of why they were wondering. Good question. Out of the mouth of babes and Tunnocks. No, I didn't go to church, though I lived by it. I went to the pub, there to sit and think myself to oblivion. I had more pressing problems than what I believed. For example, there was what I knew, aged and yellowed and intensified, as it seemed, by the passage of time.

It was not until shortly before I finished speaking that I realized Alex was in the audience. He was seated upstairs at the back, in the gallery, which the stewards kept clear unless there was a packed house. This afternoon there wasn't, but he'd gone up there anyway, because that was what he would do, and because no one would prevent him, and there he sat, resting his chin on his hands, looking expressionlessly at me. It was the dark-eyed gaze and the heavy brow I recognized. The hair was all gone, shaved to deny baldness, the grizzly stubble giving him a Balkan aspect. He seemed milled down.

How this feeling resembles love, I thought. He was not looking at me, but then his eyes shifted and focused, and we gazed at each other. All the while I went on talking fluently. What should I do? Denounce him from the lectern? The setting was dramatic enough – a theatre, really, with a stage, an audience, or a courtroom, where an evildoer might be pointed out in all his glittering isolation so that the assembled community could focus their sudden righteous, vengeful wrath and drag him to the place of execution. But this was Divott, an outrageously ordinary place, where life went on in the tiny details of kindness and gossip and habit, and where for matters to be otherwise was unthinkably exceptional. Exton's life and Jane's death could have nothing to do with Divott, no matter that they had taken place hereabouts. Divott, you might have said, was a late example of ideology in action. If I could hide there, so could Alex, though he felt no need for concealment. To sit apart was to invite notice. Women in the audience had detected him, somehow, as had Molly's young assistant.

In the event I did nothing. I completed my talk. The audience applauded and Alex joined in, but abstractedly, as though out of good manners, like a politician at an arts event, always about to slip away to meet some more serious obligation, mentally already taking stock of the next venue. The chairman asked for questions. A couple of hands were raised, I began to answer, and by the time I looked up again Alex had gone.

He is ruined, I thought. He has gone bald. There is no need for you to do anything. Not that you would. As I left, copies of Alex's *Durable Fire: the Life of Jane Jarmain* were shouldering Exton aside on the display table. It was just business. The day would pass – Alex's talk, the accompanying film (though I found it hard to imagine there was any usable material) and the concluding *In Conversation*. It would pass.

The narrow street outside the hall was busy now with people moving between venues, carrying bags of books, local cheese and the watery thing that passed for wine 'of the region'. I needed a drink, so I made my way slowly past the churchyard and round the corner to the Green Man. A pub should always be out of sight round a corner, Gwyther used to say: it discourages the frivolous. Lunch was over. In the dim, varnished light of the bar a couple of old boys sat in companionable silence or – let's face it – senile torpor, over pints of Ansells mild. I checked my briefcase to make sure I'd got the *TLS*. The crossword would provide me with a stay against confusion while I decided what I wasn't going to do. I ordered a pint of Guinness and put a vodka in it, then stepped across the corridor into the dimness of the snug.

'Come in,' said Alex. 'It's okay. There's plenty of room.' He was occupying Professor Gwyther's end of the bench. A pint of Tapeworm stood on the table before him. The cunt was wearing an earring. He was ruined but it suited him. The little girls would understand.

I sat down on the stool opposite. I hate having my back to a room, as he was well aware.

'Back on the holy ground, eh?' he said.

I don't know why I had imagined that if we had to encounter each other he would be less direct in his approach. Why should he be shy?

'This your local, then?' he asked. There was something amiss with his voice. It was mid-Atlantic round the edges, as if he'd suffered a head injury. 'I'll say one thing. It's peaceful. Like the grave. Though not all graves are quiet, of course.'

'What are you doing in here?'

'Someone recommended it. A matey called Puttock or something.'

'Tunnock. Again, though, why here?'

'He said it was the local poets' pub, so after all this time I had no option but to have a look.'

'And now you've had one.'

He glanced over my shoulder as someone came into the room, then he rose, smiling. A blonde girl who at first sight looked about fourteen had appeared at my shoulder, wearing a tiny strappy pink cotton dress and ridiculous high heels. She had a handbag the size of a suitcase, into which she began to peer. She found her mobile phone, made a listening gesture at Alex and turned away.

'That's Sophie. She's from the publishers. My tour guide, as it were,' he said, tilting his head to look past me at Sophie's long brown legs. 'Assigned for the duration of the tour.'

'You're not, are you?' I asked. I couldn't help myself.

'Haven't quite decided yet,' he said, thoughtfully. 'Slightly complicated.'

'They're sending a photographer for the graveyard bit,' said Sophie, turning back. Alex nodded and rose. He went through to the bar to get drinks. Sophie sat on the bench and squinted at the display on her mobile. For God's sake, wear your glasses, you silly girl, I thought. But that was perhaps the least of her problems.

'Are you here for the festival?' she asked.

'I'm on the committee. My name is Martin Stone.' It meant nothing to her. 'Alex and I go back a long way.'

'You must be thrilled,' she said. I looked at her quizzically. 'I mean, the way it's livened up this year, with all the—' She broke off, at a loss.

'You mean the reburial of Jane Jarmain? I hadn't thought of it quite like that.'

'You sort of – well, yes, sorry – you know what I mean.'

'I sort of do, yes. So how well do you know Alex?'

'Well, his fame sort of goes before him. And he is, you know, amazing. And a bit naughty.'

'Isn't he? And what about Jane?' She looked at me uncertainly. 'I mean, have you read the poems?'

'Dipped in – it's been really busy.' She smiled, eager to please if possible. We both knew there wasn't much to go on.

'I bet Alex asked for you in person to accompany him while he's over here, didn't he?'

She gave a beautiful smile.'How did you know that?' she asked.

Alex's return with a tray of drinks spared me. 'Martin's an ogre, Sophie,' he said. 'I hope he hasn't been depressing you with all his gloomy Exton schtick.'

'Sorry. Who's Exton again?' she asked.

Alex and I exchanged a glance, each offering the other the honour. I expected a gumshield of orange rind to materialize in my mouth. 'A seventeenth-century poet from these parts. A parish priest who thought he was going to hell,' I said.

'That's really interesting.' Sophie was helpless to resist an upward inflection at the end of the sentence.

'I like to think so. I could show you some of his work in manuscript,' I said. 'In my office. It's just round the corner.' I'm sorry: my cruelty was misapplied.

'Time's a bit tight, actually,' she said.

We sat there. Alex drained his new pint in one and leaned back with a satisfied sigh. 'Get some in, then, pet,' he said, in a fake Geordie accent. Sophie was about to say something but caught his look and went to do his bidding, the mobile once more clamped to her ear.

'So what do you think?' he asked.

'About what?'

'Young Sophie.'

'I think you should leave her alone. Her dad's younger than you.'

'You're still jealous, then.'

'That must be it.' I should have got up and left long since, but the familiar electricity was in the air and made me want to see what was coming next. The feeling was almost one of detached interest, as the process of reeling-in got under way.

'I remember very little, you know,' he said.

'I imagine you'd need to. But you've managed to write a book about it.'

'Not quite the same thing, is it? Memory and imagin-ation, and so on. And I had the benefit of Jane's rather comprehensive diary. Had to be a bit selective there to spare one or two people's blushes, right?

'I remember very clearly anyway.'

'Do you think so? Don't you find it changes the further away you get?'

'No. It gets clearer.'

'Jane was always doomed, you know.'

'We haven't had a chance to find out otherwise, have we?'

'Come on. You thought the same. All that feyness.'

'She wasn't fey.'

'You see what I mean? It changes.' I shook my head. 'No? You think? Then we must agree to differ.'

Sophie came back with the drinks on a tray. As she stood handing them round, Alex ran a finger down her leg.

'Alex,' she said, more worried by the indiscretion than the touch.

'Don't mind me, lovey. I'm easily old enough to be your dad, apparently.'

She smiled sweetly at him, then gathered herself. 'I've got to deal with these calls and it's going to be all interruptions, so I'll just shoot off and get on with it.'

'I'll be here when you want me, probably,' said Alex. Once more Sophie looked as if she was about to say something, but thought better of it and left.

'I should get going as well,' I said.

'I've missed you.'

'Fuck off.'

'No, really. We had a lot of laughs, with the magazine and so on. What was it called?'

'I remember things differently.'

'Of course.' Alex inclined his head. 'And you're still here. Still on the holy ground. You dug your grave and you've been lying in it, whining quietly, ever since. Almost but not quite inaudible.'

'Your book doesn't mention that you burned Jane's manuscript.'

'You've read the book, then.'

'It wouldn't have come across very well, that particular episode, I suppose.'

'There you are – that's what I mean, remembering things differently.'

'I saw you come running out of the trees and throw the poems in the fire, Alex. I rescued one or two when you'd run off again. I gave them to Jane.'

'That's a very neat account you have there. But you were tripping off your head, let's not forget. I bet you don't tell your students that, do you?'

'You spiked the drinks.'

'Did I? Can you prove it?'

'You and your German chums.'

'They were Diane's chums, actually. Their names have gone, I'm afraid.'

'Dieter and Irmgard. You don't mention them either.'

'Ephemeral figures.' Like me, I thought, unable to prevent myself. 'Dead now, I shouldn't be surprised,' he said. He shook his head and shrugged. 'What can you do?'

'Tell the truth and shame the devil.' He smiled. 'And how is Diane?' I asked. 'Or has she fallen off the world as well? I see she made the film for you.'

'Not so good. Still around, though.' He looked at his watch. 'Resting at the hotel, I guess. She's kind of fucked up now, healthwise. Always lived pretty hard.'

I raised an eyebrow.

'There were casualties, as we know,' he said, and nodded. 'Unavoidably, in a time of change and discovery.'

'Jane, for example. And Luke.' He looked puzzled at
the name. 'You seem quite well on it.'

'I've been very blessed.' *I'm invulnerable*, his expression
said. *But try if you feel you must.*

'You destroyed Jane. Can you live with that?' I hadn't
meant to say this.

He smiled. 'What do you want me to tell you, Martin?
That's ridiculous. Destroyed? It was sad, that whole thing
with the scene back then, and the book makes it sad.
Makes it clear it was sad. That's what the readers get. And
the viewers. You need to see the film.'

'Diane's contribution to the sum of knowledge.'

'She doesn't let anything go to waste, not even now
she's sick. I haven't seen it, so it's really the première.' For
his accent alone I wanted to hit him with an ashtray. 'But
it's bound to have something to tell us about the old days.
I see they're putting it on in the old fleapit.'

'The Star's become a community arts centre. There's a
film on every week.'

'Of course. And I imagine the carpet's like Velcro. Arts
centre, my arse. Day centre, more like.' His contempt was
a reflex now, like a swing door in his head.

'And I suppose the film will make you sound sad, and
look sad, and a bit brave and tragic, won't it? Here, folks,
this is what sadness is like. But you're not sad, are you,
Alex? You could still just own up.'

'Are you crazy? As I say, we disagree. I don't know

about you, but I have to live with things as they are. Anyway, I'll sign your copy if you like. We could swap – Exton for Jane, just like writers do.' He took a copy of Exton's *Selected Journals* from his bag and passed it across the table for me to sign. I looked at him. 'And here's one of mine,' he said. 'I already signed it. Do you need a pen?'

I shook my head and pushed the book back towards him. He shrugged, unruffled.

'Actually,' he went on, 'I've been getting interested in Exton just lately. There's a film in there, I think, if we can just get rid of those poems. So it's kind of *Kilvert's Diary* with demonic interventions. There's money to get it made. I mean, they made a movie about the Earl of Rochester, so why not? And when it gets to the script stage I'd be needing an academic adviser, so—'

'Why didn't you tell me you'd married Jane?'

'Why not? Because it was none of your fucking business, sunshine. She was my girlfriend, remember. Anyway, she didn't see fit to tell you either, did she?'

'How on earth did you keep her for so long? You must have had some hold on her.'

'So it would appear. She wasn't the only one, was she? It's a gift.'

'Why, though? Why her?'

'Look, Martin, it's simple. They're all cock-happy in the end, whatever they say, whatever they think they think. But knowing that is one thing, of course. Making it work is another. That takes initiative, nine inches of it.'

'She left you behind. Young as she was. Twenty-three.'

'Suicide is a self-defeating way of doing that.'

'I meant in the work. Young as she was, she wrote things you couldn't even dream of.' The pomposity was leaking out again, beyond my power to control.

'Supposing I'd wanted to. Or needed to. It's only poetry.'

'Aren't you ashamed?'

'Ashamed? Not for a fucking minute, matey. I've made things happen.'

'You have indeed. What would she have thought of you inventing her poems?'

'We'll never know, will we? Anyway, are you interested?'

'What in?'

'Helping with the Exton film.'

'No. Is Diane involved in that too?'

'Too late for that, I suspect, the poor bitch, but she's certainly interested – after all, it's a film and she's made a few, festival stuff like this, maybe not where it's really at. I take note of what she has to say. Though of course, as you remember, poetry's not exactly her thing.'

'So what's her interest?'

'The powers under the earth? Evil with a big V. Anything sexy like that. The discord of what happens, maan. Anyway, time to go. See you on the red carpet, I imagine. Sure you don't want the book?'

There was another question. In fact, it was the only important question, but I was unable to imagine myself asking it, and I let him go.

22

Of course I'd read his bloody book. I wasn't going to and then I did. I'd gone into Molly's shop at lunchtime the previous day. That was what the row had been about.

'I suppose you have to stock Alex Farren's book,' I said quietly, since there were customers in the shop.

'This is a bookshop. It's my livelihood,' said Molly, not looking up from the computer screen. 'I understand how you feel' – I must have bristled – 'I mean, I think I do, I do try to, Martin, but if I excluded every book on the basis of customers' dislikes and disapprovals—' she glanced up as a grey head turned and peered abstractedly our way.

'I'm a customer, am I?'

'Well, in this instance, yes. If you had your way I'd be out of business.'

'No, I do see that.'

'There are some copies on the table near the door, with all the other festival material. As I imagine you've noticed.'

I bought and paid for a copy and went upstairs to Molly's sitting room. Her reading chair stood in the bay window looking on to the hill and across the market. I settled down with Alex's book. There was a photograph of Jane on the cover. It was her, but I hardly recognized her, even though I could tell it had been taken in the pub garden at Summer Street. The picture credit was Diane's. Jane seemed terrifyingly young and vulnerable, anticipatory, caught between delight and doubt – not a face of hers I'd ever seen. There was none of her strength in that look. The shot had been very carefully chosen. There were several others in the book – Jane and Susie sunbathing, Jane and Diane sitting on the diving board at Moon House – most tending in the direction of literary cheesecake. Except the wedding photo; Alex in a suit, Jane looking dazed in a gauzy white minidress, holding a posy of lilies on the edge of the marketplace in Cambridge. Why had I never known? Who else had known? If I had been so ignorant, what confidence could I possess? Alex had the advantage, the victor writing the history. I opened a bottle of wine left over from a book launch. The church clock struck two.

As we know, this is the age of biography. The supposedly real thing trumps the thing imagined, though there's a lot of accompanying blather about the creativity of the biographer, the power of reconstructive empathy and so on. Much of the time this work is a symptom of the English disease of Philistine curiosity – much rather the life than the work. Of course I'm implicated too, a long way down the food chain, by working on Exton. I'm a sort of biographer myself. In a few instances, I admit, I've been convinced, when the biographer's sympathies are large and selfless enough to let his subject emerge as though by her own posthumous volition. At the same time, it often seems that a complete lack of sophistication might be best: line up the stuff and let it speak for itself if it can. A bit like Exton's journals, perhaps. Or so I hope.

In any case, Alex's book was a lie, as I had known it would be. Despite what I said later to him in the pub, it was as if he had had no choice, because if he were to tell the truth he would no longer be Alex, and to be Alex was the whole point, Alex with the fame and the jailbait catnip and the durable frisson of hipness. Alex: say it soft and it's almost like praying. It was as if we had never been apart. All I could do was wait for the weekend to be over. In the meantime, from the introduction:

> As long as I knew her Jane was radically short of self-confidence. Her need for affirmation was such that you might have supposed she was an American. When I first became aware of her, as an undergraduate, she was in the group but not of it, as if waiting for admission. I was happy to oblige, but over the years people have sometimes asked whether I would have acted so casually if I had known the consequences of this casual act. My answer is: certainly, for as Shelley wrote, 'If we are to live, let us live.'

I wondered if anyone else would realize that this sort of thing was Alex's idea of a joke at their expense and Jane's. If they couldn't smell a lie, mightn't they sense an insult? Apparently not. Anyway, the book was written primarily for the American market, in a sort of American, full of selfless yet egomaniacal affirmations of the kind I quote above, whereby self-interest and the general good have undergone a mysterious and irreversible merger. The feeling in the book trade, apparently, was that the book would be getting Big Respect here, too. The Sunday commentators were tooling up. I watched with a combination of odd detachment (the whole thing was absurd and unreal) and demented fury (it was none the less taking place).

And there was this, later in the book:

It would be fair to say that Jane's verse technique was underdeveloped when first I encountered her work. I did my best to mitigate this by balancing the obvious influence of the female Confessional poets with more classically achieved examples, and it is clear to see that in her last days she made great strides – we have to remember how short her life in fact was – and managed both to achieve formal control and to move into a freer, more radical mode based on the confidence she had been given. I still remember sitting in the cottage kitchen with her, painstakingly arguing for the whole afternoon about a line ending, or the use of a colon in place of a full stop in a poem she was rather optimistically hoping to submit to the *Times Literary Supplement*. Her obduracy was, I came to see, the necessary face of her insecurity. It was of course worth the struggle to get *Night Watch* out into the light from the not immediately promising bedroom-study darkness of its adolescent origins.

Except in the chronological sense, I don't think Jane had ever been an adolescent. She had been parachuted into early adulthood with a defective map and phrasebook. Hence her impatience with people who were slow on the uptake. Alex was no fool: he must have known what she was really like, but in the service of his own will he was capable of abolishing the facts through the kind of simpli-fication that would make sense to an audience whose sympathies he could accurately predict. He knew how the world had to be, what the market would stand. He prob-ably viewed this as radical honesty – and, these days, disagreement was likely to be powerless. Culture no longer had the power, or the courage of conviction, that would enable it to instruct. The expert had become despicable by dint of being an expert.

Or again (one of my favourites):

I hadn't planned to marry. In those days, who did? And in any case I felt I still had a good deal of living and exploring to do. But when Jane asked if I would marry her, I somehow knew that for her this was a question of survival, that this fey, beautiful, talented creature could not see a way forward without the kind of security which she thought marriage would provide. In some ways she was rather old-fashioned, and so, it turned out, was I. In the end it wasn't enough to save her, but there is only so much we can do for other people, however much we try.

Or, lastly, this inimitable passage:

The formalities of the law were not designed to satisfy the need to know how and why Jane died so tragically young. Despite the rumour and speculation among some who knew nothing and others who might have known better, which I do not intend to revisit here, I have my own sense of what took place, and that too must remain private. I say this to try to forestall the possibility that the death will somehow dwarf or out-shine the brief life that was lost. For myself, I long ago decided that I would try to do my best by Jane, and much of the intervening time has been devoted to assembling, editing, interpreting and generally serving her work as it has moved from initial obscurity to the degree of recognition it currently enjoys – a status Jane too would have enjoyed, in her inimitable startled, uncertain way. There were sacrifices. My own work was long since set aside to serve her cause. But I have no complaints.

After my encounter with Alex I went back to the shop and sat upstairs in the window again, not reading, just looking idly out, killing time.

I must have fallen asleep. St Bart's clock was striking six when I stirred. Below, on the opposite pavement, a little old woman in an electric wheelchair was brusquely negoti-ating her way round the corner at the top of Market Hill. I watched her until she was out of sight, then went downstairs to help Molly close up. It was clear that she didn't want me to: the row seemed to have settled quietly in, and the pub seemed the most attractive proposition. There was nothing else requiring my attention between now and Alex's event, which I would not of course be attending.

Halfway down the hill I overtook the woman in the wheelchair.

'Hey, stranger,' she said as I went past. The shrunken

yellow creature in the blue fleece was not Diane. Only her voice and the video camera convinced me that it was her. Something violent had happened to her face, locking one side into a grimace. A stroke, I realized. But she could only have been my age.

'You could act like you're pleased to see me, Martin, since we're both here in the street.'

'It's such a surprise. How are you?' The words were out before I could catch them.

She smiled, in so far as she could. 'Is there a bar you can recommend?'

The snug of the Green Man was empty. Diane asked for a mineral water with a slice of lemon. 'I'm all fucked up, man,' she said. 'Too much fun over too long a period with too little regard to the consequences.'

'I'm sorry.'

'Not your fault.'

'Whose fault is it?'

'Alex and I are still together. So the care gets paid for. I wanted to come back here and have another look.'

'First time back?'

'And the last. I have maybe a year. '

'Jesus, Diane.'

'What's it to ya? You hated me. Anyway, the liver's shot, so at least everything matches.'

'Well, I'm here now.'

'I appreciate it. Alex is kinda busy all the time.'

I couldn't help smiling. She smiled back in that terrible diagonal way she'd been left with. Then she raised the camera. 'You don't mind?'

'Have I a choice?'

'Fuck, no. You can't turn down a dying woman's wish.' As she spoke she filmed me staring back at her. 'It stops me getting bored. That's all I've ever been afraid of, really, boredom.'

'So Alex looks after you.'

'Alex pays. I go where he goes. I'm useful. I'm the human element. That is, people see me tagging along and think he must be human.'

'I used to do that too.'

'Yeah? Meanwhile he goes on his merry way, fucking anything that can still walk, and for all I know some that can't.'

'And what's that job like, the being-human one?'

'It's boring as hell, but I'm used to it. I think he thinks I'm an example of something – a period he's deftly moved on from or some bullshit like that. I guess it's my punishment. Time was, I was supposed to be the winner. Maybe you noticed that, back then.' She cackled. 'So I aim to keep busy, as long as possible.' Whatever I thought of Diane and her vanity and her destructive stunts and what would probably now be called her (impossible) neediness, she didn't lack courage.

'He's a cruel fucker.'

'A cruel rich fucker. A girl has to eat.' If she'd ever known shame or regret, she seemed to have disposed of them. 'Did you ever think how it's always been like this – that we might as well have been sitting in this dump for the last thirty years?'

'That's more or less what I've been doing.'

'Different strokes,' she said, and cackled again. 'Fuck this, Martin – can you get me a large vodka with ice?'

'Is that wise?'

'Well, I'm not saving myself for anyone.'

I did as she asked. We sat for a while, not talking, while she savoured the drink. Eventually she nodded and I realized that the conversation, or the nearest thing we'd ever had to it, had gone away for good now. She smiled, sharing the knowledge, and shrugged.

'Time to go,' I said.

'That's fine. My curiosity's satisfied.'

'What about?'

'You survived,' she said. 'I thought you would. You didn't have very much at stake really.'

I rose. 'I'm going along past the Star,' I said. 'Would you like a push?' Off a cliff, for example?

'I drive this rig myself,' she said. We went out into the thickening evening sun. 'But walk over with me.' I held open the pub door as she steered herself on to the ramp.

We went a little way in silence. When the Star came into view, she reached out a hand to me and said, 'I'm sorry about Jane.'

'Me too.'

'If it hadn't been that it would have been something else. Some people are just born that way.' I had no reply. Diane took a deep breath. 'Let me go in there by myself – do you mind?' I shook my head.

I waited a couple of minutes, then slipped into the cinema just as the event was starting. A steward was directing Diane to a wheelchair space near the front. The

Star had been refurbished and seemed smaller than on that
strange, smoke-filled Sunday afternoon we'd spent watching *The Wicker Man*, but the redecoration had used the
reds and blues of the original fleapit and kept the barley-
sugar pillars framing the stage. The smell of rot and bodies
had gone. Somebody loved the place, but the old usherette
would certainly not have approved. For one thing, it was
packed. I found a perch on the steps beside the circle. My
grey crowd were all there, plus the same number twice
over, some of them actually existing young persons. I tried
to look as if I was there in an official capacity and would
be required elsewhere at any moment. Two could play at
that game. Nobody noticed.

Half of the public life of literature, it seems to me,
consists of embarrassment. I have been excruciated count-
less times, for my own sake, for that of others, and
sometimes with a kind of gleeful incredulity. This was an
occasion of the third sort. Simon Tunnock's mercifully
brief introductory remarks were a supreme example.
Agony, unction, empathy, ignorance. Jane, right? Wasn't it
sad? Wasn't it *terribly sad*? If there had been any loose
furniture to hand he would have chewed it in a touchingly
understated way. I found myself suppressing a laugh,
glared at disapprovingly by the grown-ups in the vicinity.
*But, look, aren't we lucky and privileged to be here and
paying for it?*

In the front row of the stalls sat Alex. On either side of
him were Sophie and the winsome Jacqui Trice, culture
correspondent from the BBC, there with a camera crew,
who were taping Simon and the audience but wouldn't be

using Simon's stuff in a million years. Jacqui normally 'did films', but apparently she was either willing or obliged to put her shoulder to the broken wheel of poetry as well and be 'in conversation' with Alex after the showing. Alex, of course, was somehow not 'just poetry', which was clearly an additional draw.

With the introduction over, Alex bowed his head modestly, then rose and went to the lectern. He read a handful of Jane's poems, interspersed with pieces of his own. You could almost hear a collective pillowy sigh from the crowd: here was the sadness, here was what it was like, here was the suffering survivor, glittering with modesty.

I knew Jane's poems backwards. Alex had been altering them again. At one point he explained that his long-term project was a complete edition of the poems, based on the latest texts. I couldn't help smiling then. How late could they be? The audience liked the stage gravitas of his delivery. He explained that he would finish with a piece of his own, written after the Irish 'Lament for Art O'Leary'. In his hands this cry of pain became a catalogue of body parts once belonging to Jane. The audience loved this equally. Some people rose to their feet to applaud. I realized all over again – always crashing in the same car – that people will take what they're given: they seek instruction on what they ought to like. They're eager to bestow their trust, to be part of the circle of almost-belonging. Divott was doomed.

Or maybe not. Alex took his seat and the film began. When the title came up – *Powers under the Earth*: *A film by Diane Eckhart* – I could tell that the event would not be quite as billed. A subtitle dedication followed, in deliberately scratchy lettering: *Alex 4 Jane 30 plus years.* The opening scene, in bleachy Super-8, showed the smouldering barn behind May Hill, with a yellow fire hose snaking round the side of the building. A policeman approached and placed his hand over the lens. Now the camera focused on a sheet of paper with three lines in Jane's handwriting:

> *Night at the window. When will you come then,*
> *As though you belong to the dark,*
> *To show me the way there, my lover?*

The audience sighed again, more at ease with these now-familiar lines. There was a cut to the mourners, Susie and me included, leaving the coroners' court in our unaccustomed formal clothes, panning to show Jane's sister, a plainer version of Jane, wearing a rather outmoded black hat and getting into a car, then staring out silently at the camera. Where had Diane got all this stuff? The audience shifted in their seats. So far there had been nothing on the soundtrack. Cut to Alex standing on the diving board, glistening with water and sunlight, all threat and promise – and here the music came in, Bo Diddley from 1956.

There was a fade to the Rakes onstage at the party, but the music track stuck to Bo Diddley while the camera moved away to take in the dancers, Susie and Jane looking baffled among them, as the acid took hold. Then there was Jane, dancing with blissful aggression on the pool's edge in her bikini, diving in but displaced by another shot of the smoking barn. Someone was stealing the memories out of my head. The music continued through a scene of Alex and Jane sitting in the pub garden, arms round each other's shoulders, before shifting to Alex, standing in the bedroom at May Cottage with a stack of paper in front of him. Jane was apparently not present. The top sheet was held up to the camera:

NIGHT WATCH

Poems by Jane Jarmain

The camera drew back. Alex was holding a lighter. He struck a flame and brought it close to the edge of the page. There was a collective flinch in the audience. Another piece of paper appeared with a handwritten caption in broad black marker pen:

IT'S ONLY BLOODY POETRY
WHO CARES, MAAN?

Now someone had contrived to get footage of Alex and Diane in Jane's bed. Clearly this film had not been through the Board of Classification. Many in the audience were waiting to see who would blink and rise first. The scene shifted to the temple on the night of the party, shot from what seemed to be Irmgard's viewpoint, as the smoke-blackened revellers, Luke's haircut recognizable among them, hauled armloads of books to dump them in the leaping flames in the dry pool. The soundtrack had switched to Rachmaninov's *The Isle of the Dead*. It was possible that no one in the audience but me saw Alex come running up out of the dark with the sheaf of pages in his hand. Here the film ran white: finished or incomplete? No credits, anyway. But the music was still ranting absurdly away before it too was cut off.

You had to admit Diane knew how to put a movie together. By this point, though, rather than debating the merits of the piece, the audience was achieving critical mass, pretending not to leave while in fact discreetly doing so.

I looked down towards the stage. Diane was nowhere to be seen, and Alex had risen to his feet, peering up towards the projection box, waving his arms. Sophie was holding up her phone as if it must contain the answer, while Jacqui Treece had moved over to join the camera crew. Alex began to push his way through the crowd towards the exit. The way parted before him as people turned to get a tactful look at the possible monster.

The exit at the rear of the circle brought me out by the door of the projection box. It stood ajar and I was anxious to have a look before anyone else arrived. There was no one inside. The finished reel still seemed to be in the machine. Alex came rushing along the corridor with an alarmed young woman who wore a badge on which was printed: 'Lisa, House Manager'.

'What the fuck is going on?' Alex shouted. He turned to me. 'Did you do this?'

'Sadly, no,' I replied, 'but hats off to whoever did. Very striking piece of work. The last art, eh? The last something, anyway, I should think.'

'It's a fake,' he said. 'Counterfeit.'

'In what sense?' I asked. He stared at me. I wondered if he might start foaming at the mouth.

'The way it's cut,' he said, weakening. 'People can tell that.'

'You think so?'

'Where's the projectionist?' he asked.

'Ms Eckhart insisted that only her team do the show-ing,' said Lisa.

'What fucking team?'

'Well, her colleagues.'

'She hasn't got any fucking colleagues. I'm all she's got,' Alex said.

'You don't need to swear,' said Lisa.

'Oh, fuck off!' Alex roared. He was actually growling now.

'Of course – now I remember,' I said. 'You didn't actually view the film in advance. Meant to be a surprise. Well you can't fault Diane on that score, can you?'

'Give me the film,' said Alex.

'I'm sorry, I can't do that,' said Lisa. 'I can only hand the film back to Ms Eckhart. That was the agreement.'

I think if I hadn't been there he might have tried to seize the film from her. I'm sure he thought about it.

'What agreement? Where the fuck is she?' Alex screamed. 'What agreement? She's a fucking cripple! How far can she have got?' He ran off again, yelling for Sophie.

'I'll just pack the, er, film up,' said Lisa.

'Is there a return address?'

She studied the packaging. 'Doesn't seem to be.'

'Then look after it. Put it in your safe and make sure that whatever happens you don't hand it over to anyone except Diane. Unless they've got a warrant.'

At that point I slipped away into the evening. Molly gave me a pained glance as I went past the deserted bookstall. Trade had not been as good as expected. The streets were oddly quiet too. Back to the Green Man for me, though I hadn't brought a thing to read, and then, in the sweaty sunset, into St Bart's churchyard to see Exton's tomb and the site beside it prepared for Jane's interment. They were roped off, awaiting tomorrow's events.

23

These days, I get up early. Sleep won't have me much after four a.m. Winter nights feel like a tomb, but it's not so bad in summer. By seven o'clock I'd been reading in my study for an hour, then I went downstairs to make some tea. Molly was already in there, sitting in the unexpectedly sunny window, reading Alex's book. I put the kettle on and we waited warily for a break in the frost between us.

'I had the Tunnocks round here last night,' she said.

'You didn't deserve that.'

'Ginny was in tears.'

'Oh dear.'

'Don't be like that, Martin. She's tried very hard, they both have, and now it's all spoilt.'

'You make it sound like a garden party. I suppose it is, in a sense. But they couldn't have known what would happen.'

'Did you?'

'Eh? How could I?'

She shook her head. 'Anyway,' she went on, 'there was a hell of a fuss with the committee afterwards. They're worried it'll get into the papers.'

'I thought they wanted publicity.'

'Oh, stop it. Think of someone else for a change.'

'You agreed with me that all this business with the reinterment and getting Alex over here was a bad idea. Remember?'

'Yes, but we have to deal with things as they are, Martin. Surely you can see that.'

'The situation is not of my making.'

'Really.'

'What the hell does that mean?'

The doorbell rang. Molly sighed and went to answer it.

'Someone for you,' she said, coming back into the kitchen, followed by Sophie. She was pale and twitchy and looked misplaced in the same pink dress she'd worn yesterday over which she'd thrown a short jacket.

'I just wondered if you'd seen Alex,' Sophie said, aiming for a light tone but crash-landing in the foothills of anxiety. Her hand was twitching to get her phone out, but even she knew it wouldn't have the answer.

'Not since yesterday evening,' I said. 'How did you know our address?'

'Sorry? Oh, Alex had it in his notebook,' she replied miserably.

'Would you like a cup of tea?' Molly asked. 'You look as if you haven't slept. You should have some breakfast.' She manoeuvred the girl into a chair but Sophie immediately stood up again, as though Alex might suddenly materialize if only she kept active.

'It's just the television people want to get on, and he seems to have wandered off. They want the early-morning light.'

'They would, wouldn't they? Have you tried his room?'
I asked.

'He wasn't there. I tried Diane's as well. Neither of
them was there. And I've rung and rung and everything's
switched off.' A tear ran down her cheek. Molly put an
arm round her.

'He'll have gone for a walk, I should think,' I said.
'Needs to think a bit and sort himself out. Understandably.
It must have been a shock.'

Sophie nodded, trying to be convinced. 'God knows
where Diane got all that mad stuff in the film,' she said. 'It
could make things really difficult.'

'Quite.'

'He hasn't been back to this place for a long time, of
course,' offered Molly. 'He probably wants to walk the
ground.'

'Yes,' I added. 'After all, it's an important day, with
Jane's reinterment this afternoon. Needs to get in the mood
for that. Revisit some of the old familiar trysting-places.'
Molly gave me a look.

'I suppose you're right,' said Sophie. 'I just panicked.
There's been sort of quite a lot to deal with. There was
such a fuss after the film. I've never seen him angry before.
What with one thing and another we didn't get to bed
until gone two. And then his phone rang and he went out,
hours ago, and there's loads of media stuff booked. I just
wish he'd ring, you know?'

'I can imagine,' I said.

Molly glared at me. 'Why don't we come back to the
hotel with you?' she said. 'He's probably back there now.'

'Would you mind? I'd be very grateful. Sorry – it's just, you know . . .'

'We haven't got time for this,' said Steve, the director, a small horse-faced skinhead. 'It's not fucking cheap, coming all the way out here. We'll lose the light if he doesn't show up. So where the fuck is he? Sleeping it off after that business last night? What the fuck was all that about?' Steve was clearly meant for better things than farting about with dead poets.

'I don't know, Steve. I've looked everywhere,' said Sophie, miserably.

'Christ. Fucking woollybacks.' Faint ancestral Scouseness there. 'Jacqui's fucked off back to London, but that's okay, unavoidable. We can't have these other cunts showing up late, though. Not fucking on. Where is he? You mean you've got no idea? This is a joke, right?'

Sophie shook her head, close to tears. Steve lit a cigarette, then remembered the law and went out through the swing doors into the street. We trailed after him. All the way up the hill the traders were setting up their stalls. It looked like the England depicted on one of those paintings over the luggage rack in an old railway carriage. The cameraman and the sound recordist sat down on a bench to wait. The cameraman tapped his watch and looked up at the sky. The sun was almost over Summer Hill.

'I fucking know, Terry,' said the director. 'Believe me. All right?'

'Yes, guv. But we'll lose it unless—'

The director raised a palm to him and turned away.

'Right, let's think again. Is there someone else we can use?'

'Well, there's Diane,' said Sophie, doubtfully.

'What – the old bird who goes round with this Farren bloke, the one who did the film?' Steve grinned. 'That could be a laugh, eh?'

'She's in a wheelchair, right?' said Terry.

'I suppose she is,' Sophie replied. 'Does that matter?'

Terry gave an impression of thinking by moving his jaw around and tilting his head from side to side. 'Not as such. Difficult for the angle, though, with the old tomb being raised quite high up. Anyway, where is she?'

'I don't know,' said Sophie. 'She must have gone out.'

'For fuck's sake,' said Steve. 'Can't you just lock 'em in? It's like keeping gorillas in a fucking paper bag.' He lit another cigarette and looked around for someone else to devour. 'Who are you?' he said, noticing at me for the first time.

'This is Professor Stone. From the university,' said Sophie.

Steve sniffed. Clearly he wasn't keen on professors. 'You know about this Exton, do you?'

'As luck would have it he's my speciality.'

'Right. Is he? Right. Before my time, I'm afraid. Byron and that . . . Always meant to, you know . . . Anyroad, maybe you could help us out. Ever done this kind of thing? Sorry, what's your name?'

'Martin. A bit. I did a programme about Exton for Radio 3 a while back.' Apparently this was also off Steve's radar. 'I can talk, if that's what you mean. I do it for a living, really.' Steve considered. 'Alex is probably just late. Slipped his mind. He's a bit starry, these days.'

'Is he? Fuck him.'

'Can we get on, Steve?' asked the cameraman.

'And I knew Jane Jarmain very well, if that's any help.'

'Well, that's good. Okay, Martin. Right. Let's have a go. Come on, Tel, we need to get round to the church before it clouds over again.'

'Can you come with us and keep Sophie company?' I asked Molly.

'What about Alex? Shouldn't we find him?'

'No time. He can look after himself.'

Sophie was grey and sweaty now, and clung to Molly's arm as we all trooped off. I went ahead with Steve, leading the way past the Green Man and into the churchyard. St Bart's loomed in dignified sandstone silence on its low eminence. At the gate a reception committee was eager to miss nothing, however painful the previous night – the vicar, the Tunnocks, plus one or two people I recognized as the local press, though the actual ceremony of reinterment wasn't due to be held until the afternoon. And there too, filming the proceedings themselves, was a silver-haired couple, whip-thin, in matching black suits. They acknowledged me with slight bows as we passed.

'Fuck,' said Steve. 'Who are all these?'

'Organizing committee,' I said. 'They're harmless. They're very proud of what's happening. And some odd and sods from the local press. Television never comes here normally. Nothing to worry about.'

'Long as they keep out the fucking road. Look, I'll give

Sean O'Brien

you this.' He rummaged in his shoulder bag and handed me Alex's book. 'You just need to hold it, for continuity. That silly cow from the publishers clearly hasn't got one – have you, darling?' Sophie shook her head. 'What's she on, by the way?'

'Search me.'

We went round to the north end of the church. Molly helped Sophie to a bench, where the girl was immediately sick on her little red shoes. Steve nodded without surprise. The crew arranged themselves and Steve took me aside. 'I'll ask some questions,' he said. 'My voice won't be in the finished piece – Jacqui will drop them in if we do run it, which is hard to say at the moment – but just answer to camera, as clearly and briefly as you can. Who was this Exton, why he's here, why we care. Who was Jane, ditto, why it matters, yeah? Then, no offence, I can get back to the actual world, okay?'

'What about the film last night? Do we want to talk about that at all?'

'Noli bargipoli, apparently. Not to be mentioned. Bit fucking lively, though, wasn't it? That Jane was fit. Anyway, sorry, no. The exec and your pal, this bloke Farren who's AWOL, go back a long way, apparently, so we're still making the piece but, like I say, nothing's certain after that. Why? Does it matter?'

'I shouldn't think so.'

He turned. 'Right, lads, let's crack on. Everyone else, please keep well back.' We walked the few yards over the grass towards Exton's tomb, the pale casket seeming to crouch on its squat legs above the plinth. Next to it lay the freshly dug grave.

'Stand at that end, yeah?' said Steve. I did as he asked, and waited while Terry made adjustments to the camera and the sound man extended the boom within range.

There was birdsong. The sky stayed blue. The sun cleared Summer Hill and hard-edged shadows formed on the dewy, lovingly barbered grass. The onlookers waited patiently by the church, under the stained-glass rose. It was heraldic, I thought, with the clock hands halted in brief admiration of this mild, anonymous scene.

'What the fuck is that?' said Steve.

'Sorry?' I said.

'In the hole,' he said, coming forward. 'Look.'

'Have I to keep filming?' asked Terry.

'Fucking hell,' said Steve.

The others were approaching over the grass.

You didn't rise like Farinata in the cemetery in hell to despise me, did you, Alex? In your case dead seemed to mean dead. For once, you had nothing to say on the matter. The last word remained out of reach. You'd had your head caved in for one thing, and person or persons unknown had doused you with petrol and set you alight, later extinguishing your overcooked, not to say carbonized, remains and carefully placing them in a body-bag, then in the open grave intended for Jane.

You were a hell of a mess with your face burned off – understandably the television blokes couldn't resist having a look before the police were called – but the earring was still there and the wide-open jaw suggested you'd been alive when the fire took hold. And the matching jewel was still in Diane's ear when they winched her out of the empty pool at Moon House. God knows how she'd got herself up there, or in there, though I can imagine why. Of course, you're not listening. You never did.

As for Jane, she had to wait to be reburied. Not that she was ever in a hurry. The site of her grave became part of a crime scene, which I suppose is apt, under the circumstances. I never stop mourning her, wherever her remains are laid. There are lots of unanswered questions, some of them aimed at me, but I dare say I'll manage. I think – I mean I *know* – that she kept going to the barn to give you a chance to finish it. She'd said that only you could do it. The next step – deliberate, accidental, who knows? – but it seems to have been necessary, inescapable. God knows why. In the end you were interred together, as though expert beyond experience.

It seems that none of the big things was meant to happen to me, other than loss, and short of death, I suppose, which is a mercy. My supporting role is to record what I know and mix it with what I think. Anyway, Alex, no one can stop you being famous when you're dead, though in your case I mean, if I can, to turn fame into notoriety. Call me old-fashioned, if you like, but I should point out that I shall be employing the most up-to-date methods in my biography, setting aside my contempt for that vulgar form in the service of a greater cause. I would toast you, but in a sense that's already been done, hasn't it?